Praise for Lorra

'Fresh, charming and wonderfully escapist'
Beth O'Leary

'Utterly charming'
Prima

'A magical modern love story'
Helly Acton

'A wonderfully engaging tale of love and self-discovery'
Mike Gayle

'A charming, romantic read'
Sophie Cousens

'The lovely descriptions made me want to take the first
post-lockdown Eurostar to Paris!'
Kate Eberlen

'A gorgeous, romantic book packed full of joy'
Laura Pearson

'Fresh, funny and just the tonic for dark winter nights'
Zoe Folbigg

Lorraine Brown previously trained as an actress and now works as a student counsellor alongside her writing. She lives in London with her partner and their 10-year-old son.

Also by Lorraine Brown

Sorry I Missed You
The Paris Connection

LORRAINE BROWN
FIVE DAYS
in Florence

ORION

First published in Great Britain in 2023 by Orion Books,
an imprint of The Orion Publishing Group Ltd
Carmelite House, 50 Victoria Embankment
London EC4Y 0DZ

An Hachette UK Company

1 3 5 7 9 10 8 6 4 2

A CIP catalogue record for this book
is available from the British Library.

ISBN (Mass Market Paperback) 978 1 3987 1108 2
ISBN (eBook) 978 1 3987 1109 9

Typeset by Deltatype Ltd, Birkenhead, Merseyside

Printed in Great Britain by Clays Ltd, Elcograf S.p.A.

www.orionbooks.co.uk

For my lovely mum.

Prologue

Nick and I stood at the very top of the Eiffel Tower, looking down at Paris laid out below us, all treetops and sweeping boulevards and skyscrapers spiking up out of nowhere in the distance.

'You get the best views from this side, apparently,' he said. 'North-west. Look, you can see the shadow of the tower reflected on the river.'

I leaned against the railings, two hundred and seventy-six metres up in the air, feeling perfectly safe thanks to the thick lattice fence curling over our heads. It took a second or two for my eyes to adjust, to pick out exactly what he meant, but then I saw it: the picture-perfect shadow of the Eiffel Tower straddling the shimmering, deep blue waters of the Seine.

'It's stunning,' I said.

'And that's the Trocadero. The Jardins and the Palais de Chaillot. Next time, when we're here for longer, I'll take you up there.'

I nodded, unwrapping the cardigan I'd tied around my waist and slipping it over my arms, which was more difficult than it sounds, as I was also holding a baseless plastic flute of champagne. It was chillier up here than it had been at street level, despite the sky being unseasonably clear and blue, and it was almost completely silent – a contrast to the rest of Paris with its honking horns and the constant roaring of traffic. If you ignored all of the other tourists on the top level with us, that was – I didn't think I'd ever heard so many different languages being spoken in one relatively small place: I'd already picked out French, Italian, English with an American twang and Japanese.

'Let me hold your drink for you,' laughed Nick, taking my 'glass' and then handing it back to me once I was sorted.

I took a sip, savouring the moment. It was just like Nick to whisk me away to Paris for a night as a surprise. When he'd asked me to meet him at St Pancras the morning before, I'd presumed he was taking me out for breakfast in Coal Drops Yard. I couldn't believe it when he'd produced my passport and a Eurostar ticket!

I wrapped my arm around his waist, tucking myself under his arm as he pulled me into him and kissed the top of my head.

'Thank you for bringing me here,' I said.

'Actually, I did have an ulterior motive.'

I frowned. 'What ulterior motive?'

Nick dropped his hand away from my shoulders, clearing his throat.

'Is it me or is it hot up here?' he asked, unbuttoning his cuffs and pushing the sleeves of his shirt up to his elbows.

A particularly strong gust of wind answered the question for me.

'Not really,' I said, feeling a pang of anxiety. What was wrong with him? 'Are you *sweating?*'

'I'm not the best with heights,' he replied, trying to smile, except that his mouth didn't seem to want to do what his head was telling it to.

'I thought it was just flying you didn't like?'

Nick had a strange look in his eyes and I could have sworn he was tearing up. My mind immediately went – as it tended to – to the worst-case scenario. Had he brought me to the top of the Eiffel Tower to tell me that it wasn't going to work out between us after all? That we were just too different (I mean, we were, but so what?)? That I was too young for him (ten years was nothing!)? That our lives were going in different directions? These were all valid points, things I'd thought about myself, on and off, but none of it mattered. I loved him and he loved me back and I'd never really had that. And no matter how much it looked like it shouldn't on paper, it worked between us.

'I wanted to do this later. Somewhere more … private,' Nick said. 'But I'm sorry, I don't think I can wait.'

'Do what?' I asked, my pulse going haywire. 'Wait for what?'

I swallowed, sweating myself now. Why would he bring me all the way to Paris to dump me, it didn't make sense. I remained confused as he fumbled in his pocket and pulled out a red velvet ring box, and I still couldn't quite compute as he dropped to one knee, looking up at me.

'Maddie,' he said earnestly, 'in the two years we've been together, I've fallen more and more in love with you every day.'

I glanced nervously around. A few people had stopped ogling the view and were now staring unashamedly at the two of us, nudging each other with voyeuristic interest. I looked at Nick and only Nick, focusing on his blond hair with a hint of a curl (and more than a hint of grey, which I didn't mind at all) and his kind eyes and his city boy shirt and his private-school accent that I found sexier than I'd thought I would. He was lovely and he was presumably, unless I'd got it completely wrong, about to tell me that he wanted to spend the rest of his life with me.

Nick took my left hand in his clammy right one and squeezed it. 'Will you marry me, Maddie?' he asked, looking up at me hopefully.

I laughed, out of embarrassment and shock and a million other things. 'Are you serious?' I spluttered.

If this was a joke, I'd kill him.

'Yes,' he said softly. 'Would you please do me the honour of becoming my wife?'

I bit my lip, hesitating. I wasn't sure why. It was a bit overwhelming, I supposed. And it felt like the entire population of the viewing platform was waiting for my answer.

'Is it a yes?' he prompted, doubt crossing his face for a second.

'Yes,' I heard myself saying at last, not wanting to keep him hanging. 'It's a yes.'

And then a huge cheer broke out and a few people raised their plastic flutes in our direction and Nick stood up, kissed me hard on the mouth and slid the biggest diamond I'd ever seen onto the ring finger of my left hand. Then he picked me up and spun me around, holding me so tightly I could barely breathe.

'You've just made me the happiest man alive!' he said.

I laughed, begging him to put me down. 'Nick! Stop, please!'

He placed me carefully back on the ground and I held on to the fence for support. It was like he couldn't stop smiling and, in response, neither could I. My God. I was going to have an actual husband, which sounded weird now, but presumably I'd get used to it. I was going to have a wedding to plan. A dress to buy. Bridesmaids to choose. A life to lead with someone.

'Does this mean I get to meet your elusive family at last?' I teased, breathless from all the spinning.

A beaming Nick ran his thumb across my cheek.

'Absolutely. How does five days in Florence next month sound?'

Chapter One

Four Weeks Later

Florence was even more beautiful than I'd imagined, I realised, as our taxi navigated the narrow streets, its wheels bumping expertly over the cobbles. Compared to London, everything looked perfectly polished and squeaky clean, and people weren't rushing around barging into anyone who dared to get in their way like they tended to at home. There weren't even any crowds scrabbling for a look at one of the famous sights like there were in Rome (which I'd visited for all of a day on a work trip once – I hadn't been able to get close to the Trevi Fountain, for example, which had been surrounded by a twenty-deep crescent of camera-wielding tourists). The pace was slow and the sun was out, which was a bonus in April. And, oh, there was just the small matter of every single building looking like it would have been a palace in a former life.

The driver braked gently and pulled in next to the kerb.

'Here we go,' said Nick. 'This must be us.'

I wound down the window even further, poking my head out and looking up at the Palazzo Continentale which was quite possibly the grandest hotel I'd ever seen in my life. Well, perhaps not ever *seen*. I mean, I'd walked past Claridge's loads and had once had afternoon tea at The Savoy (reluctantly, to celebrate my dad and stepmum's twentieth wedding anniversary. As if the fact my dad had left my mum and married somebody else was cause for celebration), but it was definitely, hands down, going to be the poshest place I'd ever actually stayed in. It had flagpoles hanging over the door and everything! And a doorman in a smart uniform with shiny gold buttons, and a designer boutique on the ground floor, in case you suddenly thought: *oh, I know, I need a Versace dress for that party tonight, let me pop down to the hotel shop.*

Nick flung open his door, got out and then marched around to open my door for me. Ever the gentleman, which was impressive given that he must feel as knackered from the journey as I was. I was desperately resisting the urge to say *I told you so.* Nobody but him had ever thought that catching the train from London to Florence was a good idea. It had taken us over twenty-four hours, with a change in Paris and then an overnight stay in Turin. Twenty-four hours! We'd got the 10 a.m. train out to Florence this morning and it was a relief to finally be here. I refused to let myself think about the fact that I had to make the same horrendous journey home. I wondered if I could persuade Nick that I simply had to get back to London as a matter of extreme urgency and would therefore need to book myself a flight.

Nick, who seemed uncharacteristically distracted, was flicking through his phone while the poor taxi driver, who wasn't exactly young and spritely, struggled to drag our suitcases out of his boot. I gave Nick a look, and when that had no effect, I stepped in to help the man myself.

'Here, let me,' I said, taking my suitcase from him and dropping it hard onto the pavement.

Damn, that wasn't the best idea. I was pretty sure that as I'd got it for half-price in the Argos sale, it was unlikely to survive such maltreatment. And it looked tiny next to Nick's,

6

which I suspected meant that he knew something I didn't. Why hadn't he said anything about the calibre of hotel we'd be staying in? My wardrobe choices were clearly going to be all kinds of wrong.

'You could have warned me it was this swanky,' I said to Nick, who was still scrolling manically, seemingly unaware that the taxi driver was waiting to be paid.

'My mother booked it,' he said, not even looking up. 'She was hardly going to book us into a Premier Inn, was she?'

I got my purse out of my bag, genuinely confused. 'What's so wrong with a Premier Inn?'

Nick didn't answer – too busy tapping a message into his phone.

'Everything all right?' I asked.

Nick sighed. 'It's my mother. Wondering where we are.'

'Oh, right,' I said.

It wasn't like him to stress over anything, except maybe work. Anyway we'd be seeing her in less than half an hour, once we'd dumped our stuff in our room and freshened up.

'How much is that, please?' I asked the driver.

'Twenty euro.'

Twenty euros for a journey that had taken all of ten minutes?! I handed him a note, and then another five as a tip. I supposed the extortionate prices weren't his fault. I had been warned that Florence wasn't the cheapest.

'Right, then,' I said to Nick. 'Looks like reception's this way.'

He made a show of putting his phone away and then sprang to attention, ushering me in the direction of the revolving doors.

'After you, m'lady,' joked Nick.

The doorman helped us through the door and I thanked him as I dragged my suitcase through to the lobby as

7

elegantly as I could manage given the half-shredded wheels, which didn't glide as easily over the plush carpet as Nick's luxury case seemed to. My jaw literally dropped as I looked around at my surroundings. I couldn't believe this was going to be my home for the next five days! I mean, I loved hotels and, thanks to my job on a TV travel channel, I'd stayed in quite a few of them, but they were never, ever anything like this. It was like I imagined the interior of The Ritz to be, except smaller and cosier and more Italian (in other words, absolutely nothing like The Ritz).

I closed my mouth, thinking I should probably make some attempt to play it cool. To act like this wasn't so far out of my comfort zone that it would be funny if it wasn't also slightly terrifying. What did this say about Nick's family? I mean, I'd picked up that they had money, but this was another level plush.

As we headed over to the front desk, I noticed a pianist playing in the corner. His dinner-jacket-clad back was hunched dramatically over the keys as he played what I thought might have been Vivaldi, although I was definitely *not* a classical music buff, so it was just a guess. Vivaldi was Italian, though, wasn't he, so that would make sense?

When I looked up at the ceiling, I spotted a huge crystal chandelier that was about the same size as the studio flat I'd lived in before I'd moved in with Nick.

'Imagine if that dropped on your head,' I said, wincing at the thought.

'Trust you to come up with the worst-case scenario,' laughed Nick, directing me over to reception, where two women wearing chic racing green uniforms were doing an excellent job of pretending that they were excited to see us.

'Good afternoon, sir,' said one in a thick, Italian accent. 'And to you, madam! I trust you had a very good journey?'

Not really was on the tip of my tongue.

Close up, their make-up was immaculate (I always felt the same way about air stewardesses) and I immediately wished I'd reapplied mine at the train station before we got in the taxi. Anyway, it didn't matter because soon I'd be able to get up to our room and make myself look vaguely presentable to meet Nick's parents for the first time. After all, they were going to be my in-laws – I wanted them to love me as much as I hoped I would grow to love them. I was excited about the prospect of having a whole new family to get to know, one which was, presumably, much more stable than my own. Nick's parents had been married for forty-five years for a start, which was why we were all here in the first place.

Nick checked us in and when the receptionist slipped the invoice across the desk, I noticed it came to a total of just over three thousand euros, which she explained we wouldn't need to pay for now, but that she'd need to take Nick's credit card details for security reasons.

I tapped Nick on the shoulder, wide-eyed. 'How much?' I mouthed.

He looked confused. 'What do you mean?'

My mouth open and shut as though I was gasping for air. 'That's, like, half our wedding fund!'

'My parents are covering the bill,' he said, giving me a weird look, as though this was obvious.

He definitely had not mentioned anything about his parents forking out for our room.

'What, the whole thing?' I clarified.

'Yes. Can we talk about this later?'

He turned back to the receptionist, all smiles.

I often wondered, with hotels like this, what constituted a room costing five hundred pounds a night as opposed to a much more reasonable two hundred? Two fifty at a push, for a city-centre place? Perhaps all would be revealed. Also, I was starting to realise that Nick was from a more privileged background than I'd thought. Still, I didn't suppose it would make any difference – if Nick's family were anything like him, I was going to love them.

I watched as the receptionist directed Nick to the lifts; our room was on the fourth floor, apparently, with a view of the city's rooftops and the Duomo, she told us with enthusiasm. This was exciting. I'd already decided that, in the morning, I was going to wake up and throw open the windows and breathe in the Florentine air, channelling Helena Bonham Carter in *A Room With A View*.

'Thanks, but we're heading into the restaurant first,' I heard Nick say. 'Can you have our suitcases taken up to our room?'

'No problem, sir,' trilled the receptionist, calling over a porter with a flick of her wrist and barking orders at him in (I thought unnecessarily) aggressive-sounding Italian.

'Um, what are you doing?' I said to Nick brightly.

'We're going straight in to meet Mum and Dad. They're waiting for us.'

I took a moment to gather my thoughts, hoping that I could air my dissatisfaction with this plan in a calm and reasonable manner.

'But I look a complete mess!' I screeched, failing dismally.

Seriously, though! I looked down at my faded jeans and my black T-shirt and my faux-suede ankle boots that were scuffed at the toe already even though I'd only bought them a couple of weeks ago (I was terrible at keeping footwear looking nice, probably because I only had about two pairs on rotation at any one time). How on earth was I going to make a decent first impression looking like this?

'You look beautiful, Maddie. You always do,' said Nick,

running his hand reassuringly down my arm. 'Come on, let's go and say hello.'

He headed purposefully towards the restaurant and I leapt into action, grabbing his arm.

'No, Nick, honestly. I can't meet your parents in this state. At least let me put some product in my hair and shove a bit of lipstick on.'

Nick sighed. 'The thing is, we've already missed lunch. And my mum hates being kept waiting. I can tell by her text that she's not happy with us.'

'Us? There's no "us" about it,' I argued. 'You do know that if we'd flown to Italy like everyone else, we could have been here last night?'

Nick groaned. 'Not this again, Mads?'

'I still don't get how you managed to fly to Chicago for work. I didn't see you insisting you'd have to sail across the Atlantic,' I said, aware that bringing all of this up moments before we were about to meet his parents was probably the worst idea I'd ever had. It's just that this was a big moment for me and I felt put out about being dropped in it like this!

Nick pinched the top of his nose. 'I had to borrow a Xanax, as you well know.'

'OK. I get how hard it is for you. But couldn't you have taken a Xanax this time?'

'Where's your sense of adventure? I thought you were a seasoned traveller. I've got no idea why you're getting so wound up about a little train journey.'

'I wouldn't call twenty-four hours little!'

I caught the eye of the receptionist, who was observing us with interest and also slight disgust. Perhaps the quiet lobby of Florence's most upmarket hotel wasn't the best place for a row, but I had all this pent-up frustration at Nick's refusal to fly and the fact we'd barely left the country together since we'd met. We'd travelled the length and breadth of the UK, which had been fine at first, because I'd enjoyed going anywhere with him in those first few months, but after a while, one rugged, pebbled, rain-soaked beach started to look much the same as the next. I'd tried to be understanding, I really had, but the problem was, I loved travelling and, by default, that meant I loved flying, too, and now I rarely got to do either unless I was on a work trip.

Realising I was fighting a losing battle, I touched my hair, trying to neaten it up, hoping it hadn't gone frizzy but assuming it probably had because, well, that was how my hair rolled. There was nothing I could do about my clothes or my make-up, since my suitcase was currently being whisked efficiently up to our room on a silver trolley with a plethora of other luggage, most of which, I'd noticed, was Louis Vuitton. I was just going to have to brazen this out. Perhaps Nick's family wouldn't even notice what I was wearing. They were probably very nice and laid-back, with a sort of 'anything goes' attitude to clothing and I was worrying for nothing.

'Let's go,' said Nick, holding out his hand. 'You can change in a bit, once we've said hello.'

'Thanks for your permission,' I replied, reluctantly linking my fingers through his.

We walked into the restaurant together. A wave of nausea swept over me as I scanned the room, wondering which table housed the people whose family I was about to become a part of. I thought it might be the sweet, older couple in the corner who were chatting happily away as they sipped espressos, but then there was a chorus of cheers and multiple counts of '*over here, darling!*' from a different direction.

My head turned. A group of ridiculously glamorous people were sitting at a table scattered with already demolished glasses of wine and bread baskets full of crumbs and not much else and they were all staring in our direction.

Nick whispered in my ear, 'I love you. And so will they.'

I smiled tightly at him, wishing I felt half as confident. I could tell by the way these people commanded the room that they were nothing like my family.

Nick nudged me towards them and I concentrated on looking pleased to see them and not falling over and on not letting my self-esteem shatter into a million pieces when I saw how dressed up they all were (designer labels, by the looks of it). Only Nick's daughter, Daisy, looked vaguely casual and was wearing the quintessential teenager's uniform of high-waisted shorts and white crop top that only looked flattering on pre-pubescents.

'Mummy!' exclaimed Nick, launching himself at a woman in her early seventies with silver walnut-whip hair and a huge brooch pinned to her emerald green blouse that I reckoned was real sapphire and diamonds. Not that I was a gemstone expert, but she didn't seem the costume jewellery type.

Also, 'Mummy'? *Really?*

'Darling!' crooned Nick's mum as they rocked back and forth in an embrace that seemed to go on at least thirty seconds too long.

Eventually, he beamed around at me. 'Mummy, I'd love you to meet my fiancée, Maddie. Maddie, meet my mother, Rosamund.'

I stepped forward with the same tense, highly charged sensations flooding through my body that I might experience if I was being introduced to the King. How to act? What to say? To curtsey or not to curtsey (I mean, obviously not, but I suspected Rosamund would probably quite like it if I did)?

Out of the corner of my eye, I could see an exquisitely dressed woman in tan trousers and a black cashmere jumper that probably cost more than I made in a week looking me up and down with a hint of a smirk on her face. I wasn't sure who she was. Nick's sister, possibly, although I didn't think she'd been able to make it in the end?

'Lovely to meet you, Rosamund,' I said, going for the handshake option. Despite her weirdly intense clinch with Nick, Rosamund didn't look like a hugger. I pumped her wrist up and down in a manner which I hoped exuded poise and self-assurance – if I wasn't feeling it, I was clearly going to have to fake it.

'Maddie. How lovely to meet you. We've heard so much about you, haven't we, Peter?' she said, turning to the man next to her who hadn't bothered to stand up and was presumably Nick's dad. He was wearing a tweed jacket that looked as old as he was.

'Indeed,' said Peter, who had his napkin tucked into the collar of his shirt and seemed a little confused about who I actually was. 'Absolutely.'

'I hope we haven't interrupted your meal?' I said, taking in the carnage on the table.

'You're much too late for that, I'm afraid,' said Rosamund, giving Nick a pointed stare.

'Oh don't give them a hard time, Ros,' said the tan-trousered goddess, getting up and circumnavigating the table to give me an awkward, socially distanced embrace. It was like the hugging equivalent of an air kiss. Had I just coined the phrase 'air hug'? 'I'm Sophia,' she announced dramatically, elongating her vowels to perfection. 'Nick's ex-wife.'

I swallowed hard, letting myself hope for a second that I'd misheard. Because why on earth would Nick's ex-wife be here? And if I hadn't imagined it and this stunning woman was in fact his ex, why hadn't he warned me?

I smiled at Sophia as authentically as I could manage and

then glared at Nick, hoping to telepathically convey that this was not OK. This was not OK *at all*.

Nick was completely oblivious, of course, and continued his overenthusiastic greetings with aplomb, launching himself at Daisy, his fourteen-year-old daughter who I'd actually met once before. She'd been staying with Nick for a couple of weeks over the summer holidays last year and he'd thought that it would be a brilliant idea for us to meet, ensuing in a disastrous trip to the theatre where Daisy had barely said a word to me all night, had glowered through the entire performance (an admittedly very pretentious take on *Hamlet*) and then had refused point-blank to let me sit in the front seat on the drive home.

'Nice to see you again, Daisy,' I said.

She grunted a hello and wiggled her fingers in my direction. I supposed that was a start. Now that Nick and I were engaged, it felt even more important that we got along. I had several missions for this weekend (making Rosamund like me suddenly seemed even more daunting than I'd built it up to be), and one of them was to get off on a better foot with Daisy. She resented me for marrying her dad, I got that – divorce was never easy on the kids, I knew that better than anyone. But I had to win her over and this trip could be the perfect time to start.

As I saw Sophia say something out of the side of her mouth to Rosamund, I began to feel the familiar prickle of self-doubt. Were they wondering what Nick was thinking, getting engaged to somebody who was clearly 'not one of them'? Were they the sort of people who would deem me not properly English because I was of mixed heritage and my dad was from St Lucia? I started imagining all the ways in which they could think I wasn't good enough for Nick and my stomach swirled with anxiety.

I twisted my engagement ring back and forth on my finger again, reminding myself that Nick thought I was good enough and that that was all that mattered. Not that he was my favourite person right now, by any means – he could have let me smarten myself up before bringing me to face this firing squad of family members, who were looking at me as though I was some kind of alien. And he didn't want to get me started on the fact his ex was here!

'Can I go out for a walk?' Daisy asked her mum in the same whiny tone I remembered from the ill-fated theatre trip.

'No, you can't, because you don't know Florence and, knowing you, you'll get lost,' snapped Sophia.

Daisy rolled her eyes. 'Mum, I live in London. I'm sure I can find my way around a city that's basically about a tenth of the size.'

'Italian men are very sleazy, you know,' piped up Peter, who didn't seem to care that he was loudly spouting unfair cultural generalisations when there were potentially quite a lot of Italian men within earshot. 'They'll be fawning all over you the second you step outside the hotel doors.'

'Don't encourage her, Peter, she'd probably quite like that,' said Sophia.

I felt for Daisy in that moment – no wonder she was always miserable if she had to put up with passive-aggressive comments like that twenty-four/seven. Sophia had custody of Daisy, but from what I could gather, they clashed constantly. Nick hadn't told me much about his marriage to Sophia, except that it had lasted seven years and that he'd been unhappy for most of it and that it had been nasty for a while, at the end. I hadn't pushed him further at the time, but now I wished I had. What had drawn him to me, I wondered, given that I was possibly the polar opposite of the elegant, blonde, immaculately groomed Sophia? Or was that precisely it – that he'd been so damaged by whatever had happened between the two of them that he'd actively gone out looking for someone who was nothing like her? Although judging by the fact she was here on the trip, she was clearly still very much a part of the family in a way that I was already beginning to worry I'd never be.

'You haven't been to Florence before either, have you, Maddie?' piped up Rosamund, just as I was about to flag down a waiter and order myself a desperately needed large glass of wine. 'Would it be too much to ask for you to take Daisy out for a little stroll? It'll be a good chance for you both to get your bearings.'

I mean, since I'd just been travelling for twenty-four hours and hadn't even seen my room yet, going for a stroll wasn't exactly top of my agenda.

'Oh good idea,' said Nick, traitor that he was. 'You can acclimatise to Florence, Mads. She's never even been to Italy,' he explained to the table, who all laughed. Loudly. As though the concept was hilarious.

'That's not true, actually. I've been to Rome and Naples,' I protested.

'Work trips don't count,' said Nick.

The whole table snickered in agreement.

I wanted to add that I may not have spent my summers in Italy like this lot, but I had been to Vietnam and Costa Rica, places they'd probably only read about in the *Sunday Times* travel supplement. Then again, if there wasn't a private beach club or a golf course, they probably wouldn't be interested.

'I should probably unpack first,' I said, eyeballing Nick.

'You can do that when you get back, darling,' he replied, settling in next to Rosamund and pouring himself a glass of very attractive-looking alcohol.

'Well, then,' announced Rosamund, patting Nick's knee, 'let's get some champagne in to celebrate your arrival.'

'And your anniversary,' crooned Nick.

Stalling for time, I pounced on the chance to engage Rosamund in conversation. That way, hopefully they'd forget about this 'stroll' altogether, or at least I might have time to down a glass of wine before I set off. 'I hear you've been married for forty-five years,' I said, a stab of jealousy pricking my stomach quite unexpectedly.

I felt that, sometimes, and it was irrational because, for all I knew, it could have been forty-five massively unhappy years. But it still hurt that my parents had only given it eight years before acrimoniously calling it a day. I wondered, often, what would have happened if they'd tried a bit harder to make it work. Whether they'd considered, even for a moment, staying together for my sake.

'Congratulations!' I said, hoping Rosamund hadn't noticed that my expression had slipped, just for a second or two. 'What an achievement!'

Rosamund nodded, the trace of a smile on her alabaster face. For some reason, I was fascinated by her hair, which was swept starkly back from the hairline, reminding me of paintings I'd seen of Mary Queen of Scots.

'That's very kind of you,' she said to me.

'I hope Daddy bought you something nice?' said Nick, winking at Peter.

Daddy, now?

'All will be revealed, my boy, all will be revealed,' said Peter, clumsily tapping the side of his nose.

'Waiter!' squawked Rosamund to a man who was carrying three very heavy-looking plates and was clearly on his way to another table. 'Can we get a bottle of your most expensive champagne?'

I wanted to go on the walk even less now, because I really wanted to try this 'most expensive champagne', which probably cost about a grand a bottle. It was that kind of place. What would such a drink even taste like? Then again, I didn't want to get roped into having to split the bill.

'Our suitcases will be in the room by now, sweetie,' said Nick casually. 'You can pop up and get changed if you like. Daisy, wait for Maddie in the lobby, will you?'

Say no, I thought to myself. *Say no, that you will not be going for a walk right at this moment. That you fancy a drink first and then maybe you might. Do not let these people boss you around as though you are a member of their household staff. Stand your ground, Maddie!*

'Um, sure. OK,' I said, pathetic people-pleaser that I was.

Chapter Two

I consulted the map the hotel had given me, wondering which of the city's attractions was generating the slow-moving queue Daisy and I were deciding whether or not to join.

'I think it's the Galleria dell'Accademia,' I said, squinting up at the white building in front of us and then back at the map. 'And if it is, it's got Michelangelo's *David* inside, which explains the crowds.'

Daisy pushed her sunglasses onto her head, looking up at it, too. '*What*, that's what they're all waiting for? To look at some ancient piece of marble?'

I laughed, softly. 'Aren't you into sculpture?'

Daisy shrugged. 'Not really.'

The queue moved forward. I wondered whether seeing *David* was worth the hype.

'I thought your dad said you were doing GCSE art?' I said.

He'd said she was really in to it. A 'total creative' was how he'd described her. I'd thought that maybe it could be something for us to bond over. I'd loved art at school, too, although I'd never been good enough to take it any further. The reality of the work I produced had never been as good as it had seemed in my head, which was something I'd noticed about my life in general.

Daisy nodded. 'I am. But I prefer painting.'

'Me too, I think,' I said, looking up at the perfect, bright blue sky and slipping off my cardigan so that I could feel the late-afternoon sun on my arms. Somewhere in the distance, a street performer was playing something rousing and romantic on the violin. When I breathed in, I could smell burnt sugar.

'He's gutted that I'm not into something more useful,' Daisy remarked. 'Like maths or chemistry, or something.'

'I'm sure that's not true,' I replied. Nick had never given me the impression he cared what Daisy was or wasn't studying. Sophia seemed to be the one in charge of all the school-related stuff. Daisy was at one of the North London private schools, of course. I was pretty sure she'd do well whatever she chose to study for GCSE. 'He said he's going to book us both a guided tour of the Uffizi Gallery. He thinks you'd be really into it.'

'Do we have to?' complained Daisy. 'I like painting myself, not looking at other people's in a stuffy old gallery.'

I sighed inwardly. 'You'd better talk to him about it.'

I gave up on the idea of going into the Galleria, not prepared to queue for hours to see the statue if Daisy wasn't that enthusiastic about it. Perhaps we'd find something else to do and I'd come back on my own.

'Fancy a gelato?' I asked, determined to find some common ground. I'd have to use a different tactic, and food seemed as good a place as any to start. I was going to be her stepmother after all (a mortifying thought, if I was honest). And everyone loved ice cream, didn't they?

'I suppose,' huffed Daisy. 'How many calories does it have, though?'

I looked at Daisy with her long, slim limbs and her minute waist and felt quite sad about the fact she clearly wasn't confident about the way she looked. She reminded me of my half-sisters, who were just as obsessed with their weight. Nick reckoned Daisy's constant worrying about food was just a phase, and that her hormones were 'going haywire', as he'd put it. Mind you, I didn't think Nick could deal with emotional outbursts of any kind. On the odd occasion I'd lost it and had had a meltdown in front of him, I'd caught him looking at me with a mixture of utter contempt and blind panic.

'You're on holiday, Daisy. Treat yourself. Plus you look great – you don't need to worry about putting on weight.'

I bought us both a gelato – Daisy had spent absolutely ages looking at the menu and I'd watched her mind ticking over, as if she was trying to work out which flavour was the least calorific. She went for black cherry in the end and I had pistachio, a decision that for me had taken, oh, about five seconds to make.

Cones in hand, we wandered in the vague direction of the Duomo. I hadn't seen it close up yet, but you seemed to be able to spot it poking out above the rooftops wherever you were in the city. I breathed in the scent of Florence, which was warm and sweet with a punch of something floral. I wanted to stay here for ever, wafting around its narrow streets like a modern-day Lucy Honeychurch.

'Shall we take a slow walk back to the hotel?' I suggested.

Daisy looked less than enthusiastic. 'If you want.'

I took a huge mouthful of my gelato, wanting to finish it before we got back. Somehow eating a messy ice cream in the street in the middle of the day seemed like something Rosamund would disapprove of.

'Oh my God,' I groaned. 'This is literally the most amazing thing I've ever tasted.'

Daisy tutted. 'Do you have to be so loud about it?' she said, strutting off ahead.

I'd said the wrong thing again. Or had just been uncool, which came as no surprise to me. As I watched Daisy walk about two metres ahead of me, bubbling away inside of me were doubts about how I was going to navigate the next five days.

Although I'd had time to change into a floral sun dress, flat sandals and my favourite oversized cardigan, I was desperate to get back to the hotel so I could trawl through the contents of my suitcase and work out what the hell I was going to wear for dinner that night. It was my chance to make a better impression. To show Nick's family that I wasn't just some shabby girl he had picked up in a bar, but a professional, confident, relatively successful woman. Then again, how was I supposed to compete with the likes of Sophia, who I suspected would look good in an actual plastic bin bag? Not that she would be seen dead in anything that hadn't cost a small fortune, I imagined. I bet *she* didn't have a wardrobe full of H&M sale items and Topshop pieces from – no word of a lie – about fifteen years ago.

I followed Daisy up an achingly pretty street which I thought would take us in the general direction of the hotel – if I wasn't trying to keep up with her, I would have stopped to look at the market to my left. A particularly enticing stall had fake designer handbags on display.

'Hold on, Daisy!' I called after her. 'Don't walk too far ahead.'

She scowled at me over her shoulder and slowed her pace a miniscule amount. I was about to run to catch her up when my phone rang. I picked up without thinking.

'Maddie! Good, you answered. I thought I might have to email you.'

Fuck. If I'd clocked it was Tim calling, I'd have let it go to voicemail. What did he want?

23

'How's Florence?' he asked faux-casually.

'I've only just got here,' I said, keen to remind him that I was officially on annual leave and that being my boss didn't give him the right to contact me whenever he felt like it.

Just because I worked in TV and because, according to Tim, 'thousands of people' would kill for my job (doubtful), it didn't mean I had to be on call twenty-four/seven. Yes, I often had to work late, or do long hours if I was away on a shoot. I got it, and that was fine. But we worked on a low-budget travel channel, it wasn't like we were making cutting-edge documentaries here. If I wanted a few days off, I should be able to take them.

'I wanted to remind you to pick up some generic Florence footage,' said Tim, in the breezy tone he adopted whenever he was asking me to do something that deep down he knew was completely unreasonable. 'It saves us doing a separate trip and we can use it to tease *City Break Week*.'

Was he seriously expecting me to work while I was on holiday? For free? Perhaps I should threaten to call HR (although both Tim and I knew I would never do any such thing).

'I'm not sure I'll have time,' I told him. 'Nick's family have put together quite a full itinerary. And this is, as you know, my annual leave ...'

'I'm sure you can negotiate an hour here and there to do some filming, Maddie. Going above and beyond is part of this job, I'm afraid. I haven't had a proper holiday for years,' he said.

Which was a blatant lie.

'New York didn't count then?' I asked.

I didn't usually answer back because, well, you know – I needed my job. But, seriously, did he have selective memory syndrome?

'That was a … family emergency,' replied Tim.

It wasn't. I'd seen pictures of him on a rowing boat in Central Park having a whale of a time.

I checked that Daisy was still in sight and was pleased to note she had stopped to take a photo of a pretty church. This was promising – perhaps she was taking a bit of interest in Florence after all. We could bond over being first-time visitors to the city.

'Look, I'll see what I can do,' I said, trying to fob him off.

'You do that. Keep me posted, yeah?'

I ended the call and threw my phone into the depths of my bag so that I wouldn't hear it ring even if he did call back. I wanted Tim out of sight and out of mind, which was surely the point of taking a holiday from work. And if Tim had been nicer, if I felt like the company appreciated all my hard work, I might have been more inclined to be amenable. After all, the thought of spending an hour or two on my own shooting pretty footage of the Arno was actually quite appealing. But I was dispensable as far as Holiday Shop were concerned, I knew I was. I'd been stuck in the same assistant producer position for a while now and had been overlooked for promotion more times than I could mention. I thought that maybe it was because I didn't big myself up enough, like some of the other assistant producers, and because I was never the loudest in the room. People didn't seem to notice the good work I was doing. And that had been OK for a while, flying under the radar, so to speak, which had basically been my technique for getting through adolescence. My time had been split between my mum, who was preoccupied with her new twin babies (my now-teenaged half-sisters), and my dad, who had been so under the thumb of his new wife/ex-mistress, Sharon, that my visits there had felt increasingly awkward as time went on. But deep down,

I had this desperate desire to succeed. To be noticed. To be excellent at something and applauded for it. I wanted to be revered for my work, my creativity, my passion, not for my 'hilarious' banter in office meetings or for my excellent sucking-up skills.

'Right,' I said to Daisy, who was tentatively licking her gelato as though it was going to poison her. Honestly, how had she managed to make it last this long? I'd wolfed mine down in about two minutes flat. 'Hotel's just up there on the left.'

Daisy grunted a reply and followed me up the narrow Via Porta Rossa, which was lovely and shady and smelled of fresh pizza. The odd vehicle forced us onto the pavement, but otherwise we meandered right down the middle of the cobbled street. Every now and again, I pointed out a particularly pretty window display – clothes, perfumes, expensive-looking jewellery – which Daisy seemed to appreciate even if it didn't exactly spark a conversation between us.

'How come your mum's here?' I asked casually as we passed a cute bakery with rows of exquisite, cream-filled cakes placed tantalisingly in the window.

Was a gelato *and* a cake too much?

She shrugged. 'Granny wanted her to come. They still hang out, sometimes.'

Of *course* they'd hit it off. I bet Sophia was exactly the sort of person Rosamund would have chosen to be her daughter-in-law. She'd probably have picked her out of a line-up, if that had been an option. Privately educated? Check. Head-to-toe designer labels? Check. Razor-sharp cheekbones? Check.

And part of me got it, but the other part – the part I kept mostly hidden – was angry. Because they had known that I was coming, and must have realised that it would be awkward for me. And the fact that they'd not cared wasn't exactly conducive to me feeling like I could be part of the family. It was like they'd already made up their minds that Nick's second wife was going to be second-rate without even having met me, and now I supposed I was going to have to embark on a one-woman mission to win them over, although I wasn't sure where to begin. Perhaps I could impress them with my job: working in TV sounded all right if I didn't go into too much detail about Holiday Shop and if they didn't realise it was essentially a cable channel that sold discounted holidays to resorts in Tenerife and the Costa del Sol (a place I imagined was their worst nightmare). Or I could find a hobby we had in common – there had to be something. I'd try books; I read a lot, and all genres, so whatever they were in to, I was sure I could cobble together something intelligent to say. Food, maybe. I mean, I liked eating it, so that was a start.

I supposed I should be asking Nick about all of this, really, but since Daisy was here and would likely be less cagey about it, I thought she was probably my best bet if I wanted the full, unadulterated truth.

'They do seem to get on well,' I said casually.

She looked at me, brandishing her gelato with a glint in her eye. I sensed she was loving the idea that there might be tension between her mum and I – teenagers were all about the drama, weren't they?

'Does it bother you?' she asked.

'Not really,' I replied, because what else could I say? 'It was a surprise to see her here, that was all.'

'I bet,' said Daisy. 'Dad should have told you.'

'Maybe.' I was surprised and strangely heartened that even a fourteen-year-old could see that. I wasn't going mad, then.

We turned a corner and The Palazzo Continentale appeared before us, standing majestically on what appeared to be Florence's most exclusive shopping street, the Via Tornabuoni. The building itself was gorgeous, like one of those villas I'd seen in films set in the Tuscan countryside, with shuttered windows and Juliet balconies and that lovely ochre stone, but right in the heart of the city, surrounded by other equally beautiful buildings and former palazzos and sandwiched between Saint Laurent and Fendi, with Gucci diagonally opposite. Out front were two tubs housing plants so perfectly manicured, I had no idea whether they were real or not.

'Do you always stay in places like this?' I asked Daisy, who had finally finished the swirly gelato bit and had reached the cone. She nibbled at it delicately.

'Usually,' she said. 'Why, don't you?'

I gave her a look. Seriously, was she that far removed from society as to think that everyone could afford to stay in five-star hotels? If that's what posh schools and big houses and tennis lessons did for you, I was glad I hadn't had any of that stuff growing up (yeah, right – who was I trying to kid?). 'No, Daisy,' I said, feeling the need to open her mind a little. 'I couldn't afford somewhere like this usually.'

She frowned at me. 'But I thought you were some big shot in TV like Dad?'

I shook my head. 'Your dad's on a whole different level. He's Director of Marketing at Sky. I'm only an assistant producer at Holiday Shop. Hardly big time.'

'Still,' said Daisy. 'You get to travel a lot, Dad told me.'

I nodded. 'Sure, and I love that part of it. But we definitely don't get put up in places like this.'

In the absence of the doorman, which I was quite relieved about because it felt much too indulgent to have someone opening doors for me, we entered the hotel, flying through the revolving doors into what I'd secretly dubbed 'the lobby of dreams'. It was quieter now; the pianist must be on a break. A small queue had formed at the reception desk – perhaps a flight (full of sensible, plane-loving people) had just got in and everyone had arrived at once.

At the front of the line, leaning on the counter, was a man wearing a black polo shirt, one of those ones that looked silky and expensive, and black jeans. For some reason, I was drawn to him. I tried to turn my head away, to focus on making my way back to the restaurant to see if Nick was still there, hoping that he wasn't so that I could go straight up to the room, but my eyes kept flickering back to this man. There was something about his arms, which were tanned and muscular and somehow familiar. As he bent down to get something from his bag, his back muscles rippled under the fabric of his top. I wondered whether he was Italian. He had that lovely golden brown complexion and the dark hair, and was tall, 6'2" at least, I'd say. When he turned slightly to the side to hand over his passport, I caught a glimpse of his profile.

My god, it couldn't be. I stopped dead, my heart slamming against my chest, my breath catching in my throat. I watched, hoping for a proper look at his face so that I could reassure myself that I'd been mistaken. Because it couldn't be him. There was no way it could be, not here in Florence; not all of these years later.

'What's wrong?' asked Daisy, appearing next to me and looking at me strangely. 'You've gone a funny pink colour.'

Why would Aidan be here, in this luxurious but slightly stuffy hotel in Florence? This definitely wouldn't be his scene: he was all about the quirky boutique hotels, the ones with graffiti on the walls or secret basement Saki bars.

'Um, nothing,' I replied, willing myself to act normal. 'Bit hot after our walk, that's all. After you,' I said, ushering Daisy towards the restaurant.

I dared to look back over my shoulder as I fell into step beside her. The man at the desk was upright again now; the receptionist was handing him a key card. I strained to hear what he was saying, to see if I recognised his voice, but the pianist had started up again and the only thing I could hear were the opening bars of Beethoven's *Moonlight Sonata*. Of all things! I'd heard that played live once before, on an evening I'd tried hard to forget all about.

Nick and Sophia were exactly where we'd left them. A little merrier, perhaps; a little louder. Clearly the most expensive champagne had gone down well. I pulled myself together. There was nothing to be concerned about. This man's hair was definitely a tiny bit lighter than Aidan's had been. I racked the recesses of my brain, trying to picture him, which was the exact opposite of what I'd tried to do for the last two years. It had been easier to pretend that we'd never met, that I didn't know how good he smelled, or what he sounded like when he laughed, or what his favourite food was (pizza, always a plain margherita). The man at the desk was a similar height, I thought, but leaner. And I didn't remember Aidan owning a single designer top, not when I'd known him. No, I was imagining things, and what I really needed to be doing was concentrating on impressing Nick's family, on getting to know them, not on dredging up stuff from the past.

I put the Aidan lookalike to the back of my mind and followed Daisy into the restaurant.

Chapter Three

After a few minutes of small talk in the restaurant, I'd been able to escape and had finally had a chance to crash in our room for the last couple of hours. It was beautifully designed, with the sort of romantic, opulent furnishings and unbelievably soft and inviting bedding you'd expect from a hotel that cost over FIVE HUNDRED POUNDS A NIGHT!! The sky had turned a dramatic dusky blue, and when I looked out of the window, the cobbled square below was bathed in the most enticing, cosy, warm glow, and peeping out from behind the rooftops was the ever-impressive Duomo.

I felt bad even thinking it, because I knew how much Nick's family meant to him, but I wished it could just be me and Nick tonight, on our way out to dinner alone. That way, I'd be free to gorge on pasta and red wine without worrying about whether or not I was making a good impression/ saying the right thing. I was still holding on to the fact that everything would be all right. That once we'd all got to know each other, I'd have the loving, welcoming, fun second family I'd daydreamed about on the (long) train journey out here. Perhaps we'd just got off on the wrong foot.

'Ready to go down in five?' asked Nick, appearing in the bathroom doorway in a puff of steam, a pristine white towel wrapped around his waist.

He might have been ten years older than I was, but he was also ten times fitter, not least because he forked out a fortune on his gym membership and twice-weekly personal training sessions. His hair was longer when it was wet, licking his shoulders in golden clumps. Toddler's hair, I sometimes thought, but of course never said. I remembered Aidan's dark hair and his buzz cut, which I used to tease him about. My friend Lou referred to him as Army Boy and I told him this once and he'd taken it as a compliment.

I pushed the thought out of my head, going closer to the mirror to apply my mascara. I refused to be thrown off course by some random guy down in the lobby who probably looked nothing like Aidan close up. My eyes were playing tricks on me, that was all. Before today, I'd very successfully relegated Aidan to the depths of my mind, with only the tiniest details filtering through when I was least expecting it. Like the memory of the first time I'd seen him, on the shores of Loch Lomond, staggering about in his wetsuit. And, funnily enough, the last time I'd seen him, when he'd kissed me goodbye that morning, his hair smelling of his lemon shampoo, his laptop bag slung over his shoulder. And the point at which I realised he'd gone, really gone, from my life as suddenly as he'd appeared in it. I thought that deep down I still hated him for the way things had ended, but it wasn't healthy to hold grudges, was it, so I barely admitted it to myself, let alone anyone else.

'So, come on then, spill. What did your parents think of me?' I asked Nick, lining my lips with a soft cerise pencil and applying a lipstick in my favourite raspberry shade. I pressed my lips together, sealing the colour on. See? I could do well-groomed, too, if I tried. My strapless dress might be Primark rather than Prada, and instead of real gemstones I was wearing fuchsia pink earrings that looked like Christmas baubles (in a good way), but I didn't *mind* what I saw in the mirror. I smoothed down my dress, turning to one side and then the other, sucking my stomach in. 'Tell me exactly what your mum said, word for word,' I said, trying not to sound too needy but desperately feeling as though I wanted some reassurance that they didn't despise me at first sight. Perhaps they just *seemed* judgemental – it could be a hang-up from my past, and possibly I had a bit of an inferiority complex about it. They might be very chilled and really nice and I was just projecting this whole stuck-up vibe onto them when actually they were anything but.

Nick came up behind me and slid his hands around my waist. 'Mum loved you,' he whispered in my ear. 'They all did.'

I looked at his reflection in the mirror. He couldn't quite meet my eye.

'You can tell me the truth, you know,' I said, reaching out behind me to ruffle his hair. 'I'm a big girl, I can take it.' Even as I said this I felt my heart drop slightly.

He moved his hands away and started getting dressed. I watched him pull on his boxers, struggling to slide them over his still-damp skin. He hadn't actually told me anything. I thought I wanted details, but I was beginning to think that they weren't going to be what I wanted to hear.

'Tell me, then.'

'It's fine, Mads. They like you, OK?' he said, plucking his shirt off its hanger.

I bit my lip, spritzing on some perfume. I didn't believe him. It was sweet of him to try to protect me, in a way, but I also thought that we should be able to be honest with each other if we were planning on spending the rest of our lives together. I needed to know what I was dealing with. He couldn't expect me to go into tonight like a lamb to the slaughter, having no idea what – if anything – I'd done wrong. Surely he could see that.

I picked up my hairbrush, running it through my long, naturally curly hair (which I always, without fail, straightened), pushing through the painful snags and then tidying up my fringe. I was glad, now, that I'd treated myself to an expensive blow dry before we'd left London. Somehow, in my gut, I must have known that the women in Nick's family would have bouncy, expensive hair.

'I get the feeling I wasn't what they were expecting, that's all,' I said, pushing the point a little.

I was making Nick uncomfortable, I could tell, but then also I thought: *welcome to my world.*

Nick coughed. 'Well, I'd told them lots about you, so there was ... nothing that would have come as a surprise.'

'Right,' I said.

'And, um, they thought you were very ... pretty,' he added.

I rolled my eyes to myself. I reckoned I knew what that meant: that they thought I was pretty, considering ...

I took a deep breath, trying to push the negative thoughts down. They were coming thick and fast now, but since I had to sit down with these people for a three-course meal this evening, maybe I should at least try to hold it together.

'So what's your mum into? We must have something in common,' I said hopefully, slipping on my one and only pair of heels.

There, I thought, looking at myself. *Much better than earlier.*

Tonight was a chance for a new start. I was going to walk into the restaurant with my head held high, feeling good about myself and ready to face the Leveson-Gower family. Yep, that was Nick's surname, and soon to be mine. My dad had cracked up when I'd told him. Well, after he'd got over the fact that Nick hadn't asked his permission for my hand in

34

marriage, that was. He'd been quite hurt, actually. When I'd mentioned it to Nick, he'd been mortified. He said that he knew I had a difficult relationship with my dad and that he thought I wouldn't like him seeking my father's permission. And it was hard to explain: that although we clashed and we didn't really understand each other, I still loved him, and it felt like asking my dad would have been the right thing to do. Nick had tried to make amends by taking all of us (well, my dad's side of the family) out for a meal to celebrate and it was nice enough, but the damage had already been done as far as my dad was concerned.

'She plays a lot of golf?' said Nick.

I laughed. Although the clubhouse scene sounded fun.

'Horses?' he offered.

'I mean, they're beautiful, but I've never ridden one, or anything.'

'*The Times* crossword?' suggested Nick, hopefully.

Why did it have to be *The Times*?

'I'm more of a *Grazia* girl. Anyway, I don't think I could organically start a conversation about crosswords.'

Nick picked up his keys. 'Look, sweetie, just be yourself, OK? They'll grow to love you.'

'Aha!' I said. 'I knew it! You said *grow* to love me.'

Nick kissed me to shut me up, a technique I'd noticed he used often and sometimes I didn't mind, but tonight I did.

'Stop being so defensive, Maddie. Everything's fine. And you look beautiful and I am very proud to call you my fiancée and that is all you need to know.'

He planted another kiss on my forehead and I felt a miniscule amount better. So what if his family were caught up in their own self-importance? Worst-case scenario, once I'd got through this trip, I'd barely have to see them, anyway, if we didn't become as close as I'd hoped. They lived miles away in Gloucestershire, hence I'd managed to avoid meeting them at all thus far. It was only after we'd got engaged that we'd both thought it would be a good idea. And, I realised, thinking about it now, that was only four weeks ago – this trip must have been planned months in advance. I wondered, now, if Nick had been planning to come on his own. And whether Sophia had been expecting him to come alone, and whether she might have felt put out, having my appearance sprung on her like this. I supposed it was just as awkward for her as it was for me.

I picked up my clutch bag and followed Nick out of the room, wishing the butterflies in my stomach would settle. Touching my hair, I prayed that it stayed as straight and sleek as it had been last time I'd looked in the mirror but also knowing that it wouldn't.

Once I'd had a glass or two of wine I'd be able to relax and enjoy myself, I was sure of it. After all, this was supposed to be a celebration – if we kept the conversation light and focused on Rosamund and Peter, it would be fine. I was overthinking things and I knew it.

The lift doors pinged open on the ground floor and we got out and crossed the lobby, me wobbling a little in my heels because of the carpet. I almost wanted to slip off my shoes and walk barefoot on it, to feel my feet sinking into the pile, but I didn't suppose that would be the done thing and it definitely wouldn't help me win over the family. Subdued classical music was being piped out through strategically placed speakers and the open fire in the bar area had been lit, even though it was relatively warm outside last time I'd checked. Perhaps the temperature dropped in the evenings. A couple were sitting next to the flames nursing glasses of wine and talking softly to each other. His hand was on her knee; her ankle was wrapped around his. If we'd been here on our own, Nick and I could have done the same thing. Although, saying that, since we'd moved in together eighteen months ago, we'd been going out less and less for drinks and dinner, and we hadn't been on anything resembling a date since we'd got back from Paris. Lou, who had married her husband Will a few years ago, had warned me about this. She said it was important to keep that spark going, but when I tried to arrange something romantic, Nick cried off nine times out of ten citing work issues. I didn't suppose you got to management level in a huge company like Sky by doing nine-to-five hours, so this was the pay-off. It was how I'd ended up living in his three-bedroom apartment in St John's Wood and why I had to fight to pay any rent at all because he said he didn't need me to (but I wanted to, because I didn't want to feel like some sort of kept woman – I had a career, too, and had always paid my own way). If it wasn't work, it was something with Daisy. He was always on the phone to Sophia – I heard him talking to her in hushed whispers, calming her down. Although Nick never enlightened me, and I was never sure whether to ask or not, it seemed as though Sophia was finding it hard to deal with having a teenager at home with her all the time, and I didn't get the impression that Nick wanted to rock the boat (or worse, have Sophia insist that Daisy live with him), and so he would listen sympathetically and reassure her that she was an amazing mother. I felt for Daisy, actually. I knew what it was like when your parents split up and you felt like you didn't belong anywhere and that neither of them really wanted you around anymore.

We turned the corner and entered the restaurant, which looked beautiful this evening with candles flickering on every available surface and immaculately dressed waiters swanning around with plates of exquisite-looking food. I was determined to try something different tonight, to be adventurous. Maybe I'd have a dish from the specials board, if I could decipher what any of them actually were. Anyway, I was going to have to get out of my comfort zone this evening because I was pretty sure that my Italian go-to, spaghetti carbonara, would not be on the menu. I'd caught sight of it earlier and there was a definite fine dining vibe.

I spotted Rosamund immediately, at a table by the window. She kind of shimmered, which I thought was probably to do with the way her diamond earrings reflected the light. She was dazzling in red, her hair even bigger and more bouffant than it had been earlier. I had to admit, she looked magnificent.

I took a deep breath. I'd got this. It was just Nick's mum, nothing bad was going to happen.

'OK?' said Nick, taking my hand.

He could obviously sense that I was apprehensive, and giving him the third degree upstairs probably hadn't helped.

'Think so,' I said, slotting my fingers between his.

I'd be all right as long as I stuck with him. In a few hours, it would all be over and we'd be back in our room and then tomorrow morning I'd be able to do that *Room with a View* thing with the window.

It was as we dropped into single file to squeeze between two tables that I saw him. Face-on, so there was no mistaking it. Sitting alone at a table to the right, looking as shocked as I was, was Aidan.

I squeezed Nick's hand tighter, feeling light-headed, suddenly, as though my body had disconnected from my brain. It had been him, I hadn't been going mad. And there he was now, staring at me with those big eyes and that perfect, perfect face. Anger surged up inside me and I felt physically sick. Trust him to show up now, after two years of radio silence, just as I was ready to move on properly. I hated him in that moment.

I snapped my head away, forcing myself to look at Rosamund and her diamonds, to smile and to think about what was important: Nick and his family and the life we were about to start together. Not Aidan and his stupid, broken promises.

Chapter Four

We had to go through the rigmarole of air kisses and hugs again – well, Nick did, I didn't. Only Sophia half-heartedly brushed her ruby-red lips across my cheek; to everyone else, I might as well have not existed as they all fawned over Nick, stroking his lapels, fussing to make sure he was seated in prime position opposite Rosamund and next to – of all people – Sophia.

And meanwhile all I could think about was Aidan. It took all my strength not to turn around and look at him. I wanted to know if he was feeling as terrible as I was. I doubted it; if he'd cared about me at all, he wouldn't have done what he did, and a long time had passed since then. Other than a brief moment of surprise, I didn't imagine that seeing me would have any impact on him whatsoever. His annoyingly perfect cheekbones were imprinted in my mind's eye, like when you looked at the sun by mistake and then you could see it for ages afterwards. He still had that tough-guy-meets-maths-nerd vibe. For some reason, I'd noticed his long fingers, wrapped around his glass; the sexy, just-enough stubble.

'Sit down, darling,' said Nick, pulling my chair out for me.

I swallowed hard. Nick was irritating me, which wasn't fair, but I kept wondering why he'd suddenly become all affected, calling me 'darling' when it was usually sweetie (which, OK, wasn't great either, but then I wasn't big on terms of endearment). Pulling my chair out for me, like Aidan used to, when Nick had never done that before in his life. All I wanted was to go back to my room and be quiet and think. Maybe I could feign a headache.

I sat down, all self-conscious, feeling like I was going to miss the seat completely and crash to the floor. That would have pleased Rosamund. And my mortification in front of Aidan would have been complete.

'How was your walk in Florence earlier?' asked Rosamund, smiling tightly at me. 'I hear you had gelato. How lovely.'

'It was,' I said, practically blinded by the dazzle from her earrings. 'Daisy's cherry flavour looked particularly good.'

I wondered what Aidan thought of these people I was with; of Nick, whose hand I'd been holding. He could hardly miss us, what with Sophia guffawing at something Nick had said and Rosamund, who might as well have had chandeliers hanging from her earlobes. I repeated a mantra in my mind: *Do not think about Aidan. Do not think about Aidan. Do not think about Aidan and how much he hurt you or, at least, not until later.* I would give myself permission to think about him for an hour, and no more, when Nick was asleep and I was lying there in the moonlight, and then I would never think about him again.

Daisy, who was on the other side of me, was slouched down in her seat, sucking manically on a straw. She looked as delighted to be there as I was.

I gathered all my resolve and ploughed on.

'We saw the Galleria dell'Accademia, didn't we, Daisy, but the queue was huge? We didn't bother waiting.' I thought if I kept talking, it would stop this desire I had to look over my shoulder.

'Oh, you should have gone in!' exclaimed Rosamund, too

loudly. She sounded quite put out. 'If this is your first time in Florence, you absolutely must see *David*. Mustn't she, Peter?'

Peter poured himself a glass of wine – not his first, by the looks of it. 'It's overhyped if you ask me.'

'I thought that might be the case,' I agreed, picking up the wine list.

Rosamund made a clacking sound. 'That's easy for you to say when you've seen it three or four times. But poor Maddie has never even been to Italy.'

Poor Maddie?

'She has been to Italy,' said Daisy, making a gurgling sound with her straw as she foraged around for more liquid at the bottom of the glass 'She said earlier.'

I glanced sideways at her. Was she sticking up for me?

'Although it's true, I do tend to travel further afield,' I said, catching the waiter's eye as he put a basket of bread on the table. 'Could I please order a glass of, um ...'

I should have looked at the wine menu beforehand. Now what the fuck was I going to order, since I couldn't pronounce a single one of the pretentious-sounding wines on here? I scanned up and down the list, the words blurring in front of my eyes as I began to panic.

'This one, please,' I said, pointing at random. 'Large glass.'

'I'll have the same,' said Nick to the waiter. 'I trust your judgement implicitly,' he said, rubbing my knee under the table.

'Which wine did you go for, Maddie?' asked Sophia sweetly, leaning forward so that she could catch my eye.

I didn't know if I was being paranoid, but it felt like she'd asked me on purpose because she knew that wine wasn't my thing and she wanted to make me look stupid.

'The, um ...' I said, desperately scrabbling around for the

name of an Italian wine. Any Italian wine. 'Montepulciano,' I replied with conviction, even though there was very a good chance it had not been that at all.

'Oh I didn't see that on the menu,' said Sophia, flinging it open.

Thankfully, Rosamund distracted her by asking her which treatment she was planning to book at the spa for the following afternoon.

I half-listened in and eagerly kept an eye out for my wine. After a bit, my mind began to wander again – could I risk a quick look over my shoulder? I could almost feel Aidan's eyes on the back of my neck. He used to have this intense way of looking at me, as though he was trying to see right inside my head. We'd had this instant connection, the kind I'd never had with anyone else – from the moment we'd met, I'd felt as though I could tell him anything. *Almost* anything. I'd held some stuff back, of course I had, which I was glad about now, but I thought I'd probably showed him more of who I really was in the month we were together than I had revealed to Nick in two years. Sometimes, with Nick, I sort of edited myself, because I knew he wouldn't get it and I couldn't be bothered to explain. Aidan always got it.

'So, Maddie,' said Sophia from the other end of the table. 'Tell us about yourself. What do you do?'

I cleared my throat, pushing all thoughts of Aidan from my mind. This was my chance to show them that I was an equal for their doted-on son/father/ex. Somebody to be respected, not the pathetic pushover I thought I was probably currently coming across as.

'I'm in TV,' I said, smiling brightly around the table. 'An assistant producer on a travel show.'

There, that didn't sound bad. Lots of people wanted to work in TV, didn't they, as Tim was forever telling me?

'Interesting,' piped up Peter, who so far hadn't said more than a few words to me and instead had seemed much more interested in the contents of his glass. I noticed that the ice bucket had conveniently been placed just behind his left shoulder. 'What do you do then, write scripts?'

I nodded. 'Yes, there's a lot of that. Then there's researching locations, coming up with interesting new ways to present them to the audience. Making sure they've got all the legal jargon right. And I get to travel a lot, which is nice.'

'I hadn't realised you had such an exciting job,' said Rosamund. 'Nick hadn't mentioned it.'

Yes! Finally I was getting somewhere. She definitely seemed impressed.

'I've told you several times, Mummy. Maddie works at Holiday Shop, remember?'

I kicked his ankle. Honestly, what had he gone and said that for? Had I really needed to spell it out to him that I wanted to make my job sound more high-profile and alluring than it actually was? These people clearly wouldn't watch Holiday Shop if it was the last channel on earth.

'Ah ...' said Rosamund, smirking. 'I do remember now. That package holiday thing, isn't it? On one of those funny cable channels?'

Just then, the waiter brought our wine and I whipped it up as soon as he'd laid it down on the table, taking three large, syrupy gulps. Montepulciano or not, wine had never tasted better.

'That's right,' I said to Rosamund. 'It's actually very popular – we get excellent viewing figures, especially at peak daytime hours.'

'All those housewives,' remarked Peter. 'With nothing better to do than watch television, I suppose.'

'That's true, we do sell a lot of family-oriented holidays,' I said, aware that this was all going down like a lead balloon. 'So you'll get mums at home with their little ones watching, that sort of thing.'

Sophie snorted.

'You weren't one of those, were you, Mum?' piped up Daisy.

'One of what, darling?' said Sophie with the snippy undertone I'd noticed she adopted every time she spoke to her daughter.

'A stay-at-home mum,' replied Daisy, plonking her empty glass down on the table.

I looked at her out of the corner of my eye, wondering whether Daisy and I could actually be comrades in this. She seemed to dislike her family as much as I was starting to. Which perhaps wasn't fair of me, since I'd known them for all of an afternoon. But I was very good at picking up on 'vibes'. Lou teased me about this wild claim of mine, said it was paranoia, not vibes, but I disagreed: if somebody didn't like me (which had happened relatively frequently over the years, for reasons I still couldn't explain), it was very obvious to me, no matter how well they tried to cover it up. And my overwhelming feeling about the Leveson-Gowers was that they weren't exactly welcoming me into their family with open arms.

The thing was, though, I was marrying Nick – I was kind of going to be stuck with them, wasn't I? And so, to make things easier all round, I was going to have to pull out all the stops and find a connection. I'd treat it like work, perhaps – even if it took years, I could just keep chipping away at it, doing my best. Which took focus and commitment – both of which were threatened by the arrival of Aidan, who annoyingly had dominated almost every single thought I'd had since the moment I'd walked into the restaurant. I could picture him sitting there at his table for one, metres away, could imagine his mind whirring with all the things he wanted to say, or, more likely, didn't know how to say. Like why he'd stopped calling. Why he'd left me out of the blue. How the heady feeling that we were falling for each other – not just me for him, but him for me – must have been a figment of my imagination.

'Some of us had actual careers to pursue, Daisy,' said Sophia. 'It's a given, is it, that women will give up everything they've worked towards just because they have a baby? That they can't possibly expect to have both?'

'Quite right, Sophia,' said Rosamund. 'You tell them.'

'Who's them?' asked Peter. 'I hope you're not talking about us men. I'm all for women getting back in to the workplace.'

Sure you are, I thought. I bet he couldn't possibly do without his secretary.

'And you're a wonderful mother, Sophia, isn't she Nick?' simpered Rosamund.

What was it with those two?

Nick nodded obediently. 'Of course she is.'

'Do you think you two will have children?' asked Sophia, directing the question at me rather than Nick. She was staring at me so hard that I felt as though I had lasers drilling into me.

My heart sank. How to answer? Because the truth was, I still wasn't sure if that was what I wanted. I'd thought something might click once I turned thirty, like I'd suddenly start feeling broody, or being interested in other people's kids, or not minding when I got seated behind a baby on a flight and finding it cute rather than irritating. But I was thirty-one now and that hadn't happened and what if it never did?

'We'll see,' said Nick, jumping in to rescue me. 'Plenty of time.'

I didn't have to make any decisions yet, did I? I had to get my head around the idea of marriage first, and once I'd successfully got through that (although I was already dreading the coming together of Nick's family and my mum and dad), then I'd give children some serious thought.

'Hmmmn,' said Sophia. 'You mustn't leave it too long, Maddie. So many friends of mine made that mistake and now they're struggling down the IVF route.'

She was older than me – in her early forties – so possibly the fact that I was younger was riling her.

I looked over my shoulder before I could stop myself. Aidan was still at his table, looking wistfully into his glass as though he had the problems of the world on his shoulders. He'd always had that look about him, I remembered that was one of the first things I'd noticed. He gave the impression that his mind was full, that he was considering something, planning something, trying to work something out. I wondered what he was thinking about right now. And then he looked up and caught my eye and I sort of knew.

Because I was startled, I think, I let myself hold his gaze for a second before whipping my head round so fast I gave myself neck ache. I rubbed at it with the palm of my hand, trying desperately to tune in to a conversation about which starter we were all having. Somebody was going for squid; somebody else for the consommé.

The menu, I'd look at the menu, that would buy me some time, give me a moment to get my head together. My cheeks felt flushed and my heart was racing, and even though I felt as though my head was going to explode, I hoped it wouldn't be obvious to anyone else, particularly Nick, because how would I even begin to explain?

And so I focused hard on the words swimming in front of me with Aidan's face annoyingly stamped in my mind's eye.

Loch Lomond, Scotland

Two Years Earlier

Lodging the clipboard with our running order on it under one arm, I used my free hand to hold the boom above Ruthie's head while Lou checked out how the shot looked on camera.

'Take a step to your right, please, Ruthie,' called Lou.

Ruthie, who had the same arsey and slightly superior attitude as every other presenter I'd ever worked with, rolled her eyes and reluctantly did what had been asked of her. The problem was, she wanted to be working on *Good Morning Britain* or *Loose Women* or another high-profile show where you became a household name instead of being our (admittedly lead) presenter on Holiday Shop, a cable channel with barely any budget but bizarrely high viewing figures.

'So we want to pan across the Loch, nice and slow, and then pause on Ruthie so she can deliver her line,' said Tim, our producer/director/wanker of a boss.

'It would be great to get that pretty pier in shot,' I suggested. 'If you start a little bit wider, Lou, we might just see it.'

Tim looked at me.

'We'll stick with my original instruction, thank you, Maddie,' he said, dismissing my suggestion as always. 'And ... action!'

My arm began to ache as I held the boom as still as I could over Ruthie's head, straining to look in the monitor to make sure it wasn't in shot. This wasn't strictly my job, but seeing as the company were too tight to send a sound engineer with us, the assistant producer – me, in this instance – had to step in and do whatever was needed. So far, I'd written scripts, fetched coffees and lunch (a task I thought I'd left behind when I'd been promoted from runner) and touched up Ruthie's make-up (with her barking orders at me non-stop: *No, not like that, here, on the apples of my cheeks! Don't you know how to apply blusher?*). I didn't mind. It got me away from my desk and out of the studio and it was stunning here in Loch Lomond. Really beautiful.

The mid-morning sun, which somehow felt bigger and closer than it ever did in London, was climbing into the sky behind the mountains, enveloping us in a sort of hazy, otherworldly light. I'd like to work here every day, with the gentle waves lapping melodically on to the pebbly beach, and the seagulls swooping over our heads and the calm, subdued chatter of tourists as they took off their socks and shoes and paddled gingerly in the ice-cold water.

'Maddie! I said can you please pin Ruthie's dress at the back? It's too billowy in the wind,' shouted Tim.

'Oh, sure. Sorry,' I said, placing the boom on the ground and getting my wardrobe kit out of my bag – another job that seemed to have fallen to me this time around. Luckily, I'd seen the wardrobe girls working on set enough times to have some grasp of what was needed.

I found a crocodile clip and approached Ruthie, trying to give the impression that I knew what I was doing.

'This is a lovely dress,' I said, pinching the flimsy fabric between my finger and thumb and securing it tentatively between Ruthie's shoulder blades. I walked around to the front

49

to check that it had had the desired effect and wasn't causing any gaping around the bust area, which Ruthie would never have forgiven me for. Rumour was she'd had a boob job a couple of years earlier. I couldn't possibly speculate (OK, it was pretty obvious she had, but each to their own and all that).

'It's silk, so you'd better not ruin it,' she warned.

Seriously, it wouldn't hurt her to be nice once in a while. I wondered if she realised that nobody at Holiday Shop could stand her. Personally, I couldn't deal with knowing everyone was slagging me off behind my back, although, saying that, I sometimes thought they might be anyway. Lou's mantra was that not everyone you meet in life is going to like you, but I couldn't see why not. If I made an effort to be nice to everyone all the time and tried my best to make their lives easier, then what would there be not to like? The only thing was, it was kind of exhausting and also sometimes I got it wrong and instead of pleasing someone, I actually massively pissed them off. Occasionally (very occasionally), I was tempted to do exactly what *I* wanted to do and to hell with the consequences.

'Ready to go again?' yelled Tim, pretending to scribble very important notes on the script that he should have written but which he actually got me to do on the train journey up. 'It'll be good practice,' he'd insisted.

'For what?' I'd asked, annoyed because I'd wanted to spend the journey reading and staring out of the window like everyone else.

'For when you're a producer,' he'd said, knowing that I'd have no choice but to comply after that.

It was hardly a secret that I was keen to move up to a producer role – within the next twelve months, hopefully.

'Yeah, about that ...' I'd said, thinking this was as good

a time as any to broach the subject of a promotion. After all, we were stuck on a train for the next four hours, he was basically a captive audience.

'Just keep doing what you're doing,' he'd replied, winking at me smugly. 'It'll happen when the time is right.'

There were rumours that one of the producers was leaving to go to the biggest name in home shopping, QVC, which meant that, there might be a chance for me to take the next step up in my television career. I was good enough, I knew I was, and although I only had a year's experience as an assistant producer under my belt, I knew the job inside out already. But still ... as I had quickly worked out, it sometimes wasn't what you knew, it was who you schmoozed with. Most of the workforce of Holiday Shop seemed to have done a media degree at East Sussex and there was a sort of cliquey alumni network, a collection of people who vaguely knew each other from getting off their faces on Brighton Beach. I'd noticed this lot seemed to get promoted at any given opportunity.

'Right, Ruthie, let's go again, please. That's much better with the dress. And ... action!' yelled Tim.

I stretched out my arm, holding the boom, doing my bit, but then my eyes wandered to a small group further along the beach who looked like they were getting ready to go diving. One guy was struggling to get his wetsuit on and was balancing precariously on one leg while he tried to drag skin-tight neoprene over the other calf. He suddenly lunged dramatically to one side, only just saving himself by hopping wildly about in all directions while he tried to regain his balance. It was actually quite impressive. When he finally put two feet on the ground and wriggled into his wetsuit so that it was over his legs and flopping around his waist, he glanced over in my direction, catching my eye. I grinned at him, which was probably very childish of me, but there was no denying that it had been comical to watch. Luckily, he appeared to see the funny side and laughed too, throwing his hands out in a *what can I say?* gesture. He had sparkly eyes, I noticed them even from this distance, and three-day old stubble and dark brown hair styled like an actor playing a soldier on TV. Perhaps he was actually in the military – he looked fit enough, and he was clearly into extreme sports. Although technically I wasn't sure you'd call diving in a Scottish lake extreme, but it felt like it was to me, considering I was more of a once-a-month Zumba class type of person.

'Cut!' shouted Tim, bringing me sharply back to reality.

I glanced around, hoping nobody had noticed that I'd drifted off for a second there. This wasn't like me at all, I was usually so involved in doing my best work and trying to impress people that nothing else mattered. But something kept drawing me back to the guy in the wetsuit. He had his arms in it now and when he turned to talk to the instructor, I could see it gaping at the back, revealing a smooth flash of skin with the kind of light tan I thought meant he probably spent a lot of time outside in the elements. I imagined walking over to him, putting one hand on the very base of his spine and zipping his wetsuit up for him.

I shook myself out of my reverie; God, what was wrong with me? I was here on a job, not to ogle very hot men I knew nothing about and who were simply minding their own business on a beach.

'Looking fabulous, Ruthie!' shrieked Tim.

A group of Japanese tourists, who were quietly and sedately taking photographs of the lake, looked over, startled, no doubt, by Tim's booming voice. Why did he have to be so loud? We were drawing enough attention to ourselves as it was, what with the camera and Ruthie caked in make-up and dressed up to the nines in her Diane von Furstenberg wrap dress. She had a whole selection of them, each in a different chic but verging on gaudy pattern. They looked great on her because she was tall and did spinning classes five times a week and pushed salads around her plate, but I suspected they would have looked terrible on me. I was all about the skinny jeans and jumper combo. My half-sisters said I was obsessed with oversized knitwear, and I held my hands up: I was.

'Maddie, can you come and retouch my make-up?' whined Ruthie.

'Be right there,' I said, scrabbling in my bag for my make-up kit.

There were parts of working in TV I loved, but doing six people's jobs at once was not one of them.

I reapplied some powder to Ruthie's already completely matte face – for a woman in her forties, she had great skin, probably due to the two hundred pound a pop 'vampire facials' she was always banging on about. Mind you, she was also always going on about how perfect my skin was, with the sense being that she was slightly annoyed about it. *I'll be thirty next year, it'll go downhill then*, I always said to make her feel better, but secretly I hoped it wouldn't. My dad still look much younger than fifty-two, and his sisters – my aunties, who were in St Lucia – all had the most amazing smooth, brown, glowing skin with barely any wrinkles. Then again, they did have tropical fruits on tap, lots of fresh air and year-round good weather – I wasn't sure London pollution levels were conducive to ageing quite that well.

'Need any help?' I asked Lou, who was looking back at the footage she'd just shot.

'Sure. What do you think of this?' she asked, moving aside so that I could see the monitor.

Lou was a brilliant camera operator and she'd framed the shot beautifully, making Loch Lomond look all enticing and gorgeous, and managing to make the sky look wispy and ethereal. If I squinted, I could almost be in Vietnam, not Scotland.

'Lovely,' I said. 'You've even got sparkles on the water.'

'Have I?' she said. 'Let's see.'

'What's going on here, ladies?' asked Tim, appearing behind me. 'I think I should be the one checking the footage, don't you?'

'Go for it,' I said, stepping aside and giving him a tight smile.

I had another little nose at the diving group while Tim was otherwise engaged. They were all kitted out now and the instructor had the tanks out. Wetsuit guy had his back to me, but I could spot him easily – he was several inches taller than everyone else for a start. He had his hands on his hips and was listening intently to the instructions being given.

'It's not grabbing me,' said Tim, crossing his arms and pouting in the style of a teenager having a tantrum. 'This place is deathly boring and it shows on camera. I mean, there's no one around, is there? No atmosphere and no sun. How come everyone else gets to go to the Canary Islands and I get stuck here? How the fuck am I supposed to make this bleak, miserable landscape look in any way exciting?'

'It's not bleak and miserable,' I protested.

'It is,' moaned Ruthie.

'It's so peaceful, though,' said Lou. 'And just smell that air – no car fumes, just oxygen with a hint of heather. I reckon our viewers would love it here.'

'But there's nothing to do!' complained Tim. 'We need to demonstrate that there's more to Scotland than lakeside walks and whisky.'

'I don't see what's wrong with either of those two things,' I said.

Tim instantly threw me daggers.

'There's tons of other stuff to do,' I carried on, determined to get my point across. 'Glasgow's only a half-hour drive away, we could go and shoot some footage there, maybe, if we can fit it in on our last day. Or what about ...' I desperately searched around for inspiration. There had to be something that would help Tim see Loch Lomond in a more positive light. 'Water sports!' I blurted out, catching Wetsuit Guy's eye again.

He was looking over his shoulder at me with a sort of bemused look on his face, probably wondering why there were loads of loud people with English accents causing a commotion on the beach. I thought he was probably Scottish – he had that sort of tall, rugged stature, a kind of *Braveheart* vibe. And I wasn't really in to men in kilts, but he looked like somebody who, if he had to wear one, could probably pull it off.

Right, I needed to stop daydreaming about Wetsuit Guy in a kilt and get back on task.

'Look!' I said to Tim, hoping to drum up some enthusiasm. 'There's some diving or something going on over there. And I saw a sign about kayaking trips. And then at the hotel they've got leaflets about paddleboarding. We could make it very visual, get Ruthie out on the lake doing waterskiing or something.'

'I beg your pardon?' said Ruthie, looking repulsed.

On second thoughts, I couldn't imagine Ruthie doing anything that would involve getting a speck of water on her bouffant, dyed-blonde hair which never seemed to move, no matter the weather.

'It could work ...' said Tim, desperately trying not to look impressed.

On the odd occasion he gave me credit for something, I could tell it pained him.

He clicked his fingers, making sure he had everyone's full attention. 'Guys, I've had a great idea for this afternoon. Instead of yet more boring beach shots, we are going to get out on the water to do some ... activities.'

He'd had a brilliant idea?

Lou raised her eyebrows at me.

'No way,' said Ruthie. 'I'm not doing it. Water sports are not in my contract.'

'Oh come on, Ruthie,' trilled Tim, doing his best impression of being a nice person. 'Don't be like that. We can make this work, together, as a team. We'll be right there with you, supporting you, making sure you look and sound as fabulous as ever.'

Ruthie looked dubious. 'How am I going to look fabulous if I'm soaked through and wearing goggles and flippers?'

'I don't think we need to go quite that far,' said Tim, faltering.

I tried to think – we needed Ruthie to be behind this, otherwise there would be no point doing it. She had a sour face at the best of times, and we wanted to show our viewers what a good time she was having, not leave them feeling as though they'd just watched her being sentenced to life imprisonment.

'Think of it this way, Ruthie: it would look great on your showreel,' I said, coming at it from a different angle, i.e. one that would benefit Ruthie. 'Imagine this: a fun, full-of-energy segment that will prove to those big bosses over at ITV that you're not simply a static presenter who stands there looking beautiful, but that you're a real, go-getting, risk-taking reporter who will do anything, *anything*, for the best shot.'

Lou looked at me, clearly impressed.

'Hmmn,' said Ruthie, sounding more interested. 'You've got a point, actually. My showreel is a bit samey.'

'There you go,' I said. 'What about kayaking? That way, you can stay perfectly dry, and we don't need to go too far from the shore, just far enough out so that it looks like you're in the middle of the loch. Would that work, Lou?'

'Absolutely,' she replied, joining in with the pep talk. 'You probably wouldn't have to go out much further than the end of the pier.'

Ruthie sighed, touching her hair with delicate, manicured fingers. 'If you think you can get some nice shots out of it, then why not? But I don't want to be out on the water for very long. Isn't there supposed to be a monster out there?'

I smiled kindly at her. 'That's Loch Ness, Ruthie. We're in Loch Lomond.'

'Right, that's settled, then,' said Tim. 'Maddie, can you go and speak to that man over there and tell him that we need to take some kayaks out later today. Talk him into giving them to us for free in exchange for publicity.'

This was the part of the job I hated: the hustle, the asking for favours when I knew they wouldn't be getting anything in return. I just didn't understand how Tim expected these people – who had businesses to run – to disrupt everything, their whole working day, without getting so much as a token payment for their trouble. It wasn't like they'd want to do it for the glory of appearing on the UK's most popular travel channel.

'Er, and what publicity would that be?' I asked.

'Well, his kayaks will be on screen, won't they?'

I bit my lip. 'Yeah, but unless we get the name of his

kayaking school in shot, it's not exactly going to promote it, is it?'

'Fine!' huffed Tim. 'We'll do a shot of his stupid, tatty shack with all the boats inside. And tell him we'll try to get the name above the door in shot, but no promises.'

I looked over at the diving instructor, who I presumed was also the owner. 'I think he's in the middle of something,' I said. 'I can pop back in a bit.'

'You'll have to interrupt him,' said Tim. 'We need to get a schedule in place for this afternoon, there's no time to waste. Come on, Ruthie, let's go and get you warmed up in the bar, shall we?'

Lou tutted as the two of them picked their way up the beach, as though they were allergic to sand. 'Those two are fucking hard work.'

I shook my head. 'Talk about highly strung.'

Lou gave me a look as she started to pack her camera away. 'I've got a bone to pick with you,' she said.

'Another one?'

She smiled at me. 'I'm not that much of a nag, am I?'

'No comment,' I replied.

Lou always meant well and, admittedly, sometimes I needed a little push in the right direction, but she could go on a bit sometimes. We couldn't all be as vocal as she was; in fact, sometimes she could benefit from keeping things in her head and not spouting them out of her mouth before she'd had a chance to think better of it. Her road rage, for example, was off the scale.

'I was just going to say ...' she ventured.

'Here we go,' I said, bracing myself on her tripod.

'That you should stop letting Tim steal your ideas and passing them off as his own. That's how he's got to producer level, by taking other people's stuff and running with it with

58

such assurance that nobody thinks to question it. In fact, I wouldn't be surprised if he'd convinced himself it was actually his idea in the first place.'

I groaned, embarrassed that she'd noticed, even if she was my friend and therefore totally on my side. 'I know. It's just that he said there's a promotion coming up and I—'

'Do you really think he's going to put in a good word for you? Tim? Do something selfless, say nice things about actual other people? No chance,' scoffed Lou.

I'd suspected as much myself but had to keep the faith that when it came to it, Tim would do the right thing. He was my boss after all, the person I worked alongside day in, day out. If somebody was going to give me a glowing reference, it sort of had to be him.

'I need to keep him on side,' I said. 'Just in case.'

Lou zipped up her camera bag, picking it up and putting it over her shoulder.

'Don't sell yourself short, Maddie, that's all I'm saying. You'll never get anywhere in life if you try to please other people all the time at the expense of what you want.'

I watched her walk back towards the hotel. She'd hit a nerve with that comment. I'd been thinking about that a lot lately, how my main motivation for doing almost everything seemed to be to keep other people – Tim, my parents, my step-parents, my friends – happy. And I was terrible at it, because they often seemed irritated by me, despite my best efforts.

I massaged my temples for a few seconds, put my confident face on and switched into work mode to take my mind off all the other stuff. I strode over to the diving instructor at the exact moment he started handing out equipment to his terrified-looking clients. Even Wetsuit Guy looked as though he was having second thoughts.

'Um, hello? Hi?' I said, waving from the sidelines like a soccer mom who wanted to know why her little darling hadn't been picked for the team.

Eventually, the instructor noticed me and came over, all relaxed and weather-beaten. It seemed like a pretty stress-free life running a water sports business and the idea of working for myself instead of a hierarchy of corporate hounds like Tim and the senior management team above him suddenly appealed on many different levels.

'Can I help?' asked the diving instructor in a heavily accented Scottish rumble.

He probably thought I was interested in joining the session. That would be a no.

'I hope so,' I said, holding out my hand and introducing myself. 'I'm Maddie Campbell, assistant producer on Holiday Shop, the discounted travel channel on cable. Not sure if you've ever watched it, or—'

The man shook his head. 'I'm Finlay. What can I do for you? Only, I'm sort of in the middle of something,' he said.

Bloody Tim. I told him now wasn't a good time.

'I can see that, yeah, sorry.'

I could also see Wetsuit Guy looking over with interest. He really was very good-looking close up, with the sort of dreamy pretty-boy face I fell for every single time and then wondered why it all went badly wrong. You'd think I'd learn. Saying that, this guy had something different about him, something more than just a strong jawline and a sweet smile. He looked very earnest, like he had a lot going on inside his head. I bet he was into books or maths or something. A pretty-boy geek with an almost-beard. In any case, it was very attractive, and annoyingly, it was distracting me from what I was actually supposed to be doing. I tried my best to focus on Finlay.

'So, we – my producer and I – were wondering whether it would be possible to do some filming with you this afternoon? We were thinking kayaks? Having our presenter in one doing a few lines of script? Perhaps some shots of a small group of you out on the water?'

I metaphorically crossed my fingers. Tim would go mad if the guy said no, and I'd probably end up trawling around the perimeter of the lake looking for another water sports school because I'd be too scared to go back to the hotel with bad news.

Finlay laughed. 'I feel like a bloody celebrity today. One minute I'm doing an interview for a newspaper down in London and the next I'm being asked to go on national television.'

'Well, I wouldn't exactly call it *national* television,' I said, not wanting to make my proposition sound more exciting than it actually was. I wondered what he meant about the newspaper, but didn't get any further with that thought, because, oh God, what was Wetsuit Guy doing walking in my direction?

'Hello,' he said, smiling at me, lighting up his face and probably mine. 'I'm Aidan, travel reporter at the *Hampstead and Highgate Express*. And you are ...?'

I cleared my throat, shaking his hand and wondering why I was suddenly boiling hot. It was probably the massive roll-necked jumper I'd decided it was a brilliant idea to wear this morning, even though I had a tendency to overheat when I was rushing around working. And when I met super-fit men and they were standing so close to me that I could see the dimple on their left cheek when they smiled and that one eyebrow was ever so slightly higher than the other.

'I'm Maddie, assistant producer on Holiday Shop,' I said,

my voice sounding strange, as though I was listening back to it on a voice note. 'Nice to meet you.'

I looked to Finlay to bring me back to reality. I was here to organise a shoot. I was not here to go all funny while talking to cute men in wetsuits.

'Why don't you and your crew come out with us this afternoon? Aidan here is doing the same,' said Finlay.

'Certainly am,' said Aidan, holding up a notebook. 'I'm doing a story on British sporting holidays,' he explained to me.

He wasn't Scottish, then, judging by his accent. More Home Counties, perhaps.

'Oh, fun!' I said. This was not something I'd normally say. 'Where else have you been?'

He thought about it for a second or two. 'Let's see, what have I got so far … I've done cycling in the Pennines and mountain climbing in Wales. After this, it's surfing in Cornwall.'

'From one end of the country to the other.'

He laughed. 'Are you into your sports, then?'

'Um, does Pilates count?' I joked.

'Right,' said Finlay, 'can I get back to my group and see you later? Say 2 p.m.? You can brief me then on what you need.'

I nodded gratefully. 'That sounds perfect, thank you, Finlay. It'll be me, our camera operator, Lou, our presenter, Ruthie, and our producer, Tim. Ruthie can be a little …'

'Difficult?' suggested Aidan.

I nodded, holding up my thumb and forefinger to indicate that he was right. 'Just a tiny bit.'

'We'll soon have her out on the water,' said Finlay, clearly used to people feeling a bit nervous. 'And tell her she can't be wearing one of her posh dresses,' he added with a wink over his shoulder as he headed back to the diving group.

I looked out at the lake, trying to look all relaxed and as though I wasn't aware of Aidan watching me.

'I'll see you this afternoon, then,' he said.

'Sure,' I replied, keeping it very casual.

I realised that I was going to have to be the one to move and forced myself to put one foot in front of the other. It didn't feel natural, though. Not at all.

'Enjoy your dive,' I called over my shoulder.

He gave me a nervous grimace and joined Finlay and the others and I started the walk back to the hotel, looking over my shoulder about twenty-five times even though I knew that if he caught me, I would look very uncool and slightly desperate.

Chapter Five

I lay in bed with Nick snoring softly next to me. He didn't snore at home because if he did, I'd go as far as to say I would have been reluctant to move in with him. I was a bad sleeper at the best of times, but tossing and turning with someone snorting and snuffling in my ear all night had been next-level torture. I was now in that horrible limbo where I was too exhausted to get up, but not tired enough to actually sleep. I thought it must be morning, although the curtains were so thick, I couldn't tell if it was light outside or not.

I felt around for my phone (noting that even that small act took extreme effort), checking the time: 7.13. Relief. I could legitimately get up instead of lying here thinking about how strange the night before had been. The conversation around the table had gone from fine wines (which I'd strategically stayed out of after my Montepulciano disaster) to Florentine must-sees (I'd tried my hardest to chip in with this one and had even managed to give an interesting fact about the Boboli Gardens that nobody knew because I'd read it in my Rough Guide on the train) to climate change and – the worst – Meghan and Harry. Of course, Rosamund just 'didn't trust' Meghan. Based on what, it wasn't entirely clear (although I could hazard a guess). And then, of course, Peter had said he thought we 'didn't look dissimilar', which he probably thought was a compliment but hadn't felt like one.

Nick stirred next to me.

'What time is it?' he mumbled.

It was the first time he'd woken since his head had hit the pillow at just gone midnight. I envied him the ability to sleep anywhere. He'd managed to sleep through most of the train journey from Paris to Turin too, which had wound me up no end. It was all right for him: he'd practically woken up and we were there! I, on the other hand, had fidgeted around for hours on end, tried and failed to get into a new book and made endless, pointless journeys to the 'buffet car', which was essentially a vending machine full of disappointing sandwiches and Italian biscuits. I must have had at least five cups of weak, black tea, just for something to do.

'Quarter past seven,' I whispered. 'Go back to sleep.'

Yep, not only did Nick sleep like a baby all night, but he loved long, luxurious lie-ins when he got the chance. I did too, sometimes, but not if I had something on my mind. Like Aidan, who had been flashing in and out of my thoughts for hours now. If I was here on my own, I would have left the hotel immediately so that I never had to see him again.

I'd worked hard to stop thinking about him. It had been overwhelming at first, a sort of loss, I supposed, even though we'd only been together for just over a month. Other than Lou, I'd never told anyone how crap I'd felt when he'd left because I knew it sounded ridiculous – how could I have been that upset about a 'relationship' ending after four weeks? And yet, I'd had no control over it – I'd wished and wished that I could just chalk it up to experience; could have told myself that he clearly wasn't the person I thought he was and therefore I'd had a lucky escape. But nothing had worked, not for months. Meeting Nick had helped, but not entirely. And now here was Aidan, throwing a spanner in the works yet again.

I was incensed, if the truth be told. Stupid Aidan and his stupid charming personality and his ridiculously handsome face. With any luck, he'd have bolted overnight, too scared to confront me – and the truth – about what had happened between us and why he'd morphed into a different person overnight.

Nick pulled me into his arms. I tried to relax into them. *You're with Nick now*, I told myself. *You are safe and loved and getting married.*

'How did you think last night went?' he asked softly, stroking his fingers up and down my leg.

'OK,' I said.

This was my chance. I'd been wondering when – if – I should mention Aidan to Nick, and this would be the perfect opportunity to slip it in. A sort of: *the evening was great, but I was kind of thrown by seeing my ex-boyfriend sitting at the table behind us.*

'You were pretty quiet,' said Nick.

'I didn't think I was.' Anyway, what was wrong with being quiet? I hated it when people used that as a veiled insult. Were we all supposed to be guffawing loudmouths like Sophia?

'You weren't letting my mother intimidate you, were you? She's quite a ... strong character.'

That was one way of putting it. And what did that even mean? In my opinion, it was perfectly possible to be a strong woman and to not be rude. To be a strong woman and to not assume your opinions were always right. It seemed like a lame excuse for not caring about upsetting other people.

'She didn't intimidate me,' I said truthfully.

I just didn't think she was very nice, that was all, but I could hardly say that to Nick, could I? My vibes were at play again and let's just say I was picking up on a LOT of negative ones.

I cleared my throat lightly. 'Does Sophia always talk to Daisy like that?'

'Like what?'

'You know ... snippy. Like Daisy can't do or say anything right.'

I was having to tread carefully, but I'd actually found it really uncomfortable to watch. Daisy wasn't the easiest person to be around at times, but that was teenagers for you, wasn't it? And if I could clearly see that she was struggling to find her footing with Sophia, how come Nick couldn't?

'It's not easy being a single mum,' said Nick. 'I only have Daisy every other weekend, so most of it falls to her. And she's not the most patient person.'

Nick had worked his way around so that his fingers were now trailing up the inside of my thigh.

'Did you know she was coming?' I asked, burying my face in the soft, fleshy part of his shoulder.

He was silent for just a few moments too long. He knew.

'It wasn't definite. But then she does business in Florence, sometimes, so it made sense for her to combine the two.'

'Right.'

'Do you mind?'

My instinct was to reassure him. To tell him that it was a little awkward at first, and that she probably felt the same, but that, no, it didn't matter at all. But then I thought about what Lou always said to me about standing up for myself and I decided to tell him how I really felt for once. I'd test the waters. See how it went down.

'I think that, yes, I do mind,' I said.

Silence.

See, this was why I avoided conflict at all costs.

'That she's here, or that I didn't tell you?' asked Nick.

He'd taken his hand off my thigh and had rolled over

67

onto his back with his hands behind his head. I must have really annoyed him. Oh well, I'd started this – there wasn't much I could do about it now.

'Both,' I replied.

Nick sighed. I braced myself for him to flip out.

'You're right, I'm sorry. I should have given you a heads-up that she was going to be here,' he said.

Oh.

'Mum insisted on her coming, if the truth be told. When we separated, Mum was devastated. Sophia had been like a second daughter to her, and they're so similar. Tabitha – my sister – has always been in her own little world. She and mum never really saw eye to eye. But Mum and Sophia ... they're alike. They're into the same things, I suppose.'

'Like what?'

'Oh I don't know. Fashion. Shopping. Interior design. They go to Wimbledon together every year.'

'Don't tell me, Centre Court, front row?' I teased.

'Usually,' he said, without a hint of irony.

Top-priced tickets were clearly a given for Nick's family.

'But, yeah, I should have given you some warning. Can you forgive me?' he asked.

I felt a little sliver of annoyance, but it wasn't worth ruining the day over.

'I already have,' I said, kissing him lightly on the mouth. Then I rolled over and got out of bed. 'I might get up. Go for an early walk.'

I'd spent a lot of time on my own when I was younger and so being in a group felt overwhelming sometimes. It was a running joke with my friends and family that I'd often make an excuse to slope off and have a bit of a recharge. Maybe I'd have a cup of coffee somewhere – I was sure I remembered reading something about the hotel having a roof terrace. It was a bit of a risk, because what if I bumped into Aidan, who was the very last person I wanted to see? He might have changed, of course, but he'd never been able to sleep, either. He'd always been up before me; loved getting out in the fresh air before everyone else.

I eyed the video camera I'd put on the desk. Perhaps I should take it. Much as I didn't feel like working for no money at seven in the morning, if I passed somewhere particularly evocative, it seemed a shame not to capture it on camera.

'Don't leave,' said Nick, mock pathetically.

He grabbed my hand, pretending to refuse to let it go. I laughed lightly, pulling it gently away.

'I can't sleep anyway,' I told him. 'I've been awake for hours already.'

'Are you sure you're OK about this whole Sophia thing?' he asked, turning over and getting comfortable, scrunching into the foetal position.

He was so going to go back to sleep.

'I'm sure,' I said.

I heard his breathing deepen, watched the rise and fall of his body under the duvet. I went over and peeped out of the gap between the curtain and the window, wondering what the weather was like. I imagined April in Italy would be like June in the UK, especially if yesterday was anything to go by, but I supposed you could never be too sure. There were blue skies, though, and the few people out on the street seemed to be wearing long sleeves but no coat. I should be fine in a dress with something over the top. I picked out another Primark special, my favourite, a navy blue and white polka-dot skater dress. Then I rummaged in my (silly, too-small) suitcase and pulled out my sandals. Grabbing a cardigan just in case it was colder than it looked, I left the room, shutting the door gently behind me and then immediately realising I'd left my key inside. Damn. Now I'd have to wake Nick up when I got back – depending on how long I was going to be, he'd probably still be dead to the world. He slept like someone who had no conscience – I'd never, ever felt him tossing and turning, trying to solve a work problem at two o'clock in the morning, or scrolling through his phone at 3 a.m. because his mind wouldn't settle and he couldn't sleep. Considering his high-powered job, this always surprised me. He compartmentalised, he said. Whereas, for me, everything seemed to spill into the next thing – work and family and love and friends. If I felt bad about one thing, I seemed to feel bad about all of them.

I padded down the carpeted corridor, wondering what everyone else was doing behind their closed doors. Sophia and Daisy were somewhere on our floor, but Rosamund and Peter had a suite at the top of the hotel. I supposed it was their anniversary, but still: a suite! Part of me was desperate to engineer an excuse to go to their room so that I could have a nose around and another part of me found the idea of being alone with Rosamund terrifying. I imagined her cornering me, interrogating me about my intentions with her son, accusing me of being after his money, or something. I supposed she had no idea how much money I earned or had, but I assumed it was glaringly obvious that the answer was very little. I'd noticed how Nick's family swanned around the hotel, completely comfortable, their clothes and jewellery a clear indication that they had a certain amount of funds in the bank. I thought everyone could probably tell that I didn't have any such thing, and never had done.

I dreaded them asking what my parents did. It didn't usually matter; I'd just say my dad was a caretaker in a school and my mum was a beauty therapist and nobody would bat an eyelid. But I imagined with Rosamund that where you came from, your heritage, if you like, was a sort of currency – Nick had been to uni at Oxford, for example, whereas I'd been to the University of Hertfordshire, which I'd be surprised if Rosamund had ever even heard of. He'd been to a swanky private school and I'd been to my local comp.

I pressed the button for the lift, annoyed at myself. Why was I letting these people make me feel bad about everything I'd worked hard for, that my parents had worked hard for? It was almost as though they were projecting their antiquated ideas on to me and I, as usual, was sucking them up like a sponge: *You're not good enough. You're not good enough for someone like Nick.*

I pushed the thought from my mind, but then another one came back in its place: *You weren't good enough for Aidan, either.*

Chapter Six

The terrace of the Hotel Palazzo Continentale was an oasis of calm, surrounded by shrubs with a dusting of pretty little flowers, whites and yellows and pinks, and a view of Florence's ubiquitous terracotta rooftops. If I went right into the far corner, I could just make out the sun rising over the River Arno, which was much calmer than I'd imagined and nothing like the busy, undulating Thames. I put my video camera on the ledge and sat on one of the high stools facing the river, picking up a menu. All these breads and pastries – I was in hotel breakfast heaven! I ought to eat with Nick et al., even if I was starving already.

I tuned in to the sounds of Florence waking up: the joyous bells from a nearby church, the clinking of bone china being set up in the hotel restaurant, the revving of a moped engine somewhere down on the square – somebody delivering fresh ingredients to one of the restaurants, maybe. My mind immediately turned to pasta, possibly my favourite food in the world, which seemed to be strangely absent from the ostentatious menu at the hotel restaurant. Sometimes I just needed a big bowl of spaghetti with butter and a ton of cheese and I couldn't see what was wrong with that, despite what I could imagine Rosamund and Sophia would say. I was determined that at some point on this trip, I was going to sneak out alone and indulge my pasta habit without fear of it being frowned upon. I could always use art as an excuse to get away, since no one in my party seemed to have any interest in seeing any, having supposedly seen every piece of art Florence had to offer 'hundreds of times'. I didn't think I'd ever get tired of it, whether I'd been here one time or twenty.

The highlight of their week appeared to be the trip out into the Chianti region to visit a vineyard, which we'd all been booked onto for the following day, whether we liked it or not. I immediately pulled out my phone and googled Italian wines – following last night's epic fail with the wine list, I ought to memorise a couple of key facts in case somebody asked me a question.

I was busy wondering how to pronounce *Franciacorta*, which apparently was a sparkling wine from Lombardy, when someone opened the door leading from the restaurant to the terrace. Without thinking, I turned to look, which was stupid really because I should have known it would be Aidan. That was the kind of luck I had.

He stopped dead when he saw me, both of us startled into silence. My heart jolted so hard that I thought I might actually be about to throw up. I focused on my breathing: in and out. In and out. But it all came flooding back, how he used to tell me I was beautiful and funny. How we used to lie, tangled up in each other, talking for hours – I'd never felt alone when I was in bed with him because if I was awake, invariably he was, too. He'd said he'd never felt this sort of instant connection before; that he'd known I was something special the second he saw me on the banks of Loch Lomond with a weird, frumpy anorak on and windswept hair and nightmare Tim barking orders so loudly at me that the whole beach could hear.

'Don't bother trying to talk to me,' I said, my voice catching annoyingly in my throat.

'Don't worry, I wasn't planning to,' he replied, his tone ice-cold, not at all how I'd remembered.

He turned, flung open the door and headed back into the hotel.

I watched, my mouth hanging open. He was the one who'd broken my heart, and here he was acting like the wounded party. There was no excuse for what he'd done, or at least not one that I could think of. And maybe it had all happened for a reason, because if Aidan hadn't done what he did, I'd never have gone on a date with Nick. It had turned out for the best in the end, I told myself. Except that as I looked at the drinks menu, the words were all spinning in front of my eyes and my heart was still racing. I didn't want him to have this effect on me anymore. I wouldn't let him.

I stepped out onto the street, pulling my cardigan tightly around myself. The sky above me was a pure, bright blue, and I was sure it was going to warm up, but at the moment the air was chillier than it had looked from the window of our hotel room. A room that I wish I'd stayed in. What had I thought I was doing, going up on to the terrace alone? If I'd just stayed where I was, in bed with Nick, I wouldn't have had to speak to Aidan and everything would have felt much less unsettling than it did now.

A café with racing green umbrellas was setting up its tables outside on the street. It looked like a deli as well as a café, with olde-worlde bay windows filled with enticingly displayed truffle oil, truffle chocolate, truffle paste and other truffle-based foodstuffs. Who knew you could do so much with a truffle?!

'You like to sit?' said a passing waiter, who was whisking two cups of espresso over to a couple already seated.

'Sure. Yes, please,' I replied.

He dropped off the coffees and circled back to show me to a table. I took a seat facing down the road, towards the Arno, and the round castle-like building at the bottom of the street. I ordered a coffee with milk. I'd lost my appetite since seeing Aidan and didn't know how I was going to get through breakfast with everyone. Then I sat back in my chair, enjoying the way that the air felt fresh and clean and nothing like it did in London, checking my phone. Lou had already messaged, surprisingly. She was off to Palma today, shooting footage for the Majorca special; she must have an early flight.

How's it going with the in-laws-to-be?

I went to text her back, then decided to call instead. I had the urge to hear a friendly voice. Lou never sugar-coated stuff and I *had* to tell somebody about Aidan.

Lou picked up on the second ring. 'Blimey, you're up already!' she said. 'I thought you'd be languishing in bed with Nick, sharing rustic bread and mozzarella cheese and getting crumbs all over the sheets.'

'Ha! This place is too beautiful to be lying around in a hotel room,' I said.

'How's Nick's family? Tell me all. Are they as charming as he is? Do they love you already?'

My stomach dropped.

'They're … not quite how I'd imagined,' I said, struggling to put it into words. 'They're very wealthy, which is fine, obviously.'

'But …?'

'But Nick calls his mum "Mummy".'

'He doesn't!'

'And his ex-wife is here. Daisy's mum.'

Lou made a screeching sound. 'What the hell?'

'She's still very close with Rosamund – Nick's mum – apparently.'

'But this was about you bonding with them. How are you supposed to do that with her hanging around? Talk about awkward.'

The waiter brought my coffee which smelled divine. I picked up the cup and blew on the surface, taking a tiny sip.

'His dad reckons I look like Meghan Markle,' I said.

'Oh for God's sake.'

'Am I setting the tone for you?'

'Very much so,' said Lou.

I could imagine her rolling her eyes.

'And that's not the worst of it,' I added.

'There's more?'

I hesitated. While Lou had supported me every step of the way, I could sense that she'd found the whole thing with Aidan a bit much. Ever cautious, she couldn't understand how we'd got so close so quickly, and why I was so cut up about it afterwards. I could tell she'd got fed up with me being utterly miserable every time we went out and eventually she'd told me – gently – that I needed to snap myself out of it and 'get back on the horse'. It had been her who'd encouraged me to hit up Tinder and say yes to a date with Nick, even though I really wasn't ready and was secretly holding on to the hope that there'd been some terrible mistake and Aidan was going to come swooping back into my life any moment and tell me that he couldn't live without me. This I didn't share with anyone.

'Come on then, what else has happened?' asked Lou. 'Nothing interesting ever happens to me anymore and therefore I am living my life vicariously through you.'

'A quiet life sounds very appealing right about now,' I said.

'How come?'

'Aidan is here. Staying at the same hotel.'

A beat. Lots of beats.

'Lou? Are you still there?' I asked, thinking that maybe we'd been cut off.

'Sorry, yes. I was speechless for a second there. What the fuck?'

'I saw him in the restaurant last night and then again on the roof terrace this morning. Briefly, because he took one look at me and bolted.'

'Oh my God,' said Lou. 'What was it like to see him? Did you feel anything?'

'Fury?'

'Does he look the same?'

I couldn't lie to Lou. 'He still looks good, yeah.'

Lou sighed. 'He messed up, though, didn't he? And it doesn't really matter what his reason was, does it, because short of being dead, which he clearly isn't, there's really no way he can explain his way out of what he did?'

'I know. I definitely know that.'

But there was part of me that wanted to hear his explanation, anyway.

'Look, I've got a taxi coming in a minute,' said Lou. 'I'd better go and finish packing. When are you back?'

'Saturday, but then I'm going straight up to Leicester to see my dad. It's his birthday, so I thought I'd make an effort.'

'Let's hope he doesn't double-book himself this time,' said Lou, who knew exactly how flaky my dad could be. 'Oh, and Maddie? Don't let Nick's family get to you. They should be trying to impress you as well, not just the other way round.'

'Not sure they see it that way,' I replied, laughing lightly.

It felt as though I'd been fine-tuned to assess what people thought of me, what their first impressions were. Whether they were judging me. Whether they were making assumptions about my background or my schooling or my family. I think I did this to protect myself and I would usually retreat immediately if things didn't feel right, but, of course, Nick's family were going to be stuck with me and vice versa, so I couldn't.

'You're good enough for them, Maddie. More than good enough. In fact, they're probably secretly intimidated by what a smart, confident, beautiful woman you are,' said Lou.

I wanted to believe that, really I did, but when I pictured Rosamund's face in my mind's eye, I found it impossible to imagine that she was intimidated by anything at all.

Chapter Seven

The Gucci Garden – a museum, art installation and boutique in one, apparently – sat at the far corner of possibly one of the most impressive squares I'd ever seen in my life: the Piazza della Signoria. It was huge, lined with the cobbles I was getting used to walking on and flanked by a combination of restaurants with outside terraces, palaces, arches and statues. I wanted to stop and take some pictures, to refer to my map to see what was what and why it was significant to Florence's history, but Rosamund and Sophia – who were walking arm in arm like teenagers on a school trip – were hurrying us along.

'Daisy, keep up, darling!' called Sophia, looking over her shoulder at Daisy, who was lagging behind with me.

Nick and Peter were somewhere in the middle, following orders as instructed. I was tempted to catch Daisy's eye to see if she was on the same page as I was (i.e. I'd rather snatch a few hours to myself and sit at a pavement café reading my book and sipping cappuccino), but her moods were so unpredictable that I didn't want to chance it. One minute it felt as though she was on my side and the next, she was glaring at me as though I was public enemy number one.

'Look at that delightful pink!' exclaimed Rosamund, looking up at the Gucci Garden logo, which was printed on a dramatic candy-pink banner tumbling down the side of the palazzo.

Rosamund and Sophia marched straight through the entrance as though they owned the place and the rest of us followed at varying degrees of speed. I – of course – felt completely underdressed in my summer dress and flat sandals combo. I mean, I should have thought, really, that people might dress up to go to a Gucci museum, and also that people who loved Gucci were generally going to be much more fashion-conscious than I was (not to mention have a considerably higher level of disposable income).

Rosamund had ditched her trademark twinsets and jewels for something altogether edgier – in the way rich, older women did edgy: straight-cut jeans in the deepest indigo blue, a plain white T-shirt, huge Jackie-O-style sunglasses and a classic navy blazer that looked as though it might be Chanel, although that was just a guess. I didn't think I'd ever seen anyone actually wearing Chanel in real life, but her jacket was definitely not something you'd find on the high street. She looked great, I had to admit.

As for Sophia, she had really gone to town with ripped designer jeans, some sort of jazzy bomber jacket covered in sequins and patches and sky-high heeled boots. Nick was channelling his inner Italian and had on a shirt (always) with a jumper tied around his shoulders, jeans which he'd rolled up to his ankles and tan suede loafers that I swore I'd never seen before. And Peter, well, he was just wearing what seemed to be his staple uniform (i.e. tweed).

Rosamund had reserved us all tickets, so we swept through the foyer and up an enclosed, white-walled staircase daubed with the chicest-looking graffiti I'd ever seen, seemingly in French (I wasn't sure why, given we were in Italy and I was pretty sure Gucci was an Italian brand): words like *liberté*, *égalité* and *sexualité* were thrust provocatively in our faces. Rosamund and Sophia gushed over it and I couldn't help thinking that if they'd seen this graffiti on some random London wall, they'd have been turning their noses up at it. Sophia was very keen to get Daisy enthused and kept calling her over to look at things.

'Darling, this is a name you must remember. Alessandro Michele! He's the artistic director of Gucci and an absolute genius.'

Although Daisy had her arms crossed tightly across herself in a defensive stance, I could see that she was vaguely interested in her surroundings. And, actually, I was too, if I hung back so that I could discover it for myself instead of hearing Rosamund's running commentary. I managed to lose them for a few minutes in a room full of mirrors that gave the illusion of being in a sort of trippy maze, with the central point being a video of one of Gucci's cruise collections. I didn't know what a cruise collection was, exactly, but the clothes were beautiful and for a second I longed to be able to afford a pair of emerald green sequinned trousers (that I'd clearly never wear and probably cost about ten grand).

I caught up with the others in the Gucci Collectors room, which I didn't understand until I read the blurb and then I thought it was quite cool. The room was inspired by Gucci's Fall/Winter 2018 collection, which in turn had been inspired by collectors of weird and wonderful objects.

Rosamund stood beside me as I looked at a collection of 182 cuckoo clocks and watched birds popping out all over the place. I remembered a school friend's parents had had one in their hall and I'd been fascinated by that, too.

'How are you finding Florence?' asked Rosamund, cocking her head to inspect the clocks.

'Lovely,' I said. 'Thanks so much for inviting me along.'

'Well, we thought it was about time we met you. We suspected Nick was going to propose at some point.'

I hid my surprise. 'What made you think that?'

Rosamund laughed lightly. 'My son is a romantic, as you've probably worked out by now. No idea where he gets it from.'

'Well, being married to the same man for forty-five years is pretty romantic,' I said.

Rosamund shook her head. 'It's different with Nick. He never holds back when it comes to love, to his detriment at times. And he hasn't stopped talking about you since you met. I could tell he was head over heels for you a long time ago.'

This was nice. Rosamund was making an effort, which was promising. And she seemed to love Nick very much, so surely there was no reason why she couldn't also learn to love me. I wondered, though, why Nick had waited so long to introduce me to his family if they'd known about me all along.

I followed Rosamund across to the next display, which was a collection of hundreds of pairs of trainers stacked neatly in a cabinet. There were mirrors on the floor and ceiling so that if you looked up or down, you could see versions of yourself getting smaller and smaller and further and further away. Rather disconcertingly, I could also see Rosamund's reflection, about a hundred identical versions of her, no matter which direction I looked in.

'What about Gucci for your wedding gown?' suggested Rosamund.

'Um, I don't think I could afford it,' I said, taking a photo of a particularly bling pair of customised trainers.

'Or you'd look lovely in Prada.'

'Maybe.'

'You've got your own ideas, of course you have,' said Rosamund. 'Feel free to tell me to mind my own business.

I love weddings and have a tendency to get a little over-excited.'

I smiled at her. 'I'm sure I'll be very grateful for any help you can offer,' I said, reassuring her.

'Good,' said Rosamund, looking pleased with herself. 'This may not be the first time my son has got married, but presumably it will be the first time you have. Remember that. You deserve to have a big fuss made of you.'

I watched her go through to the next room, wondering about the fanfare that must have accompanied Nick and Sophia's wedding. Did she wear Prada?

'What do you think?' whispered Nick in my ear, sliding his arm around my waist.

'Of what?'

'The museum.'

'It's amazing, actually,' I said, feeling the need to whisper back. 'It's crazy when you think about what inspires fashion designers. I mean, wig collectors? Clocks?'

Nick laughed.

I checked Rosamund was out of earshot and then said to him: 'I think me and your mum might finally be bonding.'

Nick did a double take. 'Why, what's she said?'

'Oh nothing major. Just talking weddings and stuff. But it's a start.'

Nick kissed me on the top of my head. 'That's great, Mads. See? She's not as scary as she likes people to think.'

I wasn't totally sure about that, not yet. But what mattered was Nick, and if getting along with his family made him happy, then I was going to have to make it happen.

'Your mum thinks I should wear Prada on our wedding day,' I said to him.

He rolled his eyes. 'Ignore her. Anyone would think she wears designer clothes twenty-four/seven the way she and

Sophia are prancing about. Let me tell you, her wardrobe is ninety per cent Boden!'

Another group came into the room and it seemed like the right time to move upstairs. As I followed Rosamund up a level, I was greeted by a vision: Sophia posing in front of a giant Gucci campaign poster. She had put herself into the same pose as the three models behind her and was absolutely loving the attention as we formed a crescent around her.

'Oh darling, you look fabulous,' said Rosamund. 'Let me take a photograph for Instagram.'

I tried to hide my surprise and whispered to Nick, who was standing in front of me: 'Your mum's on Instagram?'

'She doesn't really understand it, but she likes to feel down with the kids,' he said under his breath.

'Come on, Maddie, your turn,' trilled Sophia, waving me over.

'I'm fine,' I said, shaking my head. Absolutely not. Not in front of this lot.

'Go on, darling,' said Nick. 'I want to take a photo.'

I sighed, realising that they were only going to go on about it until I caved in. I stood self-consciously in front of the poster, my hands hanging by my sides.

'Hands on your hips, Maddie,' instructed Rosamund. 'Like this!'

She demonstrated what she meant, popping out her hip so sharply that I was worried she was going to do herself an injury. Everyone except Daisy and Peter (who looked as though he didn't know how to use a mobile phone, let alone take a picture) clicked away. Honestly, this was mortifying.

'You next, Daisy,' said Nick, nudging his daughter.

'No fucking way,' retorted Daisy, walking off.

'Daisy! Language!' Nick called pointlessly after her.

She'd said it now, hadn't she, and I didn't imagine a

half-hearted telling-off from her dad was going to make her think twice about saying it again.

After we'd finished in the museum, I skirted around the periphery of the Gucci boutique, marvelling at the exquisite hair clips and bejewelled clutch bags and the changing room that was like something out of *Bridgerton* with its frilly curtain and chaise longue. Nick was fussing over Daisy, who was pouting sulkily until he pointed out a beautiful leather bag to the sales assistant and the two of them followed her over to the till, where Daisy unsurprisingly perked up as Nick got his Amex card out.

I'd heard there was a more reasonably priced section of the shop and headed across to it, wondering whether I could afford to treat myself to a little memento. I picked up a beautiful, hexagonal case housing a pad of Post-it notes with an illustration of a tiny cat in the corner. That would look quite nice on my desk at work, I thought, until I turned it over and saw that it cost one hundred and forty euros. One hundred and forty euros? For a pack of Post-its?! I hurriedly put them down and carried on browsing, slightly shell-shocked by the thought that if Post-its were that much, how much would an A4 notepad be?

Nick made his way over to me. 'Ready to go?' he asked.

Everyone was waiting outside – Peter, who looked bored to death, Daisy, who already had her new bag on her shoulder, and Sophia and Rosamund who were each holding a beautiful olive-green Gucci carrier bag (if you could call it that – carrier bag didn't seem to do it justice).

'What did you go for?' I asked.

'A purse,' said Sophia smugly. 'I've already got it in black, but they had the most beautiful purple.'

'And I got a sun hat,' said Rosamund, opening her bag so that I could peek inside.

'It's lovely,' I said, although in truth, it looked like a slightly more robust version of any generic sun hat you could get from a beach shop in the Costas.

'Perfect for Saint Tropez this summer,' she added.

I didn't know why everything they did had to be so showy. I was glad that Nick hadn't inherited this particular trait. He never flashed his wealth around, although, thinking about it, he *had* introduced me to a different type of life. We ate in restaurants with the sort of phenomenally expensive wine lists that I'd previously have taken one look at and laughed. And he regularly bought me huge bunches of flowers from Jane Packer, a florist I'd only ever read about in glossy magazines. But it was subtle and Nick's attitude didn't bother me in the way that Rosamund's and Sophia's did. I thought that what annoyed me was that they weren't in touch with reality, not at all. I bet they had no concept that most people struggled to pay bills and worked jobs they didn't love to make the rent and had to shop in Aldi rather than Waitrose. I would bet my life on the fact that Rosamund had never set foot in an Aldi. I thought briefly of Aidan: I'd never met his parents, there hadn't been time, but I knew, just *knew*, I wouldn't have felt like this with them.

'You didn't want anything did you, darling?' Nick asked me.

I shook my head. 'Not at those prices.'

'Quality costs, Maddie,' said Sophia, giving me a sweeping look up and down.

I was seriously beginning to question if I'd ever fit into this family and even whether I'd want to.

Chapter Eight

The lift pinged open and Nick and I stepped out onto our luxurious, carpeted, deathly quiet floor. I yawned.

'I feel like I need a lie-down in a darkened room,' I said.

It had suddenly hit me, I think, the long journey and then the energy it took to be constantly upbeat/interesting/not offended when I was around Nick's family.

'Is it all getting a bit much for you?' asked Nick, looking sheepish. 'I know my family can be hard work, but they mean well.'

I followed Nick down the corridor wondering what a suitable response would be. It was tricky with families, wasn't it? I mean, I couldn't even navigate my own successfully, let alone anyone else's.

'Think I just need a nap,' I said as we arrived outside our room.

'That's a shame,' said Nick, putting his hands on my waist and spinning me around so that my back was pressed up against the door. 'I had a more adventurous way to spend the next hour in mind ...'

He kissed me hard, trailing his hand suggestively along the outside of my thigh, running it under the hem of my dress.

'Nick,' I said, laughing lightly. 'Not here.'

I didn't feel in the mood, but Lou's voice rang in my ear. *Don't get too comfortable. And have regular sex!*

Nick blindly fumbled around with the key. It would be easier, I thought, if he just let me go and concentrated on opening the door rather than trying to do two things at once.

'You look beautiful today,' he said huskily, kissing my neck, still trying to open the door.

'Even if I do look more high-street than high-end,' I said, laughing it off.

'Why can't I get this bloody key to work?' groaned Nick with frustration.

I gently eased him off me, worried that somebody would see us in the corridor. 'Here, let me,' I said, taking it from him.

I tapped the key on the pad: it worked first time.

Inside, Nick was still very much up for it and I tried my best not to overthink things and to just be in the moment and to enjoy being with him. Sex didn't need to be mind-blowing every time, not with us. We had lots of other things going for us. Lots and lots of things.

Afterwards, I thought I'd be able to drift off into a delicious post-sex slumber, but instead my mind was whirring. Should I have enjoyed it more? Why did we always do it in the missionary position? Should I tell Nick I wanted to mix things up a bit and would it hurt his feelings if I did? Eventually, to shut out the noise, I got out of bed, telling Nick I needed to freshen up.

As I stood under the rain shower head, letting it pound my shoulders and drench my face (while keeping my hair as dry as was humanly possible, of course), I decided that what I needed was a bit of space to clear my head. A nice late-afternoon walk around Florence – on my own – before dinner should do it.

Nick watched me as I got dressed. He seemed content

and pleased with himself and relaxed, all the things I wished I could be. I'd been looking forward to this trip so much. It felt like a big moment, the next step in our lives together. I'd had a tiny flutter of nerves, obviously, as anyone would meeting their fiancé's family for the first time, but I'd been hopeful. I still was, in a way, because even if things hadn't got off to the best of starts, it was early days, wasn't it? I needed to remember how great Nick and I were together, and to believe that eventually his parents would see that, too.

'Mum's pressuring me to set a date for the wedding. Are we still thinking next spring?' asked Nick, yawning and stretching.

I pulled on a pair of jeans. I felt like being casual, and the sun was going down now so it would be cooler out.

'I think so,' I said. It felt a bit too soon but then, I suppose, why wait?

'Mum thinks we ought to bring it forward. She's got a venue in mind – somewhere in Oxfordshire. She said the colours are lovely there in the autumn and it's surrounded by trees. Apparently it looks beautiful in pictures.'

'I've never even been to Oxfordshire.'

What I really wanted to say was: please could you tell your mother to stay out of it? I didn't know which was worse, Rosamund sticking her oar in, or my mum, who was so caught up with my twin half-sisters' graduation that she'd barely asked me anything about my impending wedding. She loved Nick, or, more accurately, she was impressed that I was marrying someone with money, like she had the second time around (her words, not mine), but she didn't seem particularly interested in the detail.

'She's trying to help, I guess,' said Nick.

I sighed. 'I know. But remember how we decided we didn't want a huge wedding? Small and intimate was what we said, wasn't it? I hate being the centre of attention and it would really freak me out to have hundreds of people I'd never even met staring at me as I walked down the aisle.'

Nick winced, sucking air in through his teeth. 'Thing is, we've got quite a large extended family. Mum loves weddings, and she adores you. She wants to show you off.'

'What's the rush?' I said. 'If we get married next year like we've planned, it will give us a bigger run-up. More time to organise stuff and look for dresses. That'll make your mum happy, surely?'

Nick sat up, propping himself up on the fluffiest pillows I'd ever slept on.

'Once Mum gets a bee in her bonnet about something, it's hard to change her mind.'

'But it's our day, Nick. It's for us to decide.'

'I know,' he said, changing tack. 'Let's not worry about it now. What do you feel like doing?'

My phone beeped and I picked it up, hoping it was Lou with some encouraging words or one of her wise quotes. It wasn't, it was bloody Tim.

ANYTHING TO SEND IN? WANT TO START PUTTING THE CITY BREAK TEASER TOGETHER.

Great.

'I'm going to have to pop out and shoot some footage,' I said. 'Tim's hassling me.'

Nick tutted. 'Tell him you're on holiday.'

'I've tried that.'

'Well then, I'll come with you.'

Nick threw back the covers, getting up. I'd been looking forward to going out on my own and he'd really annoyed me bringing his mum into the equation when it came to our wedding date. I could just tell she was chomping at the bit to get full control over everything from the invitations to the honeymoon. She'd probably already picked out the bridesmaids' dresses – Versace or something, no doubt.

'I think it would be easier on my own,' I said tactfully. 'It'll be boring for you.'

But Nick was already pulling on his (ankle-skimming) trousers and I realised that I didn't have a lot of choice in the matter. Maybe Nick was more like his mum than I'd realised. I hadn't noticed it before, but now I came to think about it, he didn't seem to take no for an answer, either.

I picked up my camera and my bag. 'Come on then,' I said. 'You can be my assistant. And absolutely no complaining.'

Nick grinned. 'I will follow your every command. Without a hint of a whinge.'

I gave him a dubious look. 'I thought you hated other people telling you what to do.'

He opened the door, ushering me through. 'Ah, but you're not just "other people".'

Chapter Nine

We'd found ourselves back in the same square yet again: Piazza della Signoria. I wondered why all roads led to this place, as though it had once been the central point of Florence. Tour guides were holding up coloured flags to alert their party to their whereabouts. Horses pulling carts clip-clopped across the square and the sun, which had just begun to set, was illuminating the rooftops with flashes of gold.

'Can I actually have a proper look around this time, please?' I said to Nick, strutting off in the direction of a dramatic sculpture depicting a powerful-looking man with young children all around him and horses spouting water from their mouths.

I peered at it. It *felt* important. Mind you, everything in Florence felt as though it had the potential to be a masterpiece. Loads of artists had lived or worked in Florence at one point, I'd discovered: Botticelli, Leonardo da Vinci, Michelangelo. It was amazing how creative this place had been hundreds of years ago and perhaps no surprise that it had been coined the Jewel of the Renaissance.

'What's the meaning of this statue?' I asked as Nick appeared next to me. 'Do you know?'

Since he'd been to Florence 'so many times', I imagined he must know quite a bit about the place, more than you could pick up from reading guidebooks, anyway. It was hard,

I thought, to take in all those dates and facts out of context.

'It's Neptune,' said Nick. 'Cosimo the first of the Medici family built the Palazzo Vecchio,' he explained, pointing at the huge building next to us, 'for his wife, but she came from somewhere by the sea, and she didn't like all this terracotta and stone. So he built this fountain partly for her so that she could look out of the window and imagine that she was by the ocean.'

'So romantic,' I said, getting my camera out and doing a sweeping, panoramic shot of the whole square, ending on Neptune himself. '*David!*' I exclaimed, spotting a large statue of a naked man on the other side of the palazzo. 'This is him, isn't it? But then, wasn't he at that Galleria place?'

Nick followed me, laughing.

'What are you smirking at?' I asked good-naturedly.

'This one's fake,' said Nick.

'This is a fake *David?!*'

Nick took a photo of me looking up at it with a confused expression on my face. 'Weird, isn't it? The real thing used to be here, but then they moved it to the Galleria dell'Accademia in eighteen hundred and something,' he explained. 'They built this to replace it. The real *David* is much more impressive.'

'Can we go and see it?' I asked.

Nick looked at his watch. We'd only been out for about half an hour and he was clearly chomping at the bit to get back already.

'Come on,' I coaxed. 'Even your mum said I couldn't come to Florence and not see *David*.'

Nick sighed. 'The queues are ridiculous.'

'You can head back to the hotel if you want and I'll go on my own,' I suggested, sort of hoping that he'd think that was a brilliant idea and leave me to it. Then I could go at my

93

own pace and possibly be quite late back so that I didn't have to spend an hour navigating the planned pre-dinner drinks session.

'No, no. I promised I'd come out with you so that's what I'll do. Come on, it's this way.'

I reluctantly tore myself away from the square, vowing to come for an early-morning walk the following day and experience it on my own. I wanted to waltz across the cobbles, looking up at the sky, imagining what it must have been like to be a member of the Medici family. Perhaps stopping for a *cioccolata* at one of the cute cafés lining the square. I was used to travelling on my own and almost always preferred it that way.

Nick set off at his usual speedy pace. He never ambled anywhere or – I thought – really took in his surroundings. He was rushing through Florence in the same way he rushed through life (and, come to mention it, our relationship), not truly appreciating anything because he was already thinking about the next thing. I was the opposite. I liked to savour the moment. Enjoying the feeling of just being somewhere was always more important to me than any of the photos or footage I took. Funny, then, that I'd ended up shooting videos for a travel show and often only saw places as locations rather than lapping up the atmosphere like I might if I was on holiday.

I reminded myself that this *was* supposed to be a holiday and that I was under no obligation to do anything for Tim. But then bubbling away in the back of my mind was an idea. Something I'd been thinking about a lot, recently; a venture that might just get me out of Holiday Shop. It wouldn't hurt to have some Florence footage to play around with, just in case.

I lengthened my stride to catch Nick up, veering left to

avoid a horse and carriage carrying a couple of tourists who probably hadn't realised they'd just been conned into paying about twenty-five euros to be taken a short distance they could easily have walked.

For some reason that even Nick couldn't explain, there was absolutely no queue for the Galleria dell'Accademia. We were whisked through security, with me having to have my bag checked (and subsequently apologising for the amount of useless stuff I'd accumulated and that the poor security guard had to pick through). Then we entered the main hall of the gallery, which Nick told me had been specially built to house *David*. Strange to talk about a statue as if he was a real person, but that's how 'he' felt, I thought immediately as we walked down the long corridor, with *David* standing majestically at the end.

There was something church-like about this gallery, giving me the weird sense that *David* was waiting for me at the altar. The atmosphere was magical; hushed voices, domed ceilings, just the right amount of light falling perfectly and flatteringly on *David*'s marbled body. Nick was marching ahead, of course, but I took my time. Other statues were displayed to either side and I had a quick look, but I couldn't seem to take my eyes off the main spectacle.

As I got closer, I got my video camera out. It seemed unusual to be here without hordes of people blocking my view, so I supposed I might as well take advantage. I started the shot just above *David*'s head, panning slowly down, over his curly hair, his slingshot and his very impressive abs. He was holding something in his right hand, but I couldn't see what it was through the lens. And then something caught my attention just behind it. Looking directly down the camera at me, with bright eyes that rivalled *David*'s focused expression, was Aidan.

I dropped the camera to my side. And then Nick slipped his arm around my waist and whispered in my ear.

'What do you think?' he asked. 'Worth the hype?'

Suddenly I couldn't focus on *David*. I wanted to, but it was hard to concentrate with Aidan bobbing about in the background. He had headphones in, so I assumed he must be listening to some kind of audio commentary and he seemed to be spending a lot of time looking at *David*'s right hand.

'Definitely,' I said, my voice coming out all breathy.

'Oooh, are you getting all emotional?' teased Nick, running his thumb across my cheek as though he was soaking up tears. 'There, there ...'

'Don't, Nick,' I said, pushing him away.

'People do actually cry when they see him, you know?' he said, looking up at *David*'s face with his hands wedged on his hips.

For all his high-brow visits to Florence, Nick looked like any other British tourist with his chinos and his boat shoes and his sunglasses plonked on his head. When I involuntarily glanced at Aidan before realising what I was doing and focused on *David*'s thighs instead, I noticed he looked like he always had: just the right side of edgy. Cool without trying too hard. Hair shaved at the sides but a little longer on top; a sort of *Top Gun* vibe.

Nick was now looking at a plaque on the wall, presumably gleaning some information on *David*. I made my way over to join him.

'Did you know Michelangelo made him out of an old piece of marble that nobody else wanted? It was too big, you see, and not particularly smooth. Other artists didn't know what to do with it,' said Nick, squinting to read the text.

'When was this?' I asked, having been terrible at history

and knowing barely anything about art other than whether I liked it or not.

'Fifteen hundreds, I think. Let me have a look so I can tell you for sure,' said Nick, scanning the words on the plaque. 'Yes! I was right. Built between 1501 and 1504.'

'So he's over five hundred years old?' I said, too scared to look at *David* again in case Aidan was in my eyeline.

I was still in two minds about whether to say anything to Nick about Aidan. I should, I supposed, because if he found out now, it would seem strange, as though I had something to hide. It was difficult to wedge it into the conversation, that was all. How would I start it off? *Oh, see that really good-looking guy hovering behind* David's *right shin? I had the best sex of my life with him until once day he ghosted me and I never saw him again?*

Nick looked at his watch. 'We ought to go. Mummy's booked a restaurant for eight and we'll need to get ready. She says it's not dressy, but you know what she's like, it'll be pearls galore.'

It was no good, I was going to have to say something. I tried to keep it casual. 'How come you're calling your mum "Mummy" all of a sudden?'

Nick looked embarrassed. Perhaps it was an involuntary thing and he hadn't even noticed. 'Am I?'

'Yes.'

Nick laughed hollowly. 'Oh, I don't know. Because it makes her happy, I suppose.'

I frowned at him, still not quite getting it.

'Why do you ask? Does it bother you?' asked Nick.

And I felt bad then, because it shouldn't, should it? I should find it endearing, like his accent. He wanted to please his mum, how sweet was that? And yet ...

97

'Course not. I was just surprised, that's all,' I lied. 'Shall we go?'

Nick nodded. 'We have to go out through the shop if I remember correctly,' he said, taking my hand. 'Come on, I'll buy you a memento.'

Letting him lead me towards the exit, I took one last look at beautiful *David*. And crossed my fingers that Aidan wasn't in the gift shop.

Loch Lomond

Two Years Earlier

Lou and I were down on the beach at 1.45 sharp. I liked to be super organised on shoot days and there was nothing worse than rocking up flustered, late and under-prepared (not that it seemed to stop Tim). I looked out at the water, jotting down a provisional shot list and some generic pieces to camera that might work for Ruthie, because I was pretty sure that Tim hadn't done any of this. When we'd walked past him and Ruthie on the way out of the lodge, he'd been propping up the bar with a glass of red wine in his hand. At this rate, he'd barely be coherent, let alone on top of producing the segment.

'Shall I set up down by the water?' asked Lou, unzipping her camera bag.

'Yep. We'll start with some footage of the kayaks on the shore and then once everyone's in them, you can do some travelling shots as we row out. Is it called row, in a kayak?'

Lou shrugged. 'Don't ask me. The closest I've come to doing water sports is when you and me went out on that banana boat in Faliraki.'

My body shuddered in response. 'Don't remind me.'

I'd been flung into the water so many times that at one point I'd wondered whether I'd have been better off just swimming back to the shore. Trying to stay on a yellow inflatable while being dragged across the Mediterranean at about a hundred miles an hour had looked much more entertaining from the safety of a beach towel on the sand.

'Your phone's ringing,' said Lou.

'Ooops, meant to put that on silent,' I said, feeling around for it in my pockets.

Mind you, it was probably Tim making some excuse about being late. I glanced up towards the hotel: no sign of him or Ruthie. When I looked back, I saw Finlay unlocking the doors of his 'shack', as Tim had called it. I waved at him and simultaneously answered my call.

'Maddie? Where are you?'

'Hi, Dad. Scotland. Everything all right?'

He hesitated. 'How's it going?'

I was immediately suspicious. He never usually asked how my job was going, mainly because he didn't fully understand what I did. He was always making jokes about how I got paid to go on holiday, and when I tried to explain that it was actually very hard work and that I was sitting at a desk in an office in London most of the time, he didn't seem able to grasp the concept.

'It's fine,' I said, wishing he'd get to the point. 'It's beautiful here. You should bring Sharon.'

Sharon was my step-mum and even as I said it, I knew she would have no desire to go to Loch Lomond. Her idea of a dream holiday was lying prone on a sun lounger by a pool somewhere in Spain and not moving for at least twelve hours, except to turn every now and again so that she kept her tan even.

'About Sharon ...'

I frowned. 'What about her?'

'She's gone and booked me a weekend away for my

birthday, hasn't she? We're all off to Amsterdam, apparently. Getting one of those ferries across.'

The other kayakers were heading slowly down to the beach now, including, I noticed, Aidan. He was no longer in a wetsuit, and was wearing jeans and a chunky jumper that made him look like a sexy fisherman. Seriously, I needed to get over myself and focus on my job and also find out what exactly my dad was trying to say so that I could get this phone call over with as quickly as possible. I took a few steps towards the water, hoping I'd be out of earshot. It was hardly professional of me to be on the phone.

'Right. And when's that?'

'Well. On my birthday. This weekend,' said Dad sheepishly.

'But I'm coming to visit this weekend.'

'I know. I told her that. She said she forgot.'

I felt a thud of realisation as it became clear that, yet again, Dad and his new family – except they weren't new anymore, since my half-sister and half-brother were twenty-two and twenty-four respectively – had put themselves before me and my feelings. I'd really been looking forward to seeing them all, especially Dad.

'But it's all planned,' I said, trying not to sound shrieky. I knew Dad hated it when I got all emotional – he'd told me often enough. 'My train ticket's all booked, Glasgow to Leicester. Sharon must have known I was coming because she said she'd put the others in together so that I could have my own room!'

My dad made some weird grumbling noises, which I took to mean that he didn't know what to say. 'Sorry about that. She said she didn't realise, and the Amsterdam trip's all booked.'

I sighed. This conversation was pointless, he'd already

made up his mind that he was blowing me out to go to Amsterdam, and who could blame him? It was Sharon I was fucked off with. She'd done this sort of thing before and, honestly, I didn't suppose it was malicious on her part, I just didn't imagine I entered into her sphere of thought most of the time. 'Not much I can say then, is there? Anyway, I'm needed at work, so I'll have to go.'

'We'll celebrate together some other time, eh?'

'Sure, Dad. Happy birthday and have a great time.'

I hung up, feeling like something hard and sharp was pressing into my chest. Funny how these things triggered you, even years later. Conversations like this – and there were a lot of them – took me right back to being a child again, when Mum and Dad had first split up and everything had felt tense and uncertain and I'd been worried a lot of the time. They hadn't seemed particularly bothered about spending time with me then, either, so I didn't know why I kept hoping things would change.

'Everything OK?'

I turned to see Lou beside me. She had her camera to her eye, setting up the shot. Finlay was shin-deep in water, getting the kayaks into position.

'My dad's just cancelled my trip.'

'What, the one in a couple of days' time?'

'Yep.'

Lou rubbed my arm. 'Sorry, Mads. He's crap, isn't he?'

I nodded. 'I should have known something like this would happen.'

'When are we going to get it through our heads that our parents are not miraculously going to change overnight?' said Lou, whose wedding to Will was nearly ruined when her divorced parents practically came to blows at the reception.

'Maddie! Ruthie needs her make-up touching up.'

Tim's too-loud voice snapped me out of thinking about Dad, so at least I had him to thank for that.

I turned, plastering on a smile to face Ruthie, who was wrapped in a blanket and looking decidedly pissed off. I dipped down to get my make-up kit and as I stood up, I spotted Aidan watching me. He smiled at me and I nodded back. Perhaps daydreaming about having a wild, Scottish fling with him would pull me out of my bad mood. I unzipped the make-up kit, grabbed a pot of concealer and a brush and approached Ruthie.

'Feeling all right about getting out on the water?' I asked her brightly as I dabbed beige paste onto her face and blended it in.

'No, I am not,' said Ruthie. 'What if I fall in?'

'Oh, you won't,' replied Aidan, appearing beside us. 'It's practically impossible to capsize in a kayak.'

Ruthie looked at him, her sneer instantly turning into a smile. I wondered if he had that effect on everyone. 'Oh, hello! Are you our kayaking instructor?' she asked in a throaty voice.

Aidan laughed and shook his head. 'I'm afraid not. But I am coming out on the water with you. So if you need a hand, just shout.'

Ruthie appeared to have turned into a simpering wreck. I mean, I couldn't blame her, Aidan was being particularly manly/caring right now, which I had to admit was an excellent combo.

'I might just take you up on that,' said Ruthie, regally holding out her hand so that Aidan could shake it.

To be fair to him, he picked up on her cues and did exactly what was required, taking her hand.

'Ruthie Withenshaw, lead presenter of Holiday Shop,' she said.

'Pleased to meet you, Ruthie. I'm Aidan, travel writer on the *Hampstead and Highgate Express*.'

He gave her a dazzling smile which was so infectious that I almost smiled myself, even though it wasn't aimed at me. As I put the concealer away and got out the trusty powder compact, I caught Aidan's eye. Of course, my imagination was probably running away with me, but I had a feeling that he'd introduced himself to Ruthie to lighten the mood and help me out. Which would mean he'd actually noticed I needed some assistance. Which for some reason – because I was a sucker for feeling 'seen', probably – really cheered me up after being let down by my dad. Seriously, there had to be something wrong with this guy because on first impressions, he was *much* too good to be true.

'All done,' I said to Ruthie, who stalked off, no doubt to moan to Tim about what a ridiculous idea all this was.

I bent down to put my things away, but Aidan's boot-clad feet were in my eyeline and I felt totally self-conscious crouched down, so I stood up quickly, brushing my hair out of my eyes.

'Is there anything you can't do?' he asked. 'So far, I've seen you in charge of sound, wardrobe and make-up. Any other hidden talents I'm likely to discover as the day goes on?'

I smiled. He had noticed me.

'Or, in other words, I get to do the crap jobs that nobody else wants,' I said.

'Doesn't sound quite so glamorous when you put it like that,' he replied, laughing.

I looked at the boats bobbing on the water, wondering how we were going to get through the afternoon with expensive camera equipment to keep dry and a presenter who would rather put pins in her eyes than row herself out into the middle of a Scottish lake.

'Are you an expert at this, then? Kayaking?' I asked.

Aidan shook his head, lowering his voice. 'Hardly. I've only just recovered from diving this morning. Don't tell anyone, but water sports aren't actually my thing.'

'Same,' I confessed. 'Have you ever been out on a banana boat? Because don't.'

Aidan grimaced. 'That bad?'

'Worse.'

'Right you lot. Find a kayak each and let's get you out on the water,' called Finlay, who was clearly the only person actually feeling optimistic about our impending jaunt.

Aidan and I looked at each other.

'Good luck,' he said.

'I think you're the one who might need the good luck,' I said. 'You'll be at Ruthie's beck and call now, you watch.'

There was something about his gaze that made me feel quite exposed. As though for some reason he could see right through me, to the vulnerabilities I usually went to great pains to hide.

'Is she always this demanding?' he asked, his eyes not leaving mine.

I nodded, swallowing hard. He was making me all hot and bothered again. 'Afraid so.'

I glanced down at my notebook, reminding myself I had work to do and couldn't afford to get distracted.

'OK,' said Aidan, taking a deep breath. 'I'm going in.'

'I'll be right behind you,' I said, ushering him towards the kayaks. 'Don't fall in, will you?'

'You do know that if I go in, you're coming in with me, right?' he said, giving me a sideways glance.

I laughed. 'No chance.'

I watched, amused, when, as predicted, Ruthie made a

beeline for Aidan. He helped her get into the kayak, being very attentive and holding the boat still while she sat down.

Tim, on the other hand, who was supposed to be in the kayak next to Ruthie's, set one foot into it and recoiled. 'No. Nope, I'm sorry, I don't think I can do it.'

I went closer, looking at him quizzically.

'Everything all right, Tim?' I asked.

He did look a bit green now I could see him close up.

'I get very seasick,' he said.

I looked out at the water, which barely had a ripple on it, let alone any waves.

'I'm sure it's not as bad as you think,' I said, attempting to be reassuring while secretly wondering whether it was the fact he'd been drinking at lunchtime that had made him feel nauseous.

'You're going to have to take the helm, Maddie,' he insisted, backing off. 'I'll, er, shout instructions from the shore, or something.'

I sighed internally, distracted by Ruthie, who was having trouble lowering herself down into the kayak on account of her skin-tight Whistles pencil skirt. Once she was seated, I kicked off my trainers, waded in and used a lint brush to remove any fluff from her navy jacket, powdered her face for the hundredth time and gave her hair a generous swirl of hair spray for good measure.

'It won't move with the wind now,' I said reassuringly.

Ruthie, who was gripping the sides of the kayak like her life depended on it, looked less than impressed. 'How do I get this thing to move?' she asked through gritted teeth.

'I'll show you!' said a booming Finlay, who was kitted out in a full wetsuit, which made me slightly anxious.

We weren't intending to actually get wet, were we? He wasn't going to get us doing one of those Eskimo rolls, where you go upside down in the water? Ruthie would have a fit and so would I – I had no intention of getting my hair soaked, it would be a nightmare to try to straighten it before dinner. And with Aidan in the same hotel, I suddenly felt the need to not look a total mess. Which I wish I'd worked out this morning when I'd thought it would be a great idea to put on this horror of an outfit.

'Take this!' instructed Finlay.

He handed Ruthie an oar. She looked at it, blinking, as though she had no idea what it was for.

'Hold it in the middle. Here. Like this,' Finlay demonstrated.

Ruthie tutted as he scooted her hands along the oar, putting them in the right position.

'You'll soon get the hang of it,' said Finlay.

Personally, I wasn't convinced.

I checked the others: Tim was hanging around looking all efficient but being anything but; Lou had already got into her kayak and was raring to go.

'Pass me my handheld camera, Maddie, will you?' asked Lou.

I did as I was told, taking my time and holding on to it for dear life – if I dropped it in the water, Tim would probably fire me on the spot.

'Do you want me to take the script with me?' I asked Tim. 'Has Ruthie got a copy?'

'You tell me,' he said, pretending to read something on his clipboard.

'You weren't ... Were you expecting me to write it?' I asked him, not quite believing what I was hearing.

Tim looked up, squinting at me as though he was trying to work out which rock I'd crawled out from under. 'It was your idea, was it not? I just assumed you'd like the chance to make the segment your own. You're always banging on about wanting to produce your own show. Now's your chance.'

I couldn't argue with that, not exactly. I did want to produce my own shows. But usually, whenever I suggested I take a script off Tim's hands, he'd get all territorial and give me some menial task instead. If he'd wanted me to write the script for this, which was most unusual, he should have told me!

'I haven't actually prepared anything,' I said, zipping up my anorak as a particularly icy gust of wind hit me right in the face.

He sighed dramatically. 'Well, I suggest you cobble something together. Honestly, Maddie, you're going to have to learn to work on the hop. We don't always have hours to toil over creating the perfect combination of words, you know.'

I glanced at Aidan, who was getting into his kayak. I hoped he hadn't heard all of that, because what would he think? It annoyed me that I felt so powerless to speak up, and that I didn't have the guts to do anything about it. It wasn't fair that I was having to run the whole shoot, be Tim's minion, do Ruthie's make-up and all while Tim got paid three times as much as me for doing what, exactly? Scowling at me from the sidelines?

I pulled my notebook out of my bag and scrawled a few lines on to it. I'd get Ruth talking about all the water sports you could do on the lake. Do a couple of intros and outros. Luckily she was a consummate professional and if I fed her a line, she'd remember it word for word. We didn't have the luxury of autocue when we were on location. She might be irritating, but at least she could be relied upon to do the job at hand.

I put my notebook away, slung my rucksack over my shoulder and got into my own kayak. Embarrassingly, I was the last one to get in, so everyone was bobbing about on the water staring at me as I fumbled around with the oar and tried not to flip the kayak before I'd even started.

'Need any help?' asked Aidan, who had manoeuvred his boat so that it was next to mine.

'Um,' I said, trying to compose myself. 'Well, I've got to write a script off the top of my head, so if you've got any interesting information about the lake or kayaking, feel free to lob it in my direction.'

'Follow, me, everyone!' shouted Finlay enthusiastically. 'You want to keep the movement of the kayak as smooth as possible. Dip your oars in so they're just below the surface of the water and then ease them out like this, and back in the other side. If you want to stop, paddle backwards, like this.'

His boat came to a sudden stop and Ruthie crashed straight into the back of him. Fuck. That was bound to set her off.

'Are you OK, Ruthie?' I called, wincing.

She ignored me, which I took to be a positive sign. If she'd been hurt in any way, we'd *all* have heard about it.

Finlay carried on with his tutorial. 'And to turn the kayak, it's like this.'

He started wheeling around in a circular movement and we all followed suit with varying degrees of success. Eventually, we all got the hang of it and followed Finlay out towards the end of the pier. My arms were already aching and I was worried about Ruthie, who was groaning dramatically and stabbing at the water with ineffectual movements.

'So, we're on the largest lake – by surface area – in the whole of Great Britain,' said Aidan, skimming effortlessly along beside me. He wasn't even breaking a sweat and meanwhile I was stressed out to the max, not least about trying not to fall in.

'At its deepest point it's 190 metres deep.'

'190 metres!' I said, looking down into the blackness of the water and wishing I hadn't. It suddenly looked much eerier than it had from the shore.

'The loch and the national park you can see all around us – the Trossachs – has around four million visitors per year.'

'Wow, that's more than I'd expected,' I said, checking over my shoulder for Ruthie. 'Nearly there!' I called to her.

'Do you want some facts about kayaking?' asked Aidan.

I frowned at him. 'How do you know all of this?'

He shrugged. 'I like travelling. And when I'm travelling, I try to fully immerse myself in a place. Find out everything about it. The history, the geography, the culture, the food, you name it.'

'And you retain all of that information?'

He laughed. 'Most of it.'

'I totally want you on my team next time I do a Zoom quiz night.'

'With pleasure. What's your specialist subject?'

I thought about it for a second. 'I'm not bad on literature.'

Aidan looked impressed. 'I know nothing about books, so sounds like we'd make an excellent team.'

The thought of us working together on something was not unpleasant.

'So, go on then, give me some kayaking info. If I don't have some decent facts to feed Ruthie, she will not be happy.'

'Well, I'm no expert, but I do know that the word "kayak" originates from the Greenlandic word "qajaq".'

I widened my eyes. 'I didn't even know Greenlandic was a language, never mind that other thing you said!'

'It means hunter's boat,' he told me, slowing down so that I could catch him up.

'You're good,' I said, impressed.

We'd made it to the end of the pier and when I looked back at the shore, it seemed much further away than it had the other way around. I couldn't even make out Tim's facial expressions, let alone hear him barking orders, which was probably a good thing at this point. I was on my own, then.

I let Lou take the lead with setting up the shot, she was much bossier than I was and everyone listened to her. Annoyingly, as Ruthie flailed around getting into position, she flung up a torrent of water that – of course – landed mainly over me. I tried not to look fazed, but all I could think about was that now I was going to have to go over my hair with the straighteners before dinner. As I touched it lightly, I could feel it going springy beneath my fingertips. And it didn't help that Aidan was looking all groomed yet perfectly rugged like something out of a Burberry ad while I was a frizzy-haired, pretty much make-up-free mess in an M&S anorak. I was hardly going to make an impression on him looking like this. Which surprised me, because the minute I found someone attractive I usually panicked and backed off immediately. It was a self-preservation technique I'd learned over the years because I was sick of falling for men who couldn't have cared less about me. As I caught Aidan's eye, though, I realised something with a mixture of fear and excitement: there was something different about him; something that made me *not* want to back off.

Chapter Ten

To give Rosamund her due, the restaurant was lovely. It was nestled on a tiny street just around the corner from the hotel and the walls were the sort of gorgeous deep slate-blue I'd like to paint my home one day. Once Nick and I moved out of the apartment he'd bought for himself when he split up with Sophia, that was. It was a pretty apartment in one of those mansion blocks St John's Wood was famous for, and it was definitely bigger than the studio flat I had been living in. But still, it felt like his, not ours. And all the walls were white.

We hung our coats on a stand and followed a waiter to our table. The lighting was low (just how I liked it) and the vibe was young, trendy and casual. Rosamund had on three strings of huge, shiny (presumably real) pearls which she'd placed conspicuously over a black silk blouse. The look was finished off by diamond earrings that looked so heavy I was concerned for the welfare of her lobes. As usual, I felt like the bargain-basement member of the family. Even Daisy had let me down this time in her chic and flowy boho dress, most likely from Anthropologie – another shop I was perennially walking into and promptly walking out of when I saw the price tags.

We were already two drinks in when our mains came. I'd found this menu much more user-friendly than the one in the hotel restaurant – for a start there was an English translation for each dish. Don't get me wrong, I appreciated languages and when I travelled, I liked to get to know the basics: hello, goodbye, thank you, please, where is the bathroom? That sort of thing. But you couldn't know every item on a menu, could you? And there was always the possibility – in Italy, but elsewhere in the world, too – that I could end up eating something I'd rather not. I knew they were big on rabbit here, for example, and had purposely looked the word up so that I could avoid it: *coniglia* (feminine) and *coniglio* (masculine). Which one you used when it came to a menu, I had no idea, and since I had no intention of eating a meal that used to be a living, breathing fluffy bunny, it really didn't matter.

A waiter put my margherita pizza on the table in front of me, followed by the melanzane alla parmigiana that Nick and I were planning to share. It looked out of this world, all sizzling cheese and crispy edges; I was practically salivating.

'This looks amazing,' I said enthusiastically, inhaling the aroma of basil and tomato.

Rosamund, of course, had managed to find the most pretentious-sounding thing on essentially a quite non-pretentious menu.

'Anyone else go for the beef carpaccio with Tuscan sheep's cheese and black truffle?' she asked, as though ordering this weird-sounding dish made her the envy of every single person in the restaurant.

I had a quick glance around and noticed that most people, like me, had gone for pizza.

'I did, Rosamund,' said Sophia, who was seated opposite me. 'Oooh, here's mine. Yum.'

The waiter laid her plate down in front of her. Personally, I thought mine looked about a hundred times more appetising.

I began slicing up my pizza, not able to wait to dig in.

'So Maddie was introduced to the delights of *David*, today,' announced Nick, throwing his arm casually around my shoulders.

'Isn't he magnificent!' gushed Sophia theatrically.

'He is,' I agreed, annoyingly imagining *David* with Aidan standing next to him.

I removed the thought from my mind immediately.

'We'll have you fully cultured by the end of this trip, Maddie, don't you worry,' said Rosamund.

I'd be interested to hear Rosamund's definition of 'fully cultured'.

'Mummy,' warned Nick. 'Maddie is a seasoned traveller. She doesn't need lessons in culture from us.'

'Oh I know, darling, but there's always room to learn more. Right, Maddie?'

I happened to have a mouthful of (delicious) pizza right at that very moment and there were an agonising ten seconds or so where I chewed manically while everyone stared at me. I swallowed, washing it down with a glug of water.

'Absolutely. That's part of travelling, I think. Immersing yourself in the lifestyle,' I said, deciding it was best to overlook Rosamund's patronising tone on this occasion.

Who was I kidding? I found people patronising all the time and never pulled them up on it. Tim was the worst offender. But Rosamund was scarier than everyone at work put together, so I was hardly going to use this as an opportunity to suddenly start standing up for myself. And yet, for some reason, it felt more difficult to keep it inside. Tim might be less than complimentary about my work, but I could take that, it wasn't personal. Plus he was an arsehole to everybody. But it was like Rosamund knew exactly how to push my buttons – I was sure it was unintentional, but for some reason didn't make it any easier.

'Remind us, Maddie. Where is it you're from?' asked Rosamund, poking about in her weird mound of sheep's cheese.

Oh no. Not this. Not now.

I took a sip of wine, hoping she'd give up and move on to another topic if I paused long enough, but they were all looking at me again, waiting with bated breath for my answer.

'Kent,' I said, keeping it light.

I would give them the benefit of the doubt that this was what they meant.

'Yes, but where are you *from*? Originally?'

I'd had the same question time and time again over the years and it never got any easier. I think it was the utter disbelief that got to me, the self-righteousness of thinking I wouldn't know where I was from and had clearly made some sort of mistake.

'I'm not sure what you mean, Rosamund?' I said, feigning confusion.

'Well. I mean. Where are your ...'

She was floundering. Good.

'... family from?' she finally concluded.

'Oh, I see what you mean,' I said, still feeling like playing devil's advocate. 'My mum's from Kent, too,' I replied, smiling at her.

Rosamund nodded, clearly undeterred. 'And your dad?'

'St Lucia.'

'Ah!' she said, all triumphant, like she'd finally got it out of me. 'That's what I meant!'

Yep. Course it was.

I took another mouthful of pizza, trying to enjoy it as much as I had been before, but the relaxed feeling I'd had a few moments before was gone now.

'What time's the tour tomorrow, Rosamund?' piped up Sophia, completely oblivious to the fact that I felt as though I'd just had the life sucked out of me.

'Mum, do I have to go on this wine-tasting thing?' asked Daisy. 'Can't I stay at the hotel and watch YouTube in our room?'

'No you cannot,' snapped Sophia. 'You can watch YouTube back in London. It's beautiful out in the Tuscan countryside. Why don't you bring a sketch pad, or something? Or take some photos?'

'What, while you lot chug wine all day? Hardly seems fair,' argued Daisy.

I thought she had a good point, actually. Why would she want to come on a wine-tasting tour when she was too young to actually taste any of it? I was tempted to say I'd stay behind and take her to a gallery or something, but I knew this was the highlight of the trip for Rosamund. I ought to show willing.

'The concierge said to be in the foyer at 8.30,' said Rosamund, ignoring Daisy.

'A.M.?' I said, to clarify.

'Too early for you, Maddie?' asked Peter.

'She's an early riser, Dad, so hardly,' said Nick.

Rosamund called over the waiter to order another large glass of red wine for her and Peter. Everyone else had barely touched theirs. I supposed it was their anniversary, they were clearly celebrating. But her eyes were already looking quite glassy.

'Can I at least have some wine then? If I *have* to go?' said Daisy, not giving up.

'You can have a sip or two,' replied Nick. 'The laws out here are much more relaxed.'

Sophia glared at him. 'Do you think that's a good idea,

Nick? You know what she's like, she'll get a taste for it. Next thing, she'll be swigging cider out of paper bags on park benches.'

'She won't, Sophia. Give her some credit,' said Nick.

I squeezed his knee. I loved it when he stood up for Daisy. God, the poor girl needed somebody on her side.

'I'm glad one of my parents doesn't think I'm a complete fuck-up,' said Daisy.

'Now, now,' said Rosamund. 'We don't use that sort of language.'

I could have sworn Rosamund was slurring her words. We'd met them in the hotel bar, so it was anyone's guess how much they'd had to drink before Nick and I had arrived.

'I just don't see why I have to go!' said Daisy. 'Who takes a fourteen-year-old on a wine-tasting tour?'

'Daisy, that's enough!' snapped Sophia. 'It is your grand-mother and grandfather's wedding anniversary and you will do whatever they ask you to do.'

My strained relationship with my own parents seemed quite manageable in comparison to this. Mind you, that was probably because I rarely argued back and I admired Daisy, actually, for having a go. There were some advantages, I supposed, to having had my mum and dad split up and have new families when I was very young. For a start, they were generally so preoccupied with their new lives that neither of them cared much what I was doing. It made sneaking out to parties and smoking in the park *so* much easier to get away with. On the other hand, it also made you feel kind of alone and pretty much invisible, which wasn't exactly the best thing, either. That feeling of constantly falling under the radar, of never really making an impact, was a difficult one to shake.

'Daisy,' crooned Nick, 'calm down. It's just for a few hours.'

'*Six*. Six hours, Grandma said!'

'OK, then, it's just six hours. Shall we do something nice before we go? Have a bit of a walk? We could have an early breakfast together in San Spirito. I think you'd like it there.'

Daisy sighed dramatically. 'I suppose. But I don't see why I can't just stay here on my own. I'm not a child.'

'But you're not an adult either. Plus, we all have to do things we don't want to do at times,' said Nick. 'Isn't that right, Maddie?'

Luckily I'd just swallowed my mouthful of pizza this time and didn't have the awkward chew-watch thing to deal with.

'Absolutely,' I said, meaning it emphatically.

I didn't add that, lately, I seemed to be doing things I didn't particularly want to do approximately ninety per cent of the time.

Nick and I hung back a little as we walked the five minutes back to the hotel. He laced his fingers through mine.

'It's nice to see you've chilled out. You're not thinking about work anymore, are you?' he said.

'Barely,' I replied.

Did I really have the confidence to say no to Tim? It felt like bad things would happen if I didn't do what he wanted, but then rationally I knew that he'd just moan a bit and then probably forget about it. But he'd be disappointed – I thought that was what I found hard. Disappointing people. And yet I did anyway, probably, without trying half the time.

I paused to look in the window of one of the many boutiques along the street. They certainly loved their fashion in Florence. This particular display had dresses suspended from the ceiling, like pieces of art.

'I'm a bit worried about this tour tomorrow. I don't know

anything about wine, as you've probably worked out by now,' I admitted.

'The fact you always buy Australian kind of gave it away,' said Nick.

I looked at him, genuinely confused. 'What's wrong with Australian wine?'

He reached out and ruffled my hair. 'Oh Madeleine. You have a lot to learn.'

I pushed his hand away. 'Please don't be condescending,' I said.

He made a little huffing sound. I'd heard him do it before, when he was on the phone to a colleague usually, or sometimes to Daisy. But he'd never done it to me. 'I was joking, Maddie.'

Joke or not, it had annoyed me and I was glad I'd said something. It wasn't a huge thing, but it felt huge to me, because I was usually so busy trying to please Nick that I tended to overlook the things he occasionally did to upset me. Like inviting people round without warning me first and cancelling dinner plans at the last minute because something had come up at work. It was normal to annoy each other, surely. And yet, I couldn't quite get rid of the underlying feeling that I had to be on my best behaviour for him. Or else what? I wondered.

We carried on walking, Nick a few steps ahead. I twirled my engagement ring around on my finger, suddenly finding it even more difficult than usual to imagine my wedding day. I'd spent a lot of my adolescence dreaming about what my special day might look like. How handsome and besotted by me my husband would be, how voluminous my dress. Who I'd have as my bridesmaids (this had changed many times over the years depending on who was currently my best friend – I was going to ask Lou and Daisy, but hadn't quite got round to it). But what I used to think about most was what my in-laws would be like. I'd pictured this couple, still in love after many years together. The mum loved baking and the dad loved gardening and they both loved their son and therefore, by extension, his new bride. In my daydreams they became like second parents to me. That is, parents who actually noticed I was there and who were genuinely interested in getting to know me. They wouldn't be judgemental or unkind, and they would think me extremely funny and interesting. And while I was fully aware that this was just a fantasy, that things rarely worked out like this for anyone, Rosamund and Peter were far from the second parents I'd dreamed of and this dynamic – Nick and Daisy and Sophia – was categorically not how I'd imagined it.

'You don't think I'll make too much of a fool of myself on the vineyard tour, do you?' I asked, feeling quite vulnerable, suddenly.

For the most part, I didn't have a problem with owning my lack of knowledge – I couldn't be an expert on everything, could I, nobody could (although this was probably news to the Leveson-Gower family). And at least I was getting out there and making an effort to learn. But there was a limit to how many sneery looks I could take. And Daisy was right – six hours sounded LONG!

'How do you mean?' asked Nick.

'Well. Do they ask you things? About wine? Stuff I should know the answers to?'

'It's not a quiz. They tell *you* about *their* wines.'

I relaxed a bit.

'So it's not like they give you a glass of wine and you have to say that it's got notes of this, or hints of that?'

'I mean, I don't think so. But so what if it is? You can tell if it tastes like strawberries or apples or whatever, can't you?'

'I don't know.'

'Your palate's not that underdeveloped.'

'But all wine tastes pretty much the same to me,' I protested.

'Ah. Hence the Yellow Tail Shiraz.'

I threw him a look. Now I could never buy Yellow Tail Shiraz again. Or maybe I would, because I honestly couldn't see what the problem was with it. I also thought that if Nick was harbouring these secret, snooty opinions about Australian wines, what else was he harbouring opinions on?

'I've got that same feeling I had the night before my driving test,' I said.

Nick smiled at me. 'Nobody's testing you. And I'll be there. If it seems like you're struggling – although I don't think for a second you will be – I'll step in and change the subject or something.'

I looked at him gratefully as we turned the corner into Via Tornabuoni. In the light from the street lamps, it looked all glowy and shiny and perfect, like a movie set.

'Promise you won't leave my side, not for a second?' I said to him.

He swooped down and kissed me on top of my head. 'Promise,' he said. 'Now let's catch the others up.'

Rosamund and Sophia were just in front of us. Rosamund was clutching hold of Sophia's arm and her feet were sort of criss-crossing over each other.

'Is your mum drunk?' I whispered to Nick.

'Looks like it,' he said, grimacing.

We quickened our pace. As we were just about to fall into step beside them, I tuned into their conversation. Sophia's voice was easy to hear, haughty and high-pitched and probably travelled for miles. Rosamund's was softer. Her enunciation was not as clear as it usually was, but even so, I could just about make out what she was saying.

'Oh, Sophia, I wish you and Nick were still together. Do you ever think about it? Getting back with him?'

Sophia laughed lightly. 'He's with Maddie now, Rosamund.'

Rosamund sighed. 'She's a sweet girl. But she's not a patch on you.'

'We made a good team, Nick and I, didn't we?' snickered Sophia.

'You did, darling. You did,' said Rosamund with passion.

I stopped, right there in the street, glancing at Nick to see if he'd heard, too, but if he had, he was pretending not to.

'Mummy, take it easy on the wine when we get to the bar, yes?' he called.

Rosamund spun around on her kitten heels. 'Darling! I wondered where you'd got to.'

Sophia gave me a look and I held her gaze. She knew I'd heard, and I wasn't going to let her off the hook by pretending I hadn't. She looked away first, which gave me some small triumph. But the fact was, my suspicions had been confirmed – in Rosamund's eyes, I was never going to be good enough for Nick, or a suitable replacement for the woman he'd married first.

Chapter Eleven

I pulled the end off of a piece of croissant and stuffed it into my mouth, pretty sure that a six-hour wine tasting tour on an empty stomach would be a bad idea, although apparently we would be having a 'light lunch' at one of the vineyards.

Nick had gone out for breakfast with Daisy and I'd fully intended to go down to the hotel restaurant by myself and have something substantial, but then the bed was too big and comfortable and I'd lain under the duvet and flicked through my phone, catching up with all that was happening in the world. Then I'd made myself a Nespresso and sipped it with the windows thrown open and the prettily named Piazza degli Strozzi below me. And then, before I knew it, I had ten minutes to get dressed and downstairs, ready to meet the tour bus. Brazenly, I'd ducked into the restaurant, flung a croissant into a napkin and now I was eating it while I crossed the lobby, no doubt leaving a trail of crumbs behind me. Not the classiest look, I supposed, but needs must.

Rosamund, Peter and Sophia were waiting by the reception desk. I slowed my pace, swallowed the last of my pastry, brushed flakes of it off the front of my black vest and approached them.

'Morning!' I said.

I'd decided earlier, when I was feeling particularly relaxed and content, to make a real effort today (and would put the fact they'd annoyed me with their *where you are you from?*

line of questioning the night before to the back of my mind).
Sure, we hadn't had the best of starts, and they were a little
bit stuck-up, but it didn't mean they weren't nice people.
And when Nick and I got married, they'd be my family, too.
It would be so much easier if we got along.

'How did you all sleep?' I asked brightly.

'Very well thank you, Maddie,' said Rosamund, who had
overcompensated for the fact she could hardly wear jewels
to a daytime vineyard tour by making her hair even bigger
than usual.

Sophia had gone all casual, but in the way Elizabeth
Hurley might do casual, so that even her simple white shirt
and jeans combo looked like she'd walked straight off the set
of a Ralph Lauren photo shoot.

'Any sign of Nick and Daisy?' I asked, glancing at my
watch.

They were cutting it fine – the tour was due to leave in
three minutes.

Sophia shook her head. 'Neither of them are the best
timekeepers. I bet they're gassing away to each other and
haven't realised how late it is.'

'I'll give him a call,' I said, rooting around for my phone.

'I can do it if you like?' suggested Sophia, smiling sweetly
at me.

I smiled just as sweetly back. 'It's fine. Already dialled.'

I held my phone out to show her that I was, indeed,
already calling Nick. Aware that all eyes were on me, I metaphorically crossed my fingers that Nick was going to answer
and tell me that he was just around the corner and would
be with us in less than a minute. He was bound to, he must
realise we'd all be waiting for him. Although, saying that,
when we were back in London, it was almost impossible to
get hold of him at short notice. He always seemed to be in

meetings. I'd taken to calling his PA – Gillian – who was lovely and who knew far more about what Nick was up to on a daily basis than I did

'It's gone straight to voicemail,' I said, hiding my irritation. He'd better be here. He'd given me his word.

'Bloody Nick and his terrible timekeeping,' said Peter.

'Now, now, darling. They'll be on their way. He's probably stopped to buy Daisy a little something for the journey,' Rosamund soothed.

In truth, I didn't know why he'd decided to take Daisy out when we had such an early start, and why he'd left it to the last second to come back so that we were all – especially me – standing here anxiously waiting for him.

The revolving door spun hopefully and we all turned, fully expecting to see Nick and Daisy swanning through it, flushed and full of apologies. But instead there was a bald, tanned man wearing Ray Ban-style sunglasses and a pale blue shirt tucked into jeans heading in our direction.

'You are here for the wine-tasting tour?' he said to us in a strong, sing-songy Italian accent.

We all nodded obligingly.

'That's right,' said Peter. 'Just waiting for two more.'

The Italian man looked at his watch and shook his head. 'We are on a very tight schedule. How long will they be?'

'Any minute now,' I said, convincing myself as much as anything.

'I am Gino, your guide for the day,' he said, whipping out a clipboard from behind his back. 'So. Here at the Palazzo Continentale Hotel I have a party of six and a party of one.'

'We're the party of six,' I said.

I was in my comfort zone with this, used to organising trips and keeping to schedules (unlike Nick, clearly). I decided I may as well take the lead while I had the opportunity to and Rosamund and Peter didn't seem to want to engage with Gino, anyway, probably because he'd already been relegated to minion status, alongside all the hotel employees and anyone who worked in a restaurant.

I checked my phone: nothing from Nick and it was now 8.33. I knew that these tour guides liked to keep to a strict timetable. I'd dealt with them myriad times before, and they didn't take kindly to people rocking up late, in fact they were liable to just drive off without them. This I did not want. It would be a nightmare.

I tried texting Nick.

WHERE ARE YOU? THE TOUR IS LEAVING!

True to form, Gino was already looking stressed and was pacing up and down the foyer, staring at his clipboard.

'We will get on to the van and the others, if they are not here in five minutes, we go without them. Otherwise we have less time in the wine tasting, which does not matter to me, but after all it is why you are on this trip, *si?*'

Fuck.

Sophia actually looked quite pleased at the prospect of not having to look after (if you could call it that) a bored, whiny Daisy for an entire day. 'Oh well, if they don't make it, it's their loss,' she said breezily. 'Knowing Daisy, she's wrapped Nick around her little finger and has persuaded him to go shopping for the day instead.'

Surely he wouldn't do that, knowing how I felt about this trip?

'Let's get on this damn van, then,' said Peter, following Gino out onto the street.

The van was parked right outside, and Gino ushered Rosamund, Peter and Sophia into the three seats at the back. I got in next and there was only one seat left next to me, so either Nick or Daisy would have to take one of the two passenger seats at the front.

'Let me try him one more time,' I said.

There was something slightly embarrassing about the fact that I couldn't locate my own fiancé. Surely I, if anyone, should be able to get through to him. He must know he was running late – why hadn't he let me know? If we had some clue as to how long he would be, we could persuade Gino to wait, or maybe even pick him up along the way, but clearly none of us had any idea where he'd gone, other than to San Spirito, which was presumably a large-ish district of the city.

As I listened to Nick's phone ring, over and over, I heard Gino talking to someone outside the van.

'Ah, you are the missing party of one!'

No answer from Nick again. I was feeling more pissed off by the second. Unless the two of them appeared in the next two minutes, I was going to have to navigate the delights of Chianti alone. Not that I wasn't looking forward to seeing the countryside and the vineyards, because I was. But it felt pressured, in the way that everything with Nick's family seemed to. I wondered if I'd ever be able to completely relax around them.

Gino's head popped into the van. 'OK. We go.'

'I insist we wait for my son and granddaughter!' piped up Rosamund from the back. 'If it's just us, we don't mind missing some of the tour. Do we?'

'Not at all,' piped up Peter.

'Ah, but it is not just you,' said Gino, standing aside. 'We have another paying guest and therefore we must go and begin our tour. Otherwise I get complaints. And then I lose my job.'

He was being a touch dramatic, I thought, and of course I was perfectly down with the idea of waiting until Nick and

Daisy deigned to rock up. Perhaps the party of one could be persuaded.

I checked my phone one more time (nothing!) and when I looked up, Aidan was clambering into the van. My stomach lurched.

He took one look at me and recoiled.

'Go!' instructed Gino. 'Get into the van please,' he said, herding Aidan into the seat next to me.

He looked lovely of course, all tousled, like he'd overslept and hadn't had time to shave. He was wearing a simple black shirt and blue jeans and as he took the seat next to me (couldn't he sit in the front?!), I screamed internally. It was bad enough not having Nick here, but now I was going to have to spend the whole day with *him*. I pretended to check my phone again so that I didn't have to make eye contact.

'And who might you be?' asked Sophia, leaning forward in her seat.

'I'm Aidan,' he said simply, turning in his seat so that his face was right there in my peripheral vision.

'And what do you do, Aidan?' asked Sophia.

Was this really her first question when meeting somebody new?

Aidan cleared his throat, seemingly finding it a strain to speak. I wondered if – like me – he wanted nothing more than to get out of this bus immediately.

'I'm a travel journalist,' he replied.

'Ooooh, exciting. What are you working on?' asked Sophia.

Aidan left it a couple of beats longer than was strictly necessary to answer.

'A piece on Italy out of season. I'm doing Rome next.'

'Oh, what a lovely idea,' she said, even more enthused than before.

Did it seem weird that I was completely mute, not even looking this supposed stranger in the eye? I kept my phone in the palm of my hand – perhaps they'd think I was preoccupied with getting hold of Nick. What would I do if Aidan really was nothing to me? How would I act? I had my arms crossed defensively, I realised, uncrossing them. I wouldn't be defensive with someone I'd only just met, would I?

'I have my own clothing line, so I travel here a lot on business,' Sophia went on. 'We stock in La Rinascente, Florence's premier department store.'

'Very impressive,' said Aidan.

'So, if you'd like to interview someone,' continued Sophia, 'I'd be more than happy to step in. And certainly, for my family and I, travelling out of season is an absolute must. Who wants hordes of tourists swarming the streets and clogging up the restaurants? We like the exclusivity of travelling either in the autumn or around now, just before the summer rush.'

So she still considered Rosamund, Peter and Nick her family.

Gino started the engine. 'Please put on your seat belts, it is the law here in Italy and I will get into trouble with the police if you do not.'

We all did our seat belts up as instructed. I tried not to react to Aidan as he dug around next to my thigh trying to put his belt buckle in the right slot. I shifted as far away from him as I could, shuffling to the left so that no part of me was touching any part of him.

We were soon out of central Florence, which was much smaller than I'd thought, and were speeding along the motorway at an alarming rate. In an attempt to make up for lost time (all of about six minutes), Gino was literally putting his pedal to the floor, and we were slicing in and out of lanes, overtaking other vehicles and practically screeching around bends. I tried to distract myself from the feeling that I was about to end up in a ten-car pile-up by looking out of the window at the rolling hills flanking us on both sides. It was the perfect day for it at least, with temperatures already in the mid-twenties.

'This landscape you see here, on both sides, is the ideal climate for growing grapes and olives. Cold and rainy in the winter, dry and humid in the summer,' said Gino in his Italian lilt, which would have been relaxing to listen to if we weren't bombing along at about ninety-five miles per hour.

'Travelling alone, are you?' piped up Peter from the back seat.

Since it wasn't clear who he was talking to – presumably Aidan, but I could see why it wouldn't be obvious – nobody answered.

'You at the front, there. Party of one. Are you travelling alone?'

Aidan finally cottoned on to the fact that this question was being directed at him and half-swivelled around in his seat again.

'Sorry. I was miles away there. Yes.'

'He's just explained that he's a journalist, Peter,' said Sophia.

'Well, journalists take holidays, too, don't they?' grumbled Peter.

I crushed myself up against the door, pretending to be very interested in the miles and miles of rolling hills we were passing while also secretly listening to every single thing they said.

'What an interesting career!' exclaimed Rosamund, more enamoured than I'd seen her get about anything, ever. 'Who is it you write for, may I ask?'

'A new travel magazine launching next month. We're hoping to rival *Conde Nast Traveller*,' said Aidan.

I hid my surprise. The whole Conde Nast scene had never seemed like his thing.

'That sounds fabulous,' gushed Rosamund. 'Oh do let us exchange details before the end of the day. We'd love to read the finished piece.'

I tutted quietly. I wanted Aidan out of my life again, not friending my mother-in-law-to-be on Facebook.

'There are many other things growing in these fields,' went on Gino. 'Porcini mushrooms. Wild asparagus. Truffles. And then of course there is the wildlife: rabbits, deer, pheasants, boars. Boars are very bad for vineyards. And vineyards, for us, are life.'

I surreptitiously checked my phone. Nothing.

'Anything from Nick?' asked Sophia.

'Nope,' I said, trying not to sound fucked off but failing dismally.

I could feel Aidan looking at me, fleetingly, as though he was trying his hardest not to. I always knew when his eyes were on me, it had been that way from the moment we met.

As we whizzed along the motorway, Gino told us about the legend of the black rooster, an ancient dispute between Siena and Florence to decide who would control the Chianti territory. Something about a white rooster and a black rooster and where they met in the middle being the point at which the border would be. The people of Siena starved their white rooster, thinking it would travel far and wide looking for food, so expanding the area they would control. The Florentines overfed their black rooster, giving him more energy and so he got much further and, as a result, Florence controls nearly all of the Chianti district.

'Chianti Classico wine must be eighty per cent Sangiovese,

the red grape native to this area, and it must have the black rooster seal. If it does not have these two things, it is not Chianti classico.'

'Good to know!' shouted Peter exuberantly from behind.

'You can see our first stop, there in the distance,' continued Gino. 'San Gimignano. A medieval village which stands four hundred metres above sea level and is called the New York of Tuscany on account of its fourteen towers. This village was the first producer of Saffron in the Middle Ages and is a UNESCO world heritage site.'

I shuffled in my seat, needing to stretch my legs which had been scrunched in a weird position so as not to accidentally brush my knee against Aidan's. I was still toying with the idea of saying something to him, something very casual and bland, so as not to draw attention to myself. Because wasn't it weird that I'd ignore someone when they were sitting right next to me? Then again, Nick's family probably thought I didn't know how to behave in social situations like this, anyway, so perhaps they weren't as surprised as I thought.

The van pulled off the motorway and after travelling up a country lane or two we pulled over at a grand, terracotta gateway leading into the village. It reminded me of Èze, a place I'd visited in the South of France once, and it shimmered in front of us, as enticing as the Emerald City.

'You will have forty minutes here,' announced Gino as he jumped out of the van and then came around to open our passenger door.

Light flooded the interior of the vehicle as we all unbuckled our seat belts. Aidan was the first out, me next, followed by the others. I purposely angled my body away from him.

'You must visit Gelateria Dondoli,' said Gino. 'It is an ice cream shop on the main square of the village and this has the best ice cream in not just Italy, but in the world. Their speciality is the saffron ice cream, it tastes like nothing you can imagine. Then you must look at the views.'

'Sounds delightful,' said Sophia, stretching and flipping her Fendi sunglasses on.

'See you back here in forty minutes. You must not be late, otherwise we lose time in the vineyards, you understand?' instructed Gino.

We all mumbled in agreement and set off into the village. I was mesmerised by the view to our right: miles and miles of beautiful, rolling Tuscan fields.

'He's very good-looking, that journalist guy,' said Sophia, watching Aidan as he thankfully walked off ahead.

Rosamund tittered, clearly agreeing with her. This was worse than I'd feared.

Loch Lomond

Two Years Earlier

The beach was pitch black except for the lights from the hotel behind me. Letting my eyes accustom to the darkness, I sat down near the shore, wrapping myself in the world's cosiest tartan blanket (strategically borrowed from my room). I began to pick out the shapes of the mountains on the other side of the loch. I couldn't remember which one Aidan had said was the tallest. Ben Lomond, I think he'd said it was called.

I had my trusty notebook with me and had planned to write some notes for the next day while I was down here, but I pretty swiftly worked out that it was too dark and I'd have to just think for now, and hope I remembered everything when I got back to my room and could write it down. We were going out on the lake on a water bus tomorrow and Tim had asked me to help him prep the script, by which he meant do all of the research and give him all of the information so that he could pass the whole thing off as his own work.

I clicked the end of my biro up and down, thinking. What would our viewers want to know about the water bus trip? What would persuade them to want to come to Loch Lomond?

'Hello.'

I looked up to see Aidan towering over me. He had a blanket around his shoulders, too and was clutching a tumbler in each hand.

'Mind if I join you?' he asked.

'Sure,' I said, putting my notebook down.

'You're still working,' he said, lowering himself onto the pebbles.

'Sadly.'

'Whisky?' he said, offering me a glass.

'I shouldn't.'

I'd already had two glasses of wine with dinner and the last thing I needed was a hangover in the morning. I wanted to get up early and do a recce of the pier, where we'd be catching the boat from later in the day. Then again, it was tempting. When in Rome, right?

'Go on then,' I said, taking it from him.

I twirled the glass around in my hand. I liked how the ice sounded when it clinked against the side.

'How was the footage from earlier?' asked Aidan, leaning back on his elbows and looking out across the water.

'Great, actually. Lou's really good. She somehow made Ruthie look as though she was an accomplished, confident kayaker. And, to Ruthie's credit, she managed to fake having a good time.'

'That *is* impressive,' he said, smiling.

I closed my eyes and breathed in deeply, listening to the water lapping gently on the pebbles.

'Do you smell that?' I said, still with my eyes closed.

'Smell what?' he asked.

'Heather. If you concentrate hard enough, you can smell it on the wind. It's sweet. Tangy. Go on, try.'

He was silent for a bit. I imagined him with his eyes closed, too, sniffing at the air.

'I've got it,' he said eventually.

My eyes popped open. In the distance, I could hear the soft sound of bagpipes, the evocative local music they'd been playing in the lodge's restaurant all night.

'Do you like your job?' Aidan suddenly asked me.

I leaned back on my elbows, too, lifting my face to the sky.

'Sort of. I guess it wasn't exactly what I had in mind when I decided I wanted to work in TV.'

'What did you have in mind?'

I laughed. 'I imagined myself producing one of those really cool Netflix shows. *Amazing Vacation Rentals*, or something where they have about twenty crew members and make everything look cinematic.'

'You like the big-budget stuff.'

'I like the idea of going further than Lanzarote.'

'Holiday Shop is just a starting point, isn't it?' he said. 'Nothing's stopping you doing your dream job after.'

'In theory.'

'You don't sound convinced ...' he said, leaning back further, so that we were almost perfectly symmetrical.

'I'm realistic, that's all. Exciting stuff doesn't generally happen to me. I've never been one to dream big. I think shooting kayaks on Loch Lomond or paragliding in Tenerife is probably as good as it's going to get. And that's fine. I like it. I'm lucky, right? My job's pretty exciting compared to most people's.'

Aidan rubbed at his jaw. 'I agree. I tell myself that again and again. But then, at the same time, I know I want more.'

I looked at his legs, stretched out, dangerously close to mine. Dangerous because I suddenly wanted to press my thigh into his. And he was a stranger, pretty much, and I never felt like this, so why was this happening?

'Such as?' I said, thinking that if I kept talking, my mind wouldn't wander.

'I want to find these little hidden corners of the world where hardly anyone has been and I want to write about them so brilliantly that everyone who reads my article thinks: I *have* to go there.'

'What's the most amazing place you've been to so far?' I asked him.

He turned to look at me. 'Chile, maybe. Or New Zealand? Saying that, I always find something amazing wherever I am.'

His eye lashes were really long, I could see that now that my eyes had accustomed to the dark. Stubble sprouted on his jawline, but it looked as though it would be soft if I ran my thumb over it.

'Even Loch Lomond?' I asked.

'Even that.'

I held his gaze. For some reason, it didn't feel as though I needed to look away, even though clearly I probably should. I brought my whisky to my lips and took a sip, putting one hand on my chest as the heat of it flowed down my throat, warming me as it went.

'Good?' he asked.

I nodded, taking another sip.

'For some reason I can't stop looking at you,' he said, propping himself up on one hand, holding his whisky in the other. When he smiled, I felt my breath quicken.

I reached out, tentatively, stroking his wrist. Was this me making the first move? I usually made some attempt to play it cool in situations like this, but it never really got me anywhere, so maybe changing it up was good. He was either interested in getting to know me or he wasn't; I didn't suppose it mattered who touched who first.

He looked down at my fingers and then took a sip of his own drink and I watched his Adam's apple bob up and down as he swallowed. I imagined trailing my finger under his chin, down his throat, unbuttoning his shirt, running my hand across his chest. He put his glass down and looped his fingers through my hair.

'You're very beautiful,' he said, inching closer.

'This is probably a bad idea,' I said, not meaning it. 'Because I'm supposed to—'

He kissed me mid-sentence. Lightly at first, then pulling back.

'You were saying?' he asked.

'Doesn't matter,' I said, grasping at the back of his head and pulling him into me. I still had ice on my tongue and he tasted like I did, of cold whisky. I pushed him back so that he was lying on the beach and then flipped myself over, straddling him. 'This is very unprofessional of me,' I said, letting out a soft moan as he ran his hands down my hips, pressing me harder into him, digging his fingernails into my back. He was as turned on as I was, I could feel it now. I ran my hands under his shirt, so eager to feel his body underneath that I nearly ripped it open, like you see people do in films. I fumbled with the buttons instead, tearing at them impatiently.

And then I heard a door open, the bagpipes getting louder, a door shutting behind someone. I rolled off him, instinctively touched my hair, pressed my lips together. He sat up, pulling his open shirt across him.

Somebody walked behind us, crunching on the pebbles.

'Evening,' said a male voice with a Scottish lilt.

'Evening!' I called back, making some attempt to glance over my shoulder. I felt around for my blanket, pulling it across me.

We were silent for a bit. My heart returned to its normal rhythm.

Aidan smiled. 'I don't usually do that. Kiss women I barely know.'

'Really? I thought you'd be king of the holiday romance?'

'Well, this isn't a holiday.'

'True,' I conceded.

'Anyway, I've never actually had one.'

I gave him a disbelieving look. A man who looked like that? He had to have women pining for him all over the place. 'Not even with all your travelling?'

His knee grazed against mine. I was tempted to stop talking and take up where we'd left off.

'I don't usually let myself get distracted by beautiful women while I'm working,' he said.

I tucked my hair behind my ears, self-conscious, suddenly.

'I've embarrassed you, haven't I?' he said.

I shrugged.

'You are, though. Really beautiful.'

'Thank you.'

'Are you seeing anyone? Back in London?' he asked.

I shook my head. 'Too busy.'

'Hmmn,' he said, as though thinking deeply about what I'd said, trying to work out the subtext.

I didn't even know the subtext. Well, I could probably work it out if I thought hard enough about it, but I didn't want to ruin the moment. I was having fun for once. Fun without the fear of consequences, because there was no way this was going to go anywhere. It was just a moment, on a beach, in Scotland. I bet that when I was back in London, I'd barely be able to remember it.

'Relationships scare me a bit, if I'm honest,' I said quietly. 'I can never get the balance quite right. The idea that you have to give enough of yourself so that the other person knows who you are, but not too much, in case it doesn't work out. Because you'd fall apart completely, then, wouldn't you?'

He looked as though he was contemplating this.

'I don't think you'd fall apart.'

Maybe not, but I wasn't prepared to risk it.

'What about you?' I asked.

'I'm not seeing anyone, either,' he said.

It was a bit late for me to ask now, wasn't it? This was what happened when you went around kissing people without thinking. He could have been married for all I knew, and then I would have felt terrible.

I was very aware of his arm resting against mine. I wanted to kiss him again, but I thought the moment had probably passed.

'Would you like to come back to my room?' he asked, his words piercing the air.

Although I wanted to say yes, yes definitely, I forced myself to think about Tim (of all people!). And Ruthie. And Holiday Shop.

'Better not,' I said, not convincing myself. 'Big day tomorrow.'

'Sure,' he said. 'Sorry. I shouldn't have asked.'

'It's fine. Don't feel bad about it.'

I stood up and as I did, he held on to my hand, tugging it gently, as though he was going to pull me back down on top of him, which in some ways I wanted him to. Instead I eased my fingers away.

'See you around, then,' I said.

'Actually, I was going to ask if I could join you guys on your lake cruise tomorrow? Would you mind? It could be good for my story.'

'Does a day trip around the loch count as a sport, then?' I teased.

He smiled. 'I don't see why not.'

He looked dazzling in the moonlight, his hair slightly dishevelled now.

I waved and walked back towards the lodge. I couldn't look around because I knew that if I did, I'd be going back to his room in an instant.

Chapter Twelve

We reached the main square in San Gimignano – Piazza della Cisterna – while it was still lovely and quiet. Gino had warned us that at around 9.30 a.m., coach-loads full of tourists would turn up and the place would be swarming. For now, though, it was like we had the village to ourselves. The little shops lining the promenade were just opening up, with the owners putting out baskets of trinkets, like lemon soaps and cork bottle-stoppers with bright ceramic tops. Little put-put trucks were trundling up the street, stopping to make deliveries, and a bus – which took up the entire, narrow main street – climbed the hill and swung precariously around the corner into the square. It was like going back in time.

'Who's up for trying some of this ice cream, then?' I asked, looking up at the gelateria Gino had recommended.

It was an unassuming place, much like any ice cream shop you'd find in Italy, with tempting mounds of whipped gelato housed behind a glass cabinet. It did, however, have a banner above its door stating that the shop had won the Gelato World Championship in 2018. Praise indeed, and clearly we had to see what the hype was about.

As the others were umming and aahing about whether it was too early for ice cream and exactly how many calories might be in a tub of it, Aidan appeared in the doorway. He clearly hadn't hung around (the story of his life) and was already holding a waffle cone with copious amounts of pale yellow ice cream piled on top. Our eyes met for a second before he checked himself, realised he was staring directly at public enemy number one and snapped his head in Sophia's direction. He obviously couldn't even stand looking at me. Which I still didn't get, because I hadn't done anything to him. I hadn't left him.

I remembered reading something about narcissists – about them being easily 'wounded' if you dented their ego. But how had I done that? And he'd never shown any narcissistic traits before, although maybe they were too well-hidden for me to have picked up on them, caught up as I was in believing that I'd just met the love of my life and that we were about to run off into the sunset together. How pathetic I'd been. As if I was the sort of person who would ever get the fairy-tale ending.

'Oooh. Which flavour did you go for, Aidan?' asked Sophia, using the gelato as an excuse to sidle up to him.

I wondered for a second whether she was his type. I didn't think so, but then how would I know? What I thought I'd known about him – the sort of person he'd seemed in the weeks we'd spent together – had turned out to be completely false. Because the Aidan I'd thought I'd known would never have dropped me like that without a word. We'd shared parts of ourselves with each other in the time we'd spent together, with the promise of more to come. And I supposed that what he'd kept hidden was the part of him that wasn't as sure about me as he'd made out he was.

'It's called Santa Fina Cream,' said Aidan, taking a mouthful. 'Oh my God,' he exclaimed, genuinely impressed. 'You *all* have to get some.'

I hung back moodily, torn between wanting an ice cream and not wanting to give him the satisfaction of thinking I was only getting one because he'd recommended it. As though I needed his permission! And also annoyed because it was beautiful here, in this terracotta-hued cobbled square, and he was ruining it for me.

'Oh go on then, Peter, let's get a cone to share,' said Rosamund with excitement.

We were back at the van for 9.40 sharp, mainly because Gino had put the fear of God into us about being late. Except for Aidan, that was, who was nowhere to be seen. I'd spotted him two or three times after stopping at the gelateria: once as he wandered down a narrow street flanked by gothic stone buildings with arches and little shutters and pretty red herringbone paving stones and once when Sophia and I walked a little further up the hill than everyone else because we wanted to take some photos (or some video footage, in my case, just to appease Tim). While I was shooting a pan shot of the tumbling rooftops of San Gimignano with the olive trees and the green hills beyond, I could see him in the bottom left of the shot, a little lower down, like a silhouette against the blue sky.

'Is he staying at our hotel, then?' Sophia had asked conspiratorially, nodding her head towards him.

'Not sure,' I'd said, keeping it as vague as I could.

My only hope was that he'd be leaving in the morning. Work trips were usually short and sweet, weren't they? He'd be on a tight schedule.

I put my seat belt on, hoping Gino wouldn't notice we were missing one passenger. It was bad of me, I knew, but I was sure Aidan could find his own way back to Florence. He could expense it, couldn't he?

'Where's that other man? The journalist?' piped up Rosamund as Gino tried to close the van door without Aidan in it.

Damn.

'He is not here at 9.40, so he misses the van. I am not supposed to park here. If I stay longer, I get a ticket,' said Gino, looking all stressed out again.

Well done, Aidan. Gino would be speeding again, now, wouldn't he, wanting to make up for the thirty seconds lost hanging around here.

'But we can't just leave him,' said Sophia, sounding put out.

She definitely fancied him.

Gino started huffing and puffing and pacing around. And then my phone pinged and I saw that Nick had finally texted.

So sorry!! We walked too far and couldn't get back in time. Trying to organise a taxi out to you now.

I sighed, firing off a text.

HURRY!

At least he was making some effort to get here, but if he hadn't even left Florence, he was barely going to have any time. I was most certainly going to to kick off the wine-tasting proceedings alone. I wondered how much you actually drank at these things. Was it a mouthful or a whole glass of each? Did you swill it around in your mouth and then spit it out afterwards? How many wines would we try? And would I feel drunk by the end of it? The way my day was going, I sort of hoped I would, even if I wasn't usually a fan of daytime drinking.

'Nick's on his way,' I called over my shoulder.

'Yes, he texted me a little while ago,' piped up Sophia.

Had he really contacted her before he messaged me?

'Daisy dragged him to some trendy café on the other side of Florence and then, surprise, surprise, they couldn't make it back in time,' explained Sophia to a confused-looking Peter.

'How ridiculous,' he said.

'Quite,' said Sophia.

'Never mind. He'll be here at some point,' reassured Rosamund.

I'd noticed how much she defended Nick. They were closer than I'd thought. Which perhaps made it even odder that he hadn't thought to introduce me to her before. I had an uneasy feeling, which was possibly my own paranoia, but it felt real. I couldn't get rid of the thought that maybe he was embarrassed by me. That if he waited until we were engaged, there'd be nothing she could do about it. And even if she did want to put him off, it would be too late. Although, of course, engagements were broken. All the time.

As I chucked my phone into my bag and looked up, I spotted Aidan legging it through the city gates. Great. Two minutes later and Gino would have been wheel-spinning away from the kerb without him.

'There he is!' called out Sophia.

Gino spun around, hands on hips, ready to unleash. After a brief (but amusingly harsh) scolding from Gino, Aidan leapt into the van.

'Sorry, everyone,' he said, ignoring me, as usual.

'We thought you'd deserted us,' simpered Sophia, leaning forward to touch him lightly on the shoulder.

Judging by the way Sophia looked momentarily thrown, I presumed he'd given her one of his dazzling smiles. I didn't know whether it made me feel better or worse that he had that effect on other people, too. I supposed that, in a way, I'd imagined us having this secret connection. That it had only been me who found him devastatingly attractive. I'd thought about it quite a lot, and at the time we were dating, it had made me feel less insecure about whether I was special enough to keep his attention. Which ultimately I hadn't been, of course.

Aidan sat down, fumbling with his seat belt. 'I confess, I had to go back for another ice cream,' he said.

Everyone except me laughed.

'Which flavour this time?' asked Rosamund.

'Grand Marnier Cream,' he called over his shoulder.

'Ooooh, delicious,' purred Sophia practically in my ear.

He'd had a bottle of Grand Marnier in his drinks cabinet. When we'd been together, he'd lived in a one-bedroom flat in Putney and I'd been there maybe eight or nine times. We'd had a shot of it in our coffee one night after dinner. I could still remember the taste of it, how I'd laughed and told him it had gone straight to my head and he'd joked that that wasn't a bad thing. I wondered if he remembered that, too. If, subconsciously, he'd chosen his gelato flavour because of that night. Or whether Grand Marnier was something he shared with all the women in his life, of which I could only imagine there must be many. He was a player, I supposed. And more fool me for falling for his charm in the first place.

We drove for a bit, thankfully at a slightly less frantic speed, curving into the heart of the countryside until Gino pulled up at a huge white villa swathed with pink bougainvillea.

'OK,' said Gino, turning into the driveway. 'Here we are at our first vineyard: Tenuta Torciano. This is a high-class vineyard. They sell their wines to big restaurants all over the world. They have lots of staff and lots of land.'

'This sounds like our sort of place, Rosamund,' I heard Peter say in the back.

'You have one hour and thirty minutes here,' announced Gino, letting us out. 'Not a minute more and not a minute less, otherwise you will not properly enjoy the other vine-yard. OK?'

'Yep,' I said, jumping out after Aidan.

I looked up at the sky, breathing in the floral scent in the air. Birds were chirruping but other than that, there were no sounds at all out here in the Chianti hills. No cars, no honking horns. Just silence and fields and an elderly woman working on the farm opposite, picking grapes from her vines.

'Follow me,' said Gino, leading us through a pretty garden and into a conservatory with purple wisteria draped all over the ceiling, and tables laid out with tablecloths and glasses. It was like a scene from a no-expense-spared wedding in a country hotel.

'This is very nice,' said Rosamund, touching her hair.

I felt like reassuring her that it hadn't moved an inch since we'd left the hotel. It couldn't possibly with that amount of hairspray on it.

We were introduced to our workshop leader, Carlotta, whose name I didn't catch for ages because although she was very smiley and very nice, she spoke so fast and with such a strong Italian accent that I could only understand every other word she was saying. I wondered if it was just me.

'She needs to slow down,' said Peter, too loudly.

Fine. Not just me, then.

I was the last to sit and in my determination not to end up next to Aidan, I'd faffed around so much, trying to second-guess where he was headed that I'd messed up and was, of course, sitting right next to him. Great. Sophia was on the other side of him and Rosamund was opposite me, so it pretty much couldn't get any worse.

I looked longingly at the bottle of wine Carlotta was brandishing and watched impatiently as she opened it, pouring quite a substantial amount of white wine into each of our glasses.

'This is a Tenuta Torciano, number 32. Very nice wine. Take it in your left hand, right hand, swill. Like this.'

I watched as Carlotta flung the glass of wine effortlessly from one hand to the other and then swilled it wildly in her right hand so the pale yellow liquid spun around in the glass like the contents of a washing machine.

'Impressive,' I said under my breath.

'Pretty sure I'm not going to be able to do that,' commented Aidan.

I dared to look at him out of the corner of my eye. Had he been talking to me? He'd probably worked out that if we sat here in frosty silence the whole time, then the rest of our group was going to wonder what on earth was going on. And I didn't think either of us wanted to draw attention to what had actually gone on.

I attempted to have a go at the swilling, worried about dropping the glass and then managing to slop wine over the top of the rim.

'Ooops,' I said. 'How are you getting on, Rosamund?'

Rosamund was swirling smugly away like a pro. 'Oh, it's easy when you've done this as many times as we have. Look, hold the stem here. Not the glass, because that will warm up the wine and we want it nice and chilled.'

I followed her lead, holding the glass by the stem, which felt very unstable and all kinds of wrong. It worked though, and the swilling came much easier when I tried it again.

'Good!' said Rosamund, and I perked up, as I tended to when I'd inadvertently managed to please somebody.

'Now, I want you to take a mouthful of wine and hold it for five seconds only,' commanded Carlotta.

'And then we swallow it?' I asked, realising too late that it was probably a silly question.

Everyone except Carlotta and Aidan laughed.

'You swallow it, yes, then if you like, you drink more, if you don't like, you pour what is left of your glass into this bucket here, in the middle of the table.'

I nodded sheepishly, deciding there and then that I was going to drink the entire glass, come what may.

I took a sip, held it in my mouth as instructed and then nearly laughed out loud when I caught sight of Aidan; his nose was wrinkled in disgust and he closed his eyes as he made a meal of swallowing it. Aidan hated white wine, I'd forgotten that. My own mouthful, on the other hand, slipped effortlessly down my throat.

'What do you taste? Which flavour?' asked Carlotta, waiting for an answer.

'What do you think, Maddie?' asked Sophia sweetly, leaning forward to direct her question to me.

I was almost certain she was putting me under the spotlight because she knew I'd have no idea what 'notes' it was supposed to have. Was the flavour really that developed that I'd be able to pick it out without so much as a clue?

'Um …'

I took another mouthful, buying myself some time. Somewhere in the midst of my panic, I saw Aidan doodling on his Tasting Notes card. He'd written the word: BANANA. Surely he couldn't be helping me, could he? Not intentionally, anyway. But in the absence of any better suggestions, it was all I had. I gave it a couple of beats for authenticity, pretending to mull it over.

'Is it banana?' I asked, as though it had just come to me naturally.

'Very good!' trilled Carlotta. 'You have an excellent palate for tasting wine.'

I leaned forward to smile at Sophia, who looked slightly less superior than she had sixty seconds ago.

I'd thank Aidan later. Maybe.

Carlotta shot out of her seat again, this time with a bottle of Chianti Classico. She proudly showed us the black rooster on the label, which, thanks to Gino, we knew all about.

'I'm looking forward to trying this,' I said to Rosamund.

'So am I,' she said. 'Waitrose do a very good one, apparently. Peter's already looked it up.'

Course he had.

'Are you a red or a white drinker?' I asked.

'It depends very much on what I'm eating,' she answered.

That I still did not understand. Why did it matter what you ate with what? Did it really make that much difference?

'Nick's very into his wine,' said Rosamund. 'I'm sure he's told you, already. His favourite spot at our gite in France was the wine cellar. Do you remember, Peter? We'd be wondering where he'd got to and then we'd find him down there, peering at labels and counting bottles.'

Although I wasn't going to give Rosamund the pleasure of me saying so, this was news to me. I knew Nick liked looking at the wine list when we were out for dinner, and always took the lead on choosing something (mainly because I didn't care enough), but as for him spending hours in a wine cellar, there'd been no mention. Nor of the fact his family had a second home in France. With a wine cellar! I wondered what else I didn't know about him and had this pang of not being sure that I wanted to know. Our relationship had moved steadily forward, in the way that society deemed it should: first the dating, then the declarations of love and then him asking me – quite quickly, in my opinion

– to move in with him. And now marriage. When I let myself acknowledge the part of me that wasn't sure – which wasn't often – I would wonder whether I'd rushed into something with Nick because of what had happened with Aidan. And then I pushed the thought to one side, reminded myself that I loved him despite all of that and that what I'd had with Aidan hadn't been sustainable, anyway, obviously not. And then I carried on.

Loch Lomond

Two Years Earlier

I rounded everyone together and we climbed up the steps onto the pier, just as the boat with *Loch Lomond Lake Cruise* emblazoned on the side moored up. Tim, of course, barged ahead onto the boat, paying little heed to the mostly elderly passengers trying to disembark. They were probably off for a look around the picturesque village of Luss, where we were based. I couldn't blame them, I'd had a wander around myself and it was like stepping back about a hundred years, with cute, chintzy tea rooms and adorable little houses that looked like ornaments on somebody's mantelpiece and gift shops selling tartan and fudge.

'We want to be at the front of the boat, otherwise we'll have a bunch of heads in the shot,' barked Tim, clearly expecting us to follow him.

Much to his annoyance, the rest of us took a more leisurely approach to getting on. I introduced myself to the captain and showed him the paperwork from Visit Scotland giving us permission to shoot footage on his boat. Possibly because he'd taken an instant dislike to Tim, he didn't exactly seem thrilled at the prospect of having us on board.

'You'd better not be blabbering on over the top of the commentary,' he said, pointing at the boom I was conspicuously holding.

'Definitely not,' I replied. 'We'll be very respectful. You'll hardly know we're here.'

Not for the first time, I wished Holiday Shop had a decent budget so that we could have booked ourselves a private tour. In my experience, these impromptu shoots never worked out as well as you'd hoped and the sound was usually awful. You couldn't expect paying passengers to stay quiet every time you wanted to shoot a link, could you?

As I took a seat next to Lou, I noticed a last-minute passenger sprinting up the steps of the pier and leaping on to the boat like something out of a James Bond opening sequence. OK, that was possibly a bit of an exaggeration, but it was Aidan and he was, well, impressive. He headed in my direction and grabbed the seat opposite. I noticed he was very slightly out of breath, but nothing like the hot mess I'd have been if I'd had to run up steps at that speed.

'That looked like hard work,' I said, grinning at him because I couldn't help myself. I was just so happy to see him, which was worrying, when you thought about it.

'Thought I was going to miss it,' he gasped. 'I've been looking forward to this.'

Lou glanced across at me and I knew what she was thinking so I refused to catch her eye. I pretended to check my script, getting out my pen in case I could make any last-minute adjustments when I heard the commentary. They were bound to have some interesting facts to add.

'Shall I set up for a shot as we pull away from the jetty?' asked Lou, smirking as she looked through her viewfinder.

I wished I'd never told her about my kiss with Aidan now, but I'd needed her opinion on it all. Was I going completely mad? Would Tim deem it a sackable offence? Lou had told me not to be so ridiculous and that I deserved to have a good time.

'Tim? Do you want a shot of us pulling away?' I asked.

'Yes, and we'll do at least one intro and outro at our first stop. And I don't want loads of noise in the background, although I don't see how we can avoid it with this lot,' he said, rolling his eyes.

The boat pulled away from the jetty and Lou shot some footage of a miserable-looking Ruthie looking all windswept at the bow of the boat. We could use it to tease the main show. Put some nice Scottish music over it.

'Let's have some smiles, Ruthie,' I said, projecting my voice over the sound of the boat's engine as it carved its way through the water.

Aidan leaned forward, his voice low and soft. 'She doesn't seem to be enjoying this, much.'

'Is it that obvious?' I mouthed.

The commentary had started up, so there was no chance of us doing any pieces to camera for the moment, so I sat back and enjoyed the ride. It was beautiful out here and, in some ways, if I squinted and – I imagined perhaps more so on a clear day with blue skies – it reminded me of Vietnam again. It had the same cragginess to the landscape, the same mountain peaks on the horizon.

'You can see Ben Lomond clearly now,' said Aidan, indicating the large mountain looming in front of us.

I nodded gratefully, relaying the information to Lou.

'Lou, get a shot of Ben Lomond in if you can? It's that peak there,' I said, pointing it out.

When the boat pulled up alongside Wallaby Island, the driver cut the engine and we were able to shoot some of the script I'd so painstakingly written (actually, that wasn't true, I'd bashed it out) last night. Considering my mind had been elsewhere, I was surprised I'd managed to put anything together.

'And action!' said Tim, ridiculously loudly given that Ruthie was only about half a metre away.

'And here we are at Inchconnachan, which, thanks to the Countess of Arran, houses Scotland's only wallaby colony. There are currently between fifty and sixty of them living here on the island!' trilled Ruthie, thankfully switching into professional mode.

It was impressive how she did that. Very convincing. So much so that my step-mum was a big fan. *She's just so nice and down to earth! Always so happy to get her hands dirty and muck in!* I'd tried telling Sharon on multiple occasions that this was Ruthie's television persona and that actually she was snippy, defensive and difficult and that nobody at Holiday Shop liked her, but Sharon wasn't having any of it, and now I'd given up. Let her believe what she wanted: who was I to shatter the illusion?

'Let's go straight into the next intro. And ... action!' yelled Tim.

'I'm Ruthie Withenshaw and welcome to part two of our Scotland special: Loch Lomond. Come with me to discover this magical region, the largest lake in Scotland peppered with twenty-two islands and twenty-seven islets. Wildlife is rife here, too, with everything from ospreys to wallabies, and there's so much to do, from relaxing island cruises to paddle-boarding and kayaking. Loch Lomond really has got it all!'

'She's good when she wants to be,' whispered Aidan.

'Talk about knowing how to turn it on,' I said.

I liked having Aidan next to me. He was funny and observant and I thought he might see the world of TV in the same way I did – slightly amusing, fun and full of self-importance (Tim was a prime example). Aidan didn't strike me as one of those worthy types who only watched travel shows if they were being fronted by Michael Portillo.

'How's your piece coming along?' I asked.

'Not great,' he said, looking at me. 'For some reason, I keep getting distracted. Every time I sit down at my laptop, my mind starts to wander.'

I felt my heart quicken. Surely he wasn't insinuating that it was me who was hindering his concentration? I tried to arrange my face in a nonchalant way, as though I wasn't beginning to feel my body burn from the chest up.

'What's been on your mind?' I asked, remembering how good it had felt to kiss him.

Had he been thinking about it as much as I had?

'You, actually,' said Aidan, smiling. 'Call me crazy, but I can't seem to get last night out of my head. You and me, out there on that beach ...'

'The lilt of the bagpipes ...' I said, thinking back.

'The waves lapping on the shore ...' he added.

I laughed. 'Kind of romantic, when you think about it.'

'I'd say so.'

'I don't actually do romance, usually,' I said.

'Why not?' he asked.

'I like being in control of my emotions,' I admitted.

'I see,' he said, frowning.

I looked intently at my script, crossing something out for the sake of it. I'd said too much.

'Would it feel too "out of control" to have a drink with me later?' he asked.

'Um ...'

It would, actually. I was already thinking of several reasons why I shouldn't. I could always use work as an excuse.

'I'm heading down to Cornwall tomorrow, you see. Leaving after lunch,' he said.

'Oh, right,' I said, disappointed. Annoyingly.

See, this was why I preferred to keep men at a safe

distance. I'd always been too scared to pursue the guys I was really into, instead ending up with either the guys I knew were players from the off or with the 'safe bet' types. The ones I thought were less likely to unceremoniously leave me on a whim. I mean, it didn't always work, and I'd been dumped several times regardless, but my heart had never felt too broken afterwards.

I immediately knew that it would be different with Aidan. That if things were to progress and then they were to end my heart would be shattered into a million pieces. My head was telling me that he wasn't worth taking a chance on, that I'd probably get hurt, so why bother? And I almost always listened to my head … Except, suddenly, something else was taking over. Because although the life I'd set up for myself was fine, there were no real highs and (thankfully, I supposed) no real lows. And kissing Aidan on the beach had felt like a high and I suddenly wanted more of it.

'We could raid my minibar if you like?' I suggested boldly.

I glanced at Lou, who was doing an excellent job of twiddling her lens cap and pretending not to listen.

Aidan nodded. 'Shall I give you a knock later, then? Say eight, eight-thirty?'

'OK,' I said, the thought of him knocking on my door making me bite my lip with anticipation. He really was lovely. His eyes looked the same colour as the water of the loch today, a sort of greeny brown and full of depth and mystery. His hair was too short to blow about in the wind, so, unlike the rest of us, it wasn't plastered all over his face. I purposely hadn't worn my anorak today, which I thought might be something to do with the fact that I'd hoped to see him, but now, wearing nothing more than jeans and an oversized turtleneck (although I had layered up underneath), I was freezing.

'What's your room number?' he asked.

I cleared my throat, wondering if this was the worst idea in the world. Now I'd spend the whole day thinking about what might happen later instead of focusing on shooting this footage. And then, what if I spent the evening wafting around my room with a full face of make-up on, wearing something casual yet alluring, only to be crushingly disappointed when he didn't, in fact, knock like he'd said? Because men – well, people generally, actually – were unreliable, weren't they? If my own dad could cancel plans to see me at a moment's notice, I was pretty sure a guy I'd known for less than a day could do the same.

'Twenty-seven,' I said.

'Twenty-seven,' he repeated.

'Will you remember that?' I asked, wondering whether I ought to offer him a pen and the corner of my script.

'I think so,' he said, grinning at me.

It was just after eight-thirty when I heard a knock on my door. I *really* hoped it was going to be Aidan and not Tim asking me to write another script. It would be just my luck, and of course I was already stressing that Aidan had changed his mind and wasn't going to show and I knew I'd be absolutely gutted if he didn't. I was wearing a short, denim skirt and a spaghetti-strap top and a chunky cardigan I loved because if you angled your body a certain way, it would slide seductively off one shoulder. If he didn't come, it would all have been for nothing. I opened the door in a casual manner, as though it didn't matter to me either way who was on the other side of it. To my great relief, it was Aidan, looking dazzling in the doorway dressed in blue jeans and a striped shirt, open at the neck. I didn't notice what he had on his feet.

'Come in,' I said, standing aside, giving the room a quick visual once-over, although I'd already done that several times. I'd arranged the room in a way I thought looked inviting – my book on the bedside table, my earplugs and eye mask out of sight, my laptop open on the desk, MTV playing on the hotel's TV, some hip-hop track making it look as though I had cooler taste in music than I actually did.

He came in, closing the door behind him.

'I hope I'm not interrupting,' he said, nodding at the laptop, which was open on the script I'd been trying to write. We were shooting in Luss the following day. Tim thought it would really suck in the American viewers (of which I didn't think we had many, but of course didn't bother saying).

'I think I'm done for the day,' I said. 'Drink?'

He nodded. 'Sure.'

I flung open the minibar, crouching down to look inside. 'What do you fancy? Beer? Wine?'

'I'll grab a beer.'

I pulled out a can of Brew Dog for him and a pre-mixed gin and tonic for myself. I could sense him watching me, which made me move in a jerky and unnatural way. I needed to relax, and hopefully a drink would help.

'You lucked out with your room, I see,' he said. 'You've got a lake view.'

I nodded, handing him the beer and opening my can. I ought to pour it into something. You couldn't really swig gin and tonic from a can, could you?

'Just a sec,' I said, disappearing into the bathroom to grab a glass.

I caught sight of myself in the mirror when I was in there and paused for a second, tightening my ponytail and smoothing down the fluffy hairs around the hairline that drove me constantly mad.

When I got back out, he was standing near the end of the bed. I put my glass on the side, poured the gin and tonic into it and took the biggest swig known to man. I took my time, partly scared to turn around, carefully putting the glass back down. I felt him come up behind me. He put his hands on my stomach, pulling me into him. It felt dangerous and delicious all at the same time.

'I've been thinking about this all day,' he said softly, kissing my bare shoulder.

I reached out behind me, my fingers disappearing into the velvety softness of his hair. He carried on kissing me, on my neck, on the top of my spine, and on the point I loved most, just behind my ear. I groaned and turned to face him. He wrapped his arms around me, kissing me on the mouth now, so hard I could barely breathe, his teeth grazing my lip, his tongue filling my mouth. My cardigan slipped off my shoulders and I shook it onto the floor and then, as if in one smooth, continuous movement, he hooked his fingers underneath the hem of my vest, pushing it up over my breasts, the palms of his hands skimming over them as he swept it over my head. I, in turn, undid the button of his jeans, lowered the zip, pulled them down over his hips. I stroked the inside of his thigh, trailing my fingers higher and higher up. Everything felt urgent: his breath coming in ragged bursts, me whispering into his ear.

'This feels really good,' I said.

His hands slid under my skirt, his thumb, warm and insistent.

'I want you so much,' he said, pushing me back onto the counter.

'Do you?' I asked, pulling at his jeans, forcing him to kick them off, doing the same with my underwear.

We moved to the bed. I lay down on my back, cushioned

by the tartan throw and the world's softest duvet, the faint sound of chatter and music floating up from the restaurant below. He lowered himself on top of me.

'Are you feeling out of control yet?' he asked.

'Absolutely,' I said, laughing lightly.

I closed my eyes, letting myself feel every single sensation as he put his hands on my knees and gently pressed them apart.

Afterwards, we lay star-shaped on the bed for ages, holding hands and chatting. It felt like the start of something.

Chapter Thirteen

By the time we pulled into the car park of the Maurizio Brogioni Winery, the second and final stop on our tour, I'd given up all hope of Nick joining us. The seven (admittedly small, but still!) glasses of wine at the first vineyard had begun to take effect and my confidence had grown – maybe I didn't need Nick as much as I thought I had. I hadn't made a complete fool of myself over my lack of wine knowledge (partly thanks to Aidan, I supposed) and I'd managed to make a smattering of small talk with Rosamund and to hold my own in our conversations. I was too half-drunk to worry that perhaps we should have moved on from the small talk stage by now, since I was imminently to become her daughter-in-law. The thing was, I thought that Sophia was probably so entrenched in that role that it would be difficult for anybody else to find their place. It would take time, probably, that was all.

As we got out of the minibus, a gorgeous tan and white spaniel with the most beautiful big, brown eyes came bounding up to us. He was on a lead, but it was so long he might as well not have been, given the freedom he had to run and roam. I greeted him warmly, letting him jump up and place his paws on my thighs.

'Hello! Hello there. Well, aren't you gorgeous?'

When he'd had enough of me, he got down and went to

greet Rosamund, who instantly recoiled as he stood on two feet with excitement.

'Oh no. Oh no, no, no!' she shrieked, shooing the poor dog away.

'You're not a dog person then, Rosamund?' I asked, amused.

How could she not want to stroke this adorable creature?

She brushed imaginary dog hairs off her jeans, which the dog hadn't so much as touched.

'I prefer cats,' she said haughtily. 'Dogs are too ...'

'Slobbery?' I suggested.

'Exactly,' she said, revolted. 'And smelly. I can't stand the way they're always leaping about.'

I crouched down to give the dog some more attention. He was a little bit slobbery but he wasn't smelly in the slightest.

'Come, ladies!' encouraged Gino, striding off towards a pretty house. 'Let us go and drink wine.'

He introduced us to Maurizio, a ruddy-cheeked, smiley Italian who had a lovely aura about him. Not that I entirely understood what auras were, and whether they were an actual thing, but I knew when somebody had a good one.

I glanced over at Aidan, who was pumping Maurizio's hand and attempting to talk in pigeon Italian. At least he was having a go. He had a nice aura, I thought. At least, I'd thought he had when I first met him in Scotland. Then I looked at Rosamund. Not so much.

Just as Maurizio led us down into his beautiful, sloping garden and began to point out the land that was his and explain why he'd chosen that particular area to set up his business (the forest gave the wine a distinct flavour, apparently), Nick and Daisy arrived. Of course, they couldn't do anything quietly and Nick completely ignored Maurizio and Gino and swooped straight in with the over-the-top air kisses and the booming voice which seemed to be getting louder the more time he spent with his family. Maurizio looked bemused by these new, noisy arrivals. I refused to let myself think about what Aidan must think. Nope, I was not going to go there.

'Sorry, everyone!' trilled Nick.

'Better late than never,' said Rosamund, wagging her finger at him as though he was a naughty child.

'Hey,' I said to Daisy as she skulked up next to me.

'Hey,' she grunted back, as though talking took extreme effort.

'How's it been, darling?' asked Nick, who, having done the rounds with everyone else, was finally acknowledging me.

'I've had several glasses of wine and about half a pint of olive oil, so all good,' I told him.

There was no point having a go at him, not least because I didn't want to give Sophia and Rosamund the satisfaction of doing it in front them. I bet they'd just love it if we started bickering, so reassuring themselves that their first impressions had been right and I *definitely* was not right for Nick.

'You're not mad at me, then?' asked Nick, wincing as though I was about to launch into an angry tirade at him.

I shrugged. I wasn't mad, exactly. Just resigned to the fact that his priority was and always would be Daisy. That's what happened when you had kids and that was how it should be. Their happiness mattered above all else (not that my parents had got the memo). Although I didn't think that that meant you couldn't say no to them occasionally.

I turned back to Maurizio, who was telling us enthusiastically about the different varieties of grape he grew. Nick hadn't seemed to cotton on to the fact that some of us actually wanted to listen to Maurizio rather than hearing him banging on about his 'dreadful' journey.

'Can you believe it, we had a—'

'Sssshh,' I hissed at him. 'I want to listen to this.'

Nick wasn't acting like himself, which bothered me. Was he really so heavily influenced by his family, who seemed to bring out a side of him I wasn't finding particularly appealing? He was coming across as a boisterous city boy today, the type of guy I knew that Aidan perennially couldn't stand and therefore would never in a million years be envious of.

I pinched the top of my nose. God, what was I thinking? It didn't matter what Aidan thought, did it?

I tried to concentrate on Maurizio, who had the sort of warm, kind face that centred you if you focused on it hard enough.

'I grow four different grapes here,' he was saying, his eyes lighting up as he explained. 'Sauvignon from France, Sangiovese – a red grape from Italy, Shiraz which is Eastern and Merlot from France.'

'Can you eat the grapes?' asked Aidan, who seemed as genuinely interested as I was. 'Do they taste good?'

'You can,' replied Maurizio. 'Some grapes you can eat. But they taste very different from the grapes you would buy, let's say, at the supermarket.'

I glanced over my shoulder at Nick, who was – quite rudely, I thought – whispering into Sophia's ear. Daisy was equally disinterested and was taking selfies against a backdrop of fields and trees. At least she was appreciating the countryside, I supposed.

'Come, let us see where the wine is made,' said Maurizio, leading us back up the path towards the winery.

Once we'd seen his impressive set-up of huge vats housing four to six thousand bottles of wine each, Maurizio led us to a long, wooden table under a pergoda, where we had panoramic views of the vineyards stretching as far as the eye could see. I was grateful for the shade the roof allowed us and the temperature was perfect – warm but not sticky-hot. I ended up sitting with Nick to one side of me and Daisy the other. Aidan was, perhaps worryingly, opposite Nick, who made a big show of introducing himself. I was going to have to tell Nick about Aidan at some point, but there never seemed to be a good time and I didn't want to make Nick feel uncomfortable. Which anyone would be, wouldn't they, if they found themselves sitting opposite their fiancée's ex-boyfriend? Then again, he'd never even been my 'boyfriend'. We'd been seeing each other, that was all, and just because I'd felt myself falling for him, more and more with every passing day, didn't mean he'd felt the same. He clearly hadn't, in fact.

'Hello, mate. I'm Nick,' he said, shaking Aidan's hand vigorously.

'Aidan. Glad you could make it in the end,' he replied with a smile.

'Ha! And now I am going to more than make up for it,' said Nick.

He grabbed the glass of wine that Maurizio had just poured him and downed it in one. Maurizio, good-natured as he was, laughed.

'You like more?' offered Maurizio, who I could tell was a generous soul.

'Oh yes,' said Nick.

I took a sip of mine. The effects of the previous wine tasting were wearing off and I thought I could just about drink more. Plus Maurizio's wines sounded delicious.

'Mmmn,' I said, enjoying the full-bodied red. 'Is this the Shiraz?'

'That is correct,' smiled Maurizio.

'I see we're rubbing off on you, Maddie,' remarked Rosamund. 'You'll be a wine expert at this rate.'

An amused Aidan caught my eye. Briefly, but at least we could look at each other, now. I wondered whether we'd ever have an actual conversation about what had happened between us. Whether I'd want to. When and where it would happen, given the situation with Nick and his family. If my primary aim was to make a good impression on them, sneaking off to meet another man behind their backs was hardly going to do me any favours.

'So how do you guys all know each other?' asked Aidan. 'You're all family?'

Nick nodded, wiping wine from his lips with the back of his hand.

'This is my fiancée, Maddie,' he said, patting my knee.

'Your fiancée?' said Aidan, raising his eyebrows.

I couldn't bring myself to look at him for long enough to work out whether he cared, instead beaming inanely at Nick in a desperate attempt to look happy about the fact our engagement was the topic of possibly the most awkward conversation ever.

'Congratulations,' said Aidan quietly.

This time I looked at him; this time he caught my eye.

'And this is my mother and father, Rosamund and Peter,' went on Nick, who was oblivious to the shifting dynamics around the table. Obviously it was just me with the leaden feeling in my stomach; I felt so hot, suddenly, that I had to fan myself frantically with a wine menu.

'And then there's my daughter, Daisy and my, um ... Daisy's mother. Sophia.'

Aidan looked confused. 'You've brought your ex and your new fiancée on the same trip?'

He was never one to hold back ... Except when it mattered.

Rosamund and Sophia guffawed loudly, as though this

was the funniest thing in the world. Except it wasn't, for me, and it felt insensitive of them to minimise it like that. I was sick of people not taking my feelings seriously, as though I was some silly woman with ridiculous ideas. Lots of people did it and I just let them, which I was also sick of – the fact that I put up with it. It was fine to be hurt by stuff other people did, and fine to call them out on it – and it wasn't fine that most of the time they took absolutely no responsibility for it. Not that Aidan's opinion mattered to me, particularly, but there was some comfort in knowing it wasn't just me who thought this whole situation was weird.

'We all get along surprisingly well, don't we?' said Nick jovially.

'Absolutely,' gushed Sophia. 'We're like one, big extended family.'

'Well, to be fair, I didn't know Sophia was going to be here,' I said.

It was out of my mouth before I'd worked out how to word it less abrasively or, more usefully, refrain from saying anything at all.

Everyone stared at me in shock. Nick squirmed.

'I'm sure I told you,' said Nick, trying to laugh it off.

'You didn't,' I replied. 'But anyway. We're here now, aren't we?'

Nick seemed stunned into silence. He wasn't used to me speaking up for myself and especially not on this trip – so far, it felt as though I'd lost my voice completely. I thought I was coming across as very quiet, very shy, not particularly dynamic. It was a side of myself I fell back into very easily – I'd sort of taxi along unseen, in the same way I'd done when my parents had split up and my whole world went a bit haywire. I'd decided pretty early on that the best thing, when I went to visit either Mum or Dad and their new partners and my half-siblings, was to not draw attention to myself. To not stand out, to be a nice, easy person, to not cause a fuss about anything. In case they decided they didn't want me around anymore because now they had these shiny new families to love instead. And I sort of dulled down my personality, I supposed, and blended into the background, going along with what everyone else wanted. In the end, it became second nature. I mean, just look at my job for starters: I was good at it, and yet I was being overlooked for promotion and Tim treated me like an intern. I thought briefly of the research I'd been doing on how to create my own travel content business: a website, reviews, videos of places I'd been, hotels I recommended. I'd got a bit carried away at the time, imagining sponsorship and partnerships with hotel chains and YouTube channels. I thought I had all the skills I'd need, but in order to do it properly, I'd have to leave Holiday Shop. Which felt terrifying, of course, even though I'd saved enough to cover six months' salary already. It was something I needed to speak to Nick about, I supposed. Not that what I earned really had an effect on his huge salary, but the prospect of leaving my job felt like the kind of thing I should be sharing with my husband-to-be.

An oblivious Maurizio was still talking passionately about his wine. 'A Shiraz must ferment in the barrel for one year. It is a violet colour. It has high flavour and high spice. You can taste black pepper?'

I nodded, taking another mouthful and remembering to hold it in my mouth for two seconds before swallowing, like they'd told us at the other winery – two for red, five for white.

I could feel Nick's eyes boring into me, but I didn't feel like explaining why I'd said what I had. I was already on the defensive, presuming that conflict – the very thing I went to great lengths to avoid – was about to ensue. And if Aidan thought he could worm his way back into my mind by doing nice things like drawing bananas on his tasting notes, he had another thing coming. I hated him, I reminded myself, and unless he had a very, very good excuse as to why he'd been AWOL for the last two years, it would likely be staying that way.

Chapter Fourteen

The winery was way behind us now as we headed back into Florence. I'd loved being out in the countryside and my brain was hungry for more information on wine-making in the region, which I'd found surprisingly fascinating. I'd had no idea so much thought went into the whole process and we hadn't even got to the bit about labels and marketing and sales. When Maurizio had showed us how different pasta with pesto could taste coupled with the right wine, I was converted. After all these years, I sort of understood the whole food/wine pairings thing. My dad would laugh at me if he could see me now.

We snaked along a winding road flanked by very expensive-looking houses on the outskirts of the city until Gino pulled over the van. A couple of coaches were parked up and I could see a café and an ice cream stall, as though there was some kind of tourist attraction nearby, but I couldn't yet tell what.

'Where are we?' I asked.

'From here you have the best views of Florence. It is the Piazzale Michelangelo,' announced Gino.

'Oh, I've read about this,' I said, from my spot in the van squished against the window. Although it hadn't felt so bad on the return journey. Somehow things were less fraught between Aidan and I. When his knee knocked into mine a couple of times as we went around a particularly sharp bend,

I didn't mind as much as I had on the journey there, when even the sight of him out of the corner of my eye had made anger bubble in the pit of my stomach.

Not that I wasn't still angry, but it felt more manageable. Because I wasn't sure, after all, that he was the monster I'd built him up to be. He'd treated me badly, there was no denying that, but I was beginning to put a slightly less obsessive and vaguely healthier spin on it: what if what had happened was about him, rather than about him wanting to hurt me? And also, if I'd stayed with Aidan I'd never have met Nick and I wouldn't be about to start planning my wedding. So, in other words, he'd done me a favour, really. I bit my lip. I thought that maybe that should make me feel better than it actually did.

'Can we jump out for a sec?' I asked, deciding that this was a photo opportunity I simply couldn't miss. I grabbed the video camera from my bag, too – this would impress Tim – he'd definitely be able to use it for his City Break promo.

Gino made a big deal of looking at his watch. 'OK, you have five minutes. But then I must get back and return the van so that it can be cleaned and ready for the next tour party. You understand?'

'Yes!' I said, following Aidan out of the van.

The others got out, somewhat reluctantly I thought, except for Peter, who had fallen asleep and couldn't be roused, even when Rosamund squawked, *come on, Peter!* into his ear. Nick and Daisy had had to get in the front, which I could sense had annoyed Nick because he was squeezed into the middle seat and had been forced to make stilted conversation with Gino for most of the journey back.

Nick fell into step beside me. 'Everything all right?' he asked, slipping his arm around my shoulders.

'Fine.'

'You're not too annoyed at me for missing the first half of the tour, are you?'

'It was more than the first half. More like two-thirds, I'd say.' I was trying hard to contain my irritation as it would be pointless, anyway – Nick wasn't the best at backing down or apologising. He probably didn't get why I'd made such a fuss about it in the first place.

We made our way over to the railings where Florence was laid out in front of us, shimmering in the heat. I turned the camera on, pressed record and did a three-hundred-and-sixty-degree turn, taking in the hundreds of tourists and the level above us where there seemed to be – no, I couldn't believe it – yet another version of *David*! This one was smaller, and bronze.

I watched the footage back on my viewfinder – it was a lovely shot, even if I did say so myself. I did some pan shots and took some stills, ideas buzzing in my mind. I could picture my website, evocative and classy, with a section for all the different places I'd explored in the world. Italy was always a popular one, and it would be somewhere I could come back to relatively easily.

'Please don't tell me you're working,' said Nick, shaking his head good-naturedly.

He was used to me not properly switching off and in some ways he was the same. But his work involved lots of phone calls and meetings and emails and mine was more about capturing beautiful things while I had the chance.

'It'll only take me a minute. And this view is spectacular.'

There were lots of people like me taking photos of the city, chattering softly to each other, pausing to eat an ice cream, or wandering over to the particularly well-appointed café next to us that brought drinks to your table as you enjoyed the vista in comfort.

As I looked out at Florence again, I noticed how the Duomo dominated the shot, as it seemed to wherever you were, and next to it the tower of the Campanile, which I planned to climb later, if the queues weren't too long. I panned across, taking everything in: the Ponte Vecchio, the Arno, so still and quiet. There were no boats going up and down, no floating restaurants or tour boats like you'd get on the Seine or the Thames.

'I was surprised about what you said about Sophia,' Nick remarked. 'I didn't think you had a problem with her being here?'

This was hardly the conversation I wanted to have when we had five minutes to take in possibly the most amazing view I'd ever seen in my life. When I'd dreamed of coming to Florence when I was young, I think it had been here I'd imagined myself. I must have read about it in a book, because this was exactly how I'd pictured it.

'I did say,' I insisted.

'When?'

I'd clearly not made much of an impact if he'd forgotten already.

'Look, let's not do this here,' I said, suppressing a sigh. I turned my camera off. I couldn't concentrate now.

'Did you really think calling me out in front of that Aidan guy was the best way to approach it? It was completely humiliating.'

He had a point.

'Look, I'm sorry, all right? I'm blaming the copious amounts of wine. You know I'm not the best at daytime drinking.'

'Hmmmn. I suppose that's true,' said Nick, softening.

I looked over his shoulder. Gino was standing by the door to the van with his hands pertinently placed on his hips.

'We'd better go,' I said.

Nick nodded, pulling his phone out of his pocket. 'Let me just make a really quick call and I'll be right with you. Don't let that Gino guy go without me.'

'I'll do my best,' I said, smiling at him and starting back to the van.

There, that hadn't been too bad. Nick and I had had a disagreement and I'd stood up for myself and nobody had died.

'What a view, eh?'

I did a double take when I realised Aidan had replaced Nick and had somehow fallen into step beside me. I decided that the best thing would be to ignore him. It would look strange to everyone else if I suddenly started talking to him now. Not that I wanted to, anyway. Hopefully, after today, I could get through the rest of my trip without ever setting eyes on him again.

'Look, don't you think it would be a good idea for us to talk?' he said, keeping his voice low.

I actually laughed out loud. Was this guy for real?

'Oh, so *now* you think we should talk?' I said, not trusting myself to look at him.

'Please,' he replied. 'Just for a few minutes. When we get back to the hotel.'

'Funny that you disappeared all those years ago without so much as a word and now we can't seem to *stop* meeting,' I commented. 'What's that about?'

The van was just a few metres away. My family-to-be were inside, waiting for me to join them. This was the last conversation I wanted to be having right under their noses.

'Just hear me out. Give me five minutes of your time,' pleaded Aidan.

I had to stick to my guns. There was nothing he could say that would make me feel differently about him, or make the aftermath of what he did any easier. So what was the point?

'No,' I said.

I was nearly at the van. Just a few more seconds and I'd be clambering inside and Aidan would have to stop talking. I didn't think he was going to throw me under the bus by saying anything in front of the others. He was an arsehole, yes, but he'd cared about me once (allegedly), so hopefully that would count for something.

'I'll be waiting on the bridge at the end of Via Tornabuoni,' he said hurriedly. 'The Ponte Santa Trinita. When we get back to the hotel.'

I tutted. He could wait there as long as he liked, there was no way I was going.

My legs felt shaky as I climbed back into the van. See, this was the effect he had on me, and I didn't want it and I didn't need it. So, no, even though part of me did want to find out exactly what had happened, just out of curiosity, I was not going to give him the satisfaction of going to meet him. I'd spent a long time getting over him, erasing him from my mind, and the best thing for me was to keep him there.

London

Two Years Earlier

We were gathered in the office for our usual Wednesday morning planning meeting and the whole team were expected to be present. Not turning up was punishable by ... well, I wasn't sure, because I'd always turned up. Even when I was ill and probably should have called in sick, I'd drag myself in, determined not to 'let down' my bosses. I didn't know who I thought I was kidding – they probably didn't notice whether I was there or not half the time, but it made me feel better, so I went with it.

'Danish?' said Lou, passing me a plate of dry-looking pastries. The free food was the only exciting thing about the meeting.

'Don't mind if I do,' I said, grabbing one and then passing the plate along to Kiely, the other assistant producer.

She'd only been at Holiday Shop for a few months and already she'd ingratiated herself with the SMT clique (headed up by Executive Producer, Mel). I worried constantly about whether, if a producer role did come up, it would go to her and I'd be savagely disappointed and uncontrollably angry. Not that I'd ever really lost it like that – I'd learned not to bother, it never got me anywhere – but I imagined that it would be something like this that would tip me over the edge.

'Right,' said Mel. 'Shall we make a start?'

I opened up my notebook. I rarely wrote anything in it, but it made me look on-the-ball, I thought.

'Let's start with the Loch Lomond footage. Tim has done a brilliant job of making a not-very-exciting destination look like a must-see. And Ruthie has really pushed herself out of her comfort zone with this one, which Tim tells me was something he worked hard on. We've got her on a lake cruise, we've got her eating a cream tea in a local tea room – and you know she doesn't like to eat on camera – and, best of all, we've got her on a kayak! It all makes for some very exciting footage, which we'll be using for all of our UK promos, as well as our Scotland Special. Well done, Tim!'

Everyone clapped.

Lou pressed her knee against mine.

Tim lapped up the attention and then, when he saw mine and Lou's faces, he made some attempt to include the rest of the team in this love-fest.

'Thanks to the rest of the team, too,' he said, in the tone you might use if you were agreeing to have root canal surgery.

'He's such a twat!' said Lou later when she swung by my desk to see if I wanted to go to an early-morning yoga class at the top of the walkie-talkie building on Sunday morning (that would be a no!).

'Don't get wound up, you know what he's like,' I said, worried she'd be overheard.

'And what's her excuse?' hissed Lou. 'Mel. Can she not see that Tim's completely useless and that actually what made that shoot work was mainly you but also me? Is she blind?'

I looked anxiously around the office. It was one thing to

slag Mel off in the comfort of our own homes (or at least out of earshot), but the prospect of being caught doing it was quite another.

'I'm literally going to start looking for a new job at lunchtime and I seriously advise you to do the same,' said Lou.

Luckily I was prevented from having to answer her by my phone ringing in my bag. My heart immediately started racing, as it had done repeatedly since I'd got back from Scotland (on a VERY expensive direct train, thanks to my dad and Sharon). Aidan and I had texted a couple of times. He'd sent me a photo on WhatsApp of him on a surfboard in Cornwall, which I'd found unbelievably sexy. But I knew he was back now and I didn't know if he was as desperate to see me as I was to see him because he was *all* I had thought about for the last five days.

I bent down and took my phone casually out of my bag, so as not to alert Lou to the fact that I'd turned into an Aidan-obsessed lunatic. I glanced nonchalantly at the screen and then nearly dropped the handset on my desk when I saw the words *Aidan Calling* on the screen. Aaargh! I wasn't prepared for this despite having run through the scenario again and again in my head since he'd left Loch Lomond. I stared at the phone, wondering how to answer, *if* to answer, whether it would be cooler and less obvious to let it go to voicemail or whether that might mean that he'd think I wasn't interested. I couldn't stand it when I had a running commentary in my head like this because there was never any clear answer and one thing always cancelled out the other.

'You've gone bright red,' said Lou, unhelpfully.

'It's Aidan,' I said, my voice sounding all tense and tight.

'Well, you'd better answer it, then,' she replied.

I took a deep breath.

'Hi,' I said. 'How was Cornwall?'

He came round later that evening after calling to tell me he'd be a bit late. I was usually reluctant to invite people back to my tiny studio flat. I always thought they'd be put off by the fact I lived on the fifth floor of a block of flats; that my bed was in the same room as my lounge and, for that matter, the kitchen. But I loved it here. I'd rented it when I got promoted to assistant producer, which, although it didn't pay much, gave me enough money to move out of the student house-share I was living in at the time. For the first time in my life, I felt like I had my own, proper space. It wasn't a room at my dad's that was in the basement away from the rest of the family (and which always gave me Harry Potter locked-in-a-cupboard vibes), and it wasn't a room at my mum's that also doubled as a snug for the girls when I wasn't there (which, to her great relief, it seemed, was most of the time).

'I love all these pictures,' said Aidan, looking at the framed photographs lining my walls. 'Where's this?'

'Hong Kong.'

'And this?'

'Peru.'

'Have you been to all these places?' asked Aidan.

I shook my head, opening a bottle of red. 'No. They're on my wish list. The places I want to visit. It gives me hope that one day I'll have the money to go, or that I'll somehow wangle a proper TV job and will be zipping across the world on a plethora of exciting assignments.'

'It's definitely possible,' said Aidan, watching me pour two glasses of wine. 'You've got to think big.'

'And there's only so many times I can go to Fuerteventura, right?' I said, grimacing and handing him a glass.

'Tired of Fuerteventura, tired of life?'

We laughed and then drank in silence for a second or two. It wasn't awkward exactly, but I thought I might feel the pressure of everything having been so sexy and a bit intense in Loch Lomond. Would I feel the same way? Would he?

'So, I've missed you,' he said.

Yes!

'Same,' I replied.

'Sorry I got held up on the way over.'

'No problem. Do you want to sit down?' I asked, ushering him onto the sofa. I sat next to him, my knee falling against his. 'You said you had an appointment?'

'Hmmmn. I had to have a blood test.'

I looked surprised. 'Everything OK?'

'Hopefully,' he said, breezily. 'There's some stuff going on with my mum, that's all. Everything feels a bit ... difficult at the moment.'

I put my wine down on the coffee table.

'Sorry to hear that,' I said.

'You think your parents are invincible, don't you? But then stuff happens out of the blue and it's like the rug has been pulled out from under you.'

I nodded. My parents were young still, only in their fifties. I wasn't there yet, with the worrying, but I supposed there would come a time when I would be. And I felt bad for Aidan that he was already having to deal with it.

'It might not be as terrible as you think,' I said. 'You're not googling stuff, are you?'

He shook his head vigorously. 'Course not.'

I raised an eyebrow at him.

'OK, maybe just a bit,' he admitted with a wry smile.

I reached for his hand, threading my fingers through his.

He sighed. 'Sorry. All this is a bit of a mood-kill, isn't it?'

I shook my head. 'It's fine,' I said. 'I hope you feel you

can ... you know, talk to me? Even though we haven't known each other very long.'

Aidan sat back on the sofa, resting his head against it, looking relaxed and comfortable. It was like he belonged here, in my little flat. He liked it, I could tell, and I liked him being here. It was perfect.

'I'm glad I met you,' he said, turning to me. 'Don't ask me how, because I'm not usually the most intuitive person, but I already know there's something special about you.'

Chapter Fifteen

While the van pulled up outside our hotel, I fished around in my pocket for a twenty-euro note to give to Gino. I knew that tour guides were really badly paid and that it was the tips that bumped up their salary and made it halfway decent. I was pretty sure that Rosamund wouldn't see it like this – I'd heard her berating Nick for being overly generous in the restaurant the other night. *Don't over-tip, Nick. They're only doing their job.* I'd spoken up for once, had told her that the waiting staff were probably only on minimum wage, which in a city like Florence wouldn't get them very far. Rosamund had bristled, not having any of it. She'd even insinuated we'd all had to struggle. I'd like to know exactly when in her life she had struggled financially but thought I'd be pushing it to ask because clearly she wouldn't have an actual answer.

I handed Gino my tip, and I saw Aidan do the same. Gino had spent the whole day with us and had given us loads of info we couldn't have found in our Rough Guides. He deserved a token of our thanks if you asked me. Perhaps I should give the others the benefit of the doubt: after all, Aidan and I were both in the travel industry; I supposed we knew how things worked. But, then again, wasn't it obvious?

'Thank you for being such wonderful guests on our tour,' gushed Gino. I could see he was chomping to get the van back so that he could keep to his precious schedule. He checked his watch.

'We'll let you go, Gino,' I said. 'And thanks again.'

We waved him off and then Aidan turned to Rosamund and Peter.

'And very pleasant spending the afternoon with you all,' he said. 'I'm sure I'll see you around the hotel.'

'Oooh, hope so,' smouldered Sophia.

'Don't forget to friend me on Facebook, will you?' asked Rosamund, thinking she was down with the kids but not realising that kids wouldn't be seen dead on Facebook these days. 'Rosamund Leveson-Gower. I shouldn't be too difficult to find.'

Aidan smiled kindly. 'Got it.'

He glanced quickly at me and then set off down Via Tornabuoni. When I caught myself and looked away, Rosamund and the others were already halfway inside the lobby. I ran to catch them up.

As if we hadn't had enough already, Peter insisted on buying us all a glass of Chianti Classico in the hotel bar. I desperately wanted to go up to my room, take a shower, give myself space to think. I imagined Aidan, standing on the bridge. What was it he was planning to say? Might it be better to know, so that I could finally get some kind of closure on the whole thing?

'Are you all right, darling?' asked Nick, patting my knee.

'Fine,' I said, smiling at him. 'I think I might just have a glass of water, actually.' I poured myself some from a jug.

Luckily, Peter was dominating the conversation with a running commentary of the wine-tasting tour involving him discussing the merits (or not) of every single wine we'd tried. He even had his tasting notes sheet out. It made me think of Aidan and I suddenly wanted to ask him whether he'd helped me on purpose. Perhaps he'd just been doodling bananas. Either way, I thought that maybe he was right: we needed to talk. Very briefly. It might feel better once we'd had it out, so to speak.

'The weather's lovely this afternoon,' I said, not quite believing what was coming out of my mouth. 'I'm just going to grab a little bit more footage and then I'll have enough to send over to Tim and I can forget about work for the rest of the trip.'

Nick was the only one to acknowledge me. Daisy was glowering at her phone in the corner, and Rosamund and Sophia were seemingly enraptured by Peter's self-indulgent monologue on Tuscan wines.

'Again?' said Nick.

'I won't be long,' I assured him.

That part was true, at least. If I did – and it was a big if – swing past the Ponte Santa Trinita, then it would be for a matter of minutes. Aidan could tell me why he'd disappeared off the face of the earth two years ago and I could tell him he could go to hell with his poor excuses and I'd walk away from him cleansed and free of the memories of the time we'd spent together that popped into my mind sometimes at the most inopportune moments. Like when I was lying in bed next to Nick. Or sitting at my computer at work. Or squished on the tube at rush hour. Actually, myriad places, if I thought about it.

I stood up, looping my camera around my neck to make a point. I was actually going to shoot some footage, because otherwise it would make me a liar, which I'd always prided myself on not being.

'See you in a bit, everyone,' I said. 'Just popping out for a sec. Work stuff, you know.'

Rosamund and Sophia mumbled a goodbye, but Peter was not to be interrupted.

I headed for the door, glancing over my shoulder and noticing that Sophia had moved into my seat as quick as lightning.

'Everything all right?' I heard her coo to Nick.

As I headed in the direction of the Ponte Santa Trinita with the scorching sun still high in the sky, I rubbed the back of my neck, realising I'd forgotten to put sunscreen on that morning. Sometimes it was difficult to remember unless I was physically sitting on a beach 'sunbathing' for hours on end. I'd always felt slightly removed from my friends when we'd been on those sorts of beach holidays, to Majorca or Corfu or Ayia Napa – when we were in our early twenties. Sunbathe, swim, get drunk, dance and repeat. I'd wanted to be like them, mithering about getting a tan and whether or not they'd burned. Moving down from a factor 15 to a 5 as the holiday went on. One of them using carrot oil and wondering why she'd come up in blisters a few hours later. I hadn't wanted sunburn, of course. I'd just wanted to be worried about it like everybody else.

As I crossed the road and walked onto the bridge, I saw him, right in the middle, leaning with his back against the wall. He had sunglasses on and was looking in my direction. It didn't feel real that we were about to have an actual conversation, given the amount of times I'd imagined it. Was it too late to bolt? I wondered. To turn around and go right back to the safety of the bar and Peter's wine-obsessed drone? Part of me had hoped Aidan wouldn't be here because, let's face it, he was liable to not turn up places when he said he would.

I found myself walking towards him, anyway, coming to a stop with my hands on my hips. I was not going to let him overpower me with his confidence and his charm and his general good-looking-ness.

'Let's get this over with, then,' I said. 'What did you want to talk to me about?'

Irritatingly, Aidan flipped his sunglasses onto his head and looked at me. *Really* looked at me. So intensely that every part of me began to tingle. I was horrified that he was still having this effect on me and I fought to make myself stop.

I whipped my eyes away, looking out at the Ponte Vecchio. In desperation, I turned on my camera and haphazardly shot some footage, starting with the pale lemon apartment buildings on my left which had Florence's trademark shutters and balconies. Then I twisted at the waist, panning the shot out across the Ponte Vecchio, with its three arches and the jewellery shops lining each side of the central street. I'd always thought people lived in those quaint little buildings with the windows that lit up cosily at night, but apparently nobody did. They were the back offices of the shops, then, I supposed. Gino had told us not to bother buying jewellery there, that it was sold at a premium, but I thought there might be something romantic about choosing a special piece there. Not that I could afford gold jewellery, obviously. But if I could.

'Can you see the corridor on top of the bridge?' said Aidan.

'What corridor?'

He pointed to the three arches in the centre of the bridge, and then the three windows above them. 'It's called the Vasari corridor. Built by Giorgio Vasari for Cosimo the first of Medici in the fifteen hundreds. He found it difficult to walk from the Palazzo Vecchio, where he lived, to the Palazzo Pitti, where he worked. He wasn't that popular and he'd be hassled by irate locals on the way. So he arranged for this custom-built elevated passageway to be created, which stretches from one palace to the other, across the top of the Uffizi Gallery and right over the Ponte Vecchio.'

I nodded. 'Thank you for the running commentary. You should use that for your article.'

Aidan laughed softly.

We were silent for a while. I finally put my camera down.

'You look great, Maddie. How have you been?'

No. I wasn't going to let him do this. I hated him and I wasn't about to let him forget it.

'If you're planning to go on a charm offensive, Aidan, please don't bother. I've learned a lot these past two years, and one of them is to not believe a word you say.'

Aidan had the audacity to look shocked. 'I've never said anything to you I didn't mean.'

He couldn't be serious?

I looked straight at him. 'Oh, really? What about *I've never felt like this about anyone in my entire life*? Or *I know it's early days, but I literally can't imagine my future without you*?'

It hurt to say it out loud, even after all this time. And it was also slightly mortifying that I'd recounted it word for word. It was like his declarations were etched in my brain, no matter how hard I'd tried to forget about them.

'I meant all of that,' he said.

'You didn't,' I replied, turning away from him. 'You couldn't have done.'

I might have guessed he'd try to deny everything.

We stood in silence for a moment or two. I wondered why I'd come, what I'd been hoping for; whether I should just leave.

'You're actually planning to marry that guy, Nick, then?' said Aidan.

'Yes. I am. And I've got no idea why you just said it like that.'

I allowed myself a quick sideways glance at him. From this angle, I could see his lashes, long and dark. I used to run the pad of my thumb over them sometimes.

'How long have you been together?' he asked.

I sighed. Why did he care about all of this? 'Two years.'

'Two years,' said Aidan, looking thoughtful as though he was mulling it over; working something out. 'I bet he's the romantic type. I bet he buys you huge bouquets of flowers,' he remarked, his eyes fixed on the Ponte Vecchio. 'Doesn't he?'

What was he talking about? I mean, Nick did buy me embarrassingly large bunches of flowers that probably cost more than a week's rent in the studio apartment I had been living in when we'd first met, but what did it matter to Aidan?

'Whether Nick buys me flowers or not is completely irrelevant,' I snapped. 'Nick shows up. Nick wants to spend the rest of his life with me and he doesn't just say it, he actually means it. So can you please just get to the point of us being here? You said you wanted to talk.'

Aidan leaned on the bridge, resting his stomach on the stone slabs. For a second, I remembered the abs he used to have (and probably still did have, looking at him), how well-defined they were, how I'd run my fingers over them when we were lying in bed together, or on the sofa, or in the park.

'It was never my intention to hurt you,' he said. 'Just so we're clear. In fact, when I was with you, I was the happiest I'd ever been.'

Did he think I was born yesterday?

'Tell me what happened,' I said, my voice sounding strained.

Aidan cleared his throat. He seemed to be struggling to

put things into words. Good, I thought. It *should* be difficult for him.

'That deep connection we had? I felt it too, and I've never felt it with anyone else since,' he said.

There was a 'but' coming, wasn't there, there had to be? He'd probably met someone else. I could handle that, I'd already imagined that a thousand times over. Or he found me acutely annoying in the end? That's what I'd assumed.

I opened my mouth to speak, but nothing came out. For God's sake!

I tried again. 'So why didn't you meet me, that night in my office? You sent me one text and then nothing. My calls went straight to voicemail, my texts went unanswered. You ghosted me, basically, and I've still got no idea what I did wrong.'

'You didn't do anything wrong, Maddie,' said Aidan, his voice cracking.

I swallowed hard. This was harder than I thought it would be. It was bringing it all back. The shock, the disbelief. The embarrassment. I'd told everybody. Everybody! About this wonderful man I'd met who actually seemed to like me, was falling in love with me, even. And then, with no explanation, he was gone.

St Albans

Two Years Earlier

'This looks nice,' I said as my mum laid a plate of crispy roast potatoes – the pièce de résistance and her signature dish – in the middle of the table.

'Mum! I asked you not to make roast potatoes,' moaned my half-sister, Amelia.

'How come you suddenly don't like roast potatoes?' I asked, surprised.

Last time I'd been over on a Sunday, which admittedly had been at least six months before, she'd piled her plate high with them and had then been told by Mum that she'd put on loads of weight if she continued to eat like that. I'd actually – for possibly the first time in my life – felt sorry for Amelia.

'She's on a diet,' said Amelia's identical twin sister, Natasha.

'That's really not necessary,' I said to Amelia, piling four roast potatoes on to my plate. 'You're both so slim, and you're young. You should be enjoying your food.'

Mum shot me a dirty look. 'Don't encourage them, Maddie.'

'Encourage them to do what? Eat?' I said, irritated.

My mum had been on diets her entire life even though

she'd never been larger than a size ten. Her constant mithering about weight had clearly rubbed off on these two.

'They've got their final ballet exam coming up,' said Mum, by way of explanation. 'Grade eight! And their university interviews are just around the corner. They need to look their best for them. Everything helps, that's what I've told them. The way you present yourself is important.'

I didn't think they needed to worry. They led a particularly cushy life, with everything falling into their laps and gigantic bedrooms decked out like something out of *MTV Cribs*. For their eighteenths, Mum and my loaded step-dad had even bought them a brand new Mini Cooper to share. Not that I was at all jealous, you understand.

'How's work?' asked Mum. 'Scotland, wasn't it?'

'Hmmn,' I said, wishing I hadn't put a dangerously hot potato in my mouth.

I flapped my hand around in front of my mouth, as though that was going to do any good. And then, because I didn't want to come across as being as lonely and pathetic as I usually did, I told them about Aidan.

'I met someone, actually,' I said. 'In Loch Lomond. He's a travel writer for the *Hampstead and Highgate Express* and he's very good-looking. Sort of Sebastian Stan-esque. And very ... funny. We just clicked.'

Everyone looked at me in shock.

'I love Sebastian Stan,' said Natasha, apparently in disbelief that somebody like that could be interested in somebody like me.

Never mind, she had her own preppy boyfriend who was very in to her, in fact there had been a long line of them throughout their teen years. Neither of my sisters could understand how it was possible to be single for the length of time I had been (two and a half years, give or take).

I was, for once, triumphant. I, too, had a life. And it felt great to tell them all about it.

'We had this instant connection,' I told Mum, really milking it now. 'The chemistry was just there from the off.'

Chapter Sixteen

I let the smooth waters of the Arno calm me as I waited to hear Aidan's explanation.

'It's probably best if I start at the beginning,' he said.

Fuck. I braced myself. This was going to be bad.

'Go on, then.'

'It started a week or two before that night,' he said, his voice faltering. 'I'd had a call from my mum. I don't know whether you remember, but she'd been having some tests?'

I nodded. 'You never said exactly what for, but I remember.'

'She was diagnosed with late-onset Hereditary Optic Neuropathy.'

I widened my eyes. 'What's that?' It sounded terrible, but what did it have to do with anything?

'She was basically losing her vision. She'd have bouts of not being able to see in colour, for example, and often everything would be blurred. It started in one eye and then, after six months or so, it started happening in both. That was when we – my dad and I – finally persuaded her to go to her doctor.'

The story I'd made up in my head was beginning to unravel in front of my eyes. In my scenario, it had had nothing to do with his mum's failing eyesight.

'My mum told me the diagnosis over dinner one night,' Aidan continued. 'She played it down, because that's what she does, but I knew there must be more to it. Once it had sunk in, I—'

He stopped dead as a young girl ran past us sobbing. Someone familiar, wearing denim cut-offs and a barely there crop top. Daisy. I spun around, watching as she crossed the bridge, running so fast that her limbs were flailing everywhere.

'Is that …?' said Aidan.

'Daisy!' I shouted. She either didn't hear me or chose not to. 'I'd better go after her.'

Aidan nodded. 'Want me to come with you?'

'No.'

Daisy was almost out of sight. I set off, half-running in her direction.

'Meet me back here. Tomorrow morning?' called Aidan.

I hesitated, turning to face him. 'I'm on a tour of the Uffizi tomorrow. I won't be able to get away.'

'What time? I'll come, too. We can talk there.'

I knew I should say no, but I'd been so close to getting the truth out of him. And I needed to know now, what did it have to do with his mum?

'Nine-thirty,' I said.

Aidan nodded. 'I'll be there.'

I hesitated and then turned and ran after Daisy. It wasn't easy to keep up with her. One minute I'd catch a glimpse of her bright white top and I'd sprint, trying to shorten the distance between us. But then she'd duck down a side road and my body would flood with adrenaline until I saw her again. There was more traffic this side of the river and at one point I looked the wrong way and almost got mowed down by a bike.

At last I spotted her. The road had widened out and there was a square ahead, with a palace to the left. I recognised it from my guidebook: the Palazzo Pitti that Aidan had just told me about.

'Daisy!'

She heard me this time and turned around. She didn't stop, but she did slow her pace, allowing me to lengthen my stride and catch her up. I hadn't had this much exercise since Lou had talked me into going to a spin class with her and I almost threw up. I tried to regulate my breath, searching Daisy's bright red, tear-stained face for clues about what had happened. Was it Sophia and her tactless comments? Or had she had a row with Nick about being late for the wine tasting?

'What's happened?' I managed to gasp.

Daisy's face crumpled.

'Oh, Daisy,' I said, instinctively pulling her in for a hug.

At first, it was a little awkward. She was stiff and unresponsive in my arms as I patted her back lightly. Eventually, though, her body relaxed a little and I tightened my grip.

'Tell me what's upset you,' I said, talking softly so as not to scare her away again. I didn't think I could manage any more running.

'He's ... he's told me he doesn't want to talk to me anymore,' said Daisy, launching into a new set of wails.

I pulled back, leading her over to the kerb.

'Let's sit down,' I suggested, lowering myself onto the ground.

It wasn't the most comfortable, but it was better than standing in the middle of the square with unsuspecting tourists giving us strange looks as though I'd been the one to make Daisy cry.

'Who won't talk to you, Daisy?' I asked gently.

'My boyfriend,' she said, sniffing.

I delved into my bag and pulled out a relatively clean

tissue, handing it to her. She blew her nose noisily.

'I didn't realise you were ... seeing anyone,' I said, worrying that I sounded less than clued-up.

What did they call it these days? It had been years since I'd been on the dating scene, but from watching my number one guilty pleasure – *Made in Chelsea* – I thought I recalled the early-dating situation being referred to as 'talking to'. As in 'I'm talking to Nick.' I mean, it seemed an odd turn of phrase. Obviously you would be talking to them, what would be the alternative?

'Dad doesn't know,' confessed Daisy. 'Mum said not to tell him because he'd go mad.'

I knew it might not be ideal to think about your fourteen-year-old daughter having a boyfriend, but I liked to think that Nick was more reasonable than that.

'Why does she think that?' I asked.

'Because my boyfriend's different from us.'

'Who's us?'

'I mean ... not you. Mum and Dad. And Granny.'

I frowned, not getting it.

'You mean he's ...?'

I hoped she'd fill in the gaps.

'From a really rough area. His mum's a single mum and works in the bookies. Mum reckons I can do better, but I don't want to,' said Daisy, a new set of tears filming her eyes. 'He's perfect. He's so funny and cool and he's in a band and we talk about all sorts of stuff, like writing lyrics and our shit parents.' Daisy looked up. 'Sorry,' she said, clearly worrying about having sworn in front of me.

'No need to apologise. I know all about what it's like to have shit parents.'

'You do?'

I nodded. 'He sounds nice. This boy.'

'He is. Was. But now he says he doesn't want to be in a serious relationship. He's called it cooling off, but I know what that means.'

I put my arm around Daisy. 'He's young. He probably doesn't know what he wants. But, whatever happens, you have to remember that it is no reflection on you. And that if it doesn't work out with him, it will be hard, for a little while, but then it will be OK again. And you'll meet someone else and it will be better than you'd ever imagined.'

Daisy nodded gratefully, blowing her nose again. 'Do you think?'

I mustered all my enthusiasm. 'I do.'

But if that was the case, if what I was telling Daisy was true, why did I still think about Aidan sometimes? And why didn't my life with Nick feel 'better than I'd imagined'?

London

Two Years Earlier

Aidan took my hand on the walk from London Bridge tube round to the Shard. I was clip-clopping along in my only pair of heels, having thought that a black jeans, silk cami top and nice shoes combo was the best bet to attend an event for which I had absolutely no idea what the dress code was. And Aidan was no help, but then he always looked smart. It was one of the things I liked about him, actually, an unexpected thing. Where I grew up, all the guys wore tracksuit bottoms and football shirts. That was an exaggeration, of course, but I didn't remember anyone in my hometown ever looking this good in a shirt and trousers.

'Are you sure they're not going to mind you bringing a plus-one?' I asked.

'Course not,' he said. 'Anyway, I hate going to press events on my own. Standing awkwardly in a corner, thinking that I should be making small talk with someone but not quite having the energy to approach anybody and start it off.'

I laughed. 'So, basically, I'm only here to make you feel better.'

'Basically,' he said, grinning at me.

We passed through the Shard's security in record time and got into the lift up to level thirty-five. We were moving so fast that my ears popped and when we stepped out into the foyer, it felt as though I had arrived in a different, quieter, head-in-the-clouds world over a hundred and twenty-five metres above London.

A woman with a clipboard ticked off our names.

'Welcome to the Shangri-La Hotels and Resorts press event,' she trilled. 'Help yourself to champagne and food. And don't forget to take a goodie bag on your way out!'

I raised my eyebrows at Aidan. 'You didn't mention goodie bags,' I said out of the corner of my mouth as we headed for the drinks table.

'I was keeping that as ammunition in case I needed to pull out the big guns to persuade you to come,' he replied.

'You had me at free champagne,' I teased.

'Thought so,' he said, winking at me and handing me a glass.

'Do you get to go to these things all the time, then?' I asked. 'Because, if so, I'm in the wrong job.'

Aidan shook his head. 'Sadly not. The last press event I went to was for the Essex tourist board. Slightly less glamorous. And if we do get swanky invites like this, the editor of the newspaper tends to go himself.'

'How did you manage to wangle this one, then?' I asked.

Aidan tapped the side of his nose. 'I cannot possibly reveal my sources, but let's just say there may – *may* – have been some bribery at play.'

I laughed. 'Well, whatever you did to get us here, I'm glad you pulled it off. This is stunning,' I said, going closer to the window.

We were in the Shard's highest restaurant, TĪNG, which served Asian fusion food, so basically my favourite cuisine ever. Not that I'd ever eaten here, but I'd repeatedly looked at the menu online, wondering if I would ever be able to afford to. It was all marble floors and dark wood features, the floor-to-ceiling windows allowing us the most perfect view of London in all its twinkly glory. Tower Bridge looked particularly dramatic, as it always did when it was lit up at night.

'It's like the opening sequence to *The Apprentice*,' I marvelled.

We each grabbed a perfect-looking canapé from a passing tray and when I popped it in my mouth, it was like a taste explosion, all soft, squidgy aubergine and miso and garlic.

'Oh my God,' I said, once I'd swallowed it.

'That really was something,' agreed Aidan, shaking his head in awe.

We beamed at each other, which sometimes we tended to do for absolutely no other reason than we enjoyed being together. I thought back to that moment on the beach a month before, when he'd first told me that he couldn't stop looking at me, and nothing had changed since then. Except that my feelings for him grew stronger the more time I spent in his company.

'Well, cheers,' said Aidan, clinking my glass. 'Here's to a great night.'

'You do realise this is officially our one-month anniversary,' I remarked, smiling.

'Hmmn,' he said. 'Are you counting day one from the moment we first kissed on the beach or the next night?'

'The beach. I still can't believe we did that, by the way!'

'Why not?' he teased. 'What's so wrong with kissing a perfect stranger by a lake in the pitch black with bagpipes squeaking in the background?'

I laughed softly, looking down at my champagne, self-conscious, suddenly, about the connection we'd had so instantly, by how I hadn't held back like I normally would. On the level below, I could hear a pianist playing Beethoven's

Moonlight Sonata, which I thought was quite possibly my favourite classical piece (not that I had an extensive knowledge of classical music, you understand).

'Maddie,' said Aidan.

'Yes?' I replied, forcing myself to look at him.

'I think I might be falling in love with you.'

I bit my lip. 'You do?'

He nodded earnestly. 'I do.'

I frowned a little, because this was what I wanted to hear, of course it was, but I had this punishing voice on my shoulder telling me that I didn't deserve any of this, that it was a fantasy, that there had to be something I was missing because things never went this well for me. Nobody ever liked me this much. So what did Aidan see in me that other people couldn't?

'What is it you like about me?' I asked, trying to use a tone that didn't sound too needy and desperate, but I thought it would probably sound like that no matter how I worded it.

Aidan looked into my eyes, as though he was trying to work out what was going on in my head. Which part of what he'd said I was overthinking. It was something he teased me about mercilessly. *You think too much! Switch off that big brain of yours!*

'I like that you work harder than anyone I've ever met. That you're passionate about the things you love. That you care about the state of the world, and about other people. That you've struggled a bit and have come through it and are a stronger, more brilliant woman for it. And I also think you're very beautiful. Does that answer your question?'

I suppose it was my own fault for asking, but I was seriously cringing. Despite what he might think, I hadn't been fishing for compliments, because I never knew how to react when somebody actually gave me one.

'You do realise you've gone bright red?' said Aidan.

'Yes. Yes, I do, thank you,' I replied, downing the remainder of my drink.

Aidan laughed, holding my chin between his thumb and forefinger, tipping my head so that he could swoop down and kiss me. I wrapped my free hand around his waist. It always felt so good to hold him, or to be held by him. I felt safe when I was with him, which didn't make sense when we'd only known each other four weeks.

I took a deep breath, determined to tell him how I felt, too. Because I didn't want to hold back anymore. It was a risk, but it felt like one that I wanted to take with him.

'I think I like every single thing about you,' I said, stroking my fingertips up and down his back. 'Even your questionable cooking skills and your terrible taste in films.'

He was like a big kid, all into Marvel and *Star Wars*. I joked that he needed to grow up and watch some bleak, edgy foreign films and that then there would be no going back.

'There is absolutely nothing wrong with a grown man having an *Iron Man* obsession,' he said, tickling me under the ribs, where he knew I couldn't bear it the most.

I laughed, squirming out of his reach.

'Seriously, though,' I said, 'I think I'm falling in love with you, too.'

He nodded, pressing his forehead against mine. 'Good. That's good.'

We stood there for what felt like ages with these big grins on our faces and London shimmering beneath our feet.

Chapter Seventeen

When Daisy and I got back to the hotel, the family were all sitting in the hotel bar, chortling about something so loudly that other guests, who mostly looked like they were after a quiet, pre-dinner drink, were looking over with varying degrees of irritation. It was like the Leveson-Gowers didn't care what anyone else thought. I realised that that was what really annoyed me about them. They had this overinflated sense of themselves, as though the oh-so-fabulous life they were living was one we should all aspire to. They probably thought we were all seething with envy, which I certainly wasn't, because I'd always believed that people who constantly judged other people were probably doing it to make themselves feel better.

I looked at Daisy as we went across to join them at their table.

'You OK?' I whispered.

She nodded. It was still obvious she'd been crying, but Daisy reckoned it was likely her mum would be too self-absorbed to ask. Except that Sophia was staring at the two of us walking in together and I couldn't quite work out what the look on her face meant, but she didn't exactly seem pleased. What had I done now? Which major faux pas had I unsuspectingly committed?

'Daisy? Come over here, please,' said Sophia, patting the empty chair next to hers.

Daisy gave me a *help me* look and I smiled encouragingly at her, wishing I knew how to make things easier for her. I stood there awkwardly for a moment or two, wondering whether anyone would notice if I just skulked up to my room, but then Nick waved me over.

'I'll make space for you here, Maddie. Come on.'

Dutifully, I went to sit next to him.

'We were just reminiscing about our last family ski trip to Verbier,' said Rosamund. 'Nick went off on a black run and didn't come back for hours. I was on the phone to search and rescue when he waltzed back through the door of the chalet looking worse for wear.'

'You'd had a fall?' I asked innocently.

'No, I'd been indulging in rather too much apres-ski!' Nick chortled.

Everyone found this hilarious.

'Do you ski, Maddie?' asked Peter.

'Afraid not.'

I tuned in to Daisy and Sophia's conversation, which didn't seem to be going well.

'I *insist* that you tell me what the matter is,' Sophia was saying. 'Right now. We don't keep secrets from each other, Daisy.'

'I don't want to think about it anymore,' replied Daisy, sulkily. 'Anyway, I've already talked it through with Maddie and now I feel much better.'

'You've talked it through with ... Maddie?!' said Sophia, clearly not believing what she was hearing.

I winced. She threw me one of her 'if looks could kill' sideways glances and I swiped a menu off the table and pretended to read it.

'Why on earth would you talk to *her* about your issues?' she whispered, clearly not realising that we could all hear every word. '*I'm* your mother. I'm the one you should be coming to.'

'I can talk to who I like,' said Daisy, defiantly. 'And, honestly, you'd be the last person I'd come to.'

'Wait until I tell your father about this!' snapped Sophia.

'Tell me what?' said Nick.

Sophia looked as though she might be about to explode.

'Your daughter has been talking to other people about her problems.' She glanced at me, then turned her attention back to Nick, one eyebrow raised.

'Which other people?' asked Nick.

'Maddie,' said Daisy, throwing Sophia under the bus.

In that moment, I thought I might just have found an ally in this wretched family.

Nick looked confused. 'And you're angry because ...?'

'Because,' spat Sophia, 'because Daisy should—'

'Maddie will be part of our family when she marries Dad,' said Daisy. 'And she's nice to talk to and you're not, so that's what I'm going to carry on doing and you can't stop me.'

Part of me was enjoying seeing the look on Sophia's face and part of me wished the ground would open up and swallow me.

As if sensing this terrible combo of emotions, Nick patted my knee ineffectively.

'Calm down, Sophia. And show Maddie some respect, please. We should be happy that Daisy has someone to open up to. It's not good to bottle things up, especially at that age.'

Sophia looked at him with disgust.

'Thanks,' I said to him quietly.

'Well,' said Rosamund, clapping her hands together like a class teacher. 'Sophia, dear, why don't you pop and get freshened up for dinner?'

'I am ready for dinner,' said Sophia in a strangely robotic voice, possibly because her jaw was so tightly clenched she couldn't form words properly.

Rosamund bristled. She wasn't used to people losing control, or at least, not in public.

'In that case, Nick, why don't you take Maddie upstairs to cool off?'

The waiter chose that moment to deliver my Chianti Classico. My first mouthful transported me right back to Maurizio's vineyard and it was Aidan I saw when I imagined being there, listening as intently as I was, golden brown from a few days in the sun, shirtsleeves rolled up.

'I don't need to cool off, Rosamund,' I said. 'I'm perfectly fine here.'

Nick, I noticed, was squirming. Things were probably getting much too emotional for his liking.

'I think it would be best, Madeleine,' insisted Rosamund, determined to exert her authority.

'What are you dismissing Maddie for, Granny? She's done nothing wrong,' piped up Daisy.

I loved her in that moment.

'Enough!' said Nick in a rare burst of anger. He always said that losing your temper should be avoided at all costs. 'Maddie, let's go upstairs. We need to get ready for dinner, anyway.'

'Fine,' I said, standing up.

The sooner I got away from this lot, the better.

As we walked to the lifts, Nick was seething, I could tell.

'Do you want to talk about it?' I asked as he jabbed the *Call Lift* button so hard I thought he might be about to break it.

'Talk about what?'

'You seem angry.'

That was an understatement, but I thought I'd better be subtle about it given the mood he was in.

'I'm frustrated, Maddie. There's a difference.'

The lift still was not coming.

'Frustrated about Sophia?' I prompted.

Nick groaned. 'No. Not just Sophia.'

The lift doors finally opened and we stepped inside.

'Come on, then,' I said, as the doors closed behind us. 'What's frustrating you so much?'

Nick couldn't seem to look at me.

'This wasn't how I thought it would be, that's all,' he said quietly. 'You meeting my family. I didn't think it would be so ...'

'Difficult?' I suggested. 'Explosive?'

He nodded tersely.

'They're not as awful as you seem to think, Maddie,' he said. 'And what you need to remember is that these are the people I love most in the world.'

'Of course I know that.'

'Then why can't you try a bit harder?'

I watched his facial expression carefully.

'Are you annoyed that we keep clashing? Over almost everything?' I asked.

I wanted him to be honest with me. Brutally, if necessary.

He sighed. 'I feel like ...'

'Go on.'

'Like you're all bringing out the worst in each other.'

I became aware of my chest rising and falling. Of feeling like I wanted to fight my corner and tell him a few home truths, but I thought I'd probably say things I'd regret and so I closed my eyes for a second or two, trying to stay calm. It felt like a kick in the teeth, because I'd been kidding myself that I was the most important person in his life, but it didn't seem that way anymore. I felt this panic, suddenly, engulfing me out of nowhere. My whole life mapped out in front of me, a life where I had to stifle my true self, where I felt less-than, just as I had when I was growing up. Was this my destiny, then, to replace my disinterested parents with somebody else's utterly disinterested parents?

'So what you're saying is, I need to get on better with them otherwise maybe it's not going to work between us?' I asked, making sure I hadn't got it wrong; skewed it in my mind.

Nick didn't say anything at first.

We reached our floor and the lift doors opened with a ping. Nick got out first, leaving me to follow a few steps behind.

'Is that what you're saying or not?' I called after him.

I supposed he could say I was goading him, but who wouldn't, at a moment like this? I needed to know exactly what he was thinking, I deserved to know that.

As he fumbled with the key swipe on our door, he spoke very quietly. 'No, Maddie. I love you. And that is not what I'm saying.'

So why didn't I believe him?

Chapter Eighteen

I waited with Daisy in the courtyard of the Uffizi Gallery. It was a stunning building – two long corridors, three stories high, supported by a series of marble pillars. Then, at the end, overlooking the Arno, a shorter series of archways and corridors connecting both sides. And on the top, I noticed it now, the Vasari corridor Aidan had told me about. I let myself imagine Cosimo de' Medici striding through it on his way to work in fifteen hundred and something, avoiding the minions swarming the streets below.

Daisy was in her own little world and had had her earphones in with her music on full-blast since we'd left the hotel. On the walk here – back across the Piazza della Signoria – I'd asked her what she was listening to and she'd pretended not to hear me. Something told me things were not going to go smoothly this morning. I sort of hoped that Aidan wasn't serious about turning up now, too. And then at the same time, after the night I'd had with Nick, when we'd barely spoken and I realised I'd started to develop a pathological hatred of Sophia, it felt like the grounding, familiar presence of somebody who didn't find me intensely annoying (Aidan) might be just what I needed.

'You are here for the Uffizi tour?' asked an attractive, blonde-haired Italian woman in her late-thirties.

'Yes, that's right,' I said, thrusting the booking voucher they'd given me at the hotel into her hands.

'Very good,' she said, checking something off her list. 'You are Madeleine, yes? And you are Daisy?'

I nudged Daisy, who reluctantly took her earbuds out.

'I am Francesca and I will be your guide today,' said the Italian.

Aidan chose that moment to appear, striding across the cobbled courtyard like Mr Darcy striding out of a lake. Even Daisy noticed him.

'There's that guy,' she said. 'From the wine-tasting tour.'

'Oh yes,' I said, feigning surprise.

'Hope I'm not late,' he said, coming to a stop next to us, giving Francesca one of his smiles. 'You must be our guide for the morning.'

To be fair to her, she didn't seem fazed by him. I decided to channel this composed, earthy Italian woman who seemed like the sort of person who wouldn't put up with crap in a relationship. It had dawned on me last night that perhaps this wasn't how things had to be – perhaps I didn't have to feel the way Nick's family made me feel, and even Nick, sometimes. And my parents. And Tim at work. Perhaps there were people out there who would respect me. Perhaps I could feel good about myself regardless. It felt like Francesca, whatever her situation, probably already felt that.

'And you are Aidan, yes?' she said.

'Yes,' he confirmed.

'Do I really have to come on this tour?' said Daisy.

'Yes, you do, because your dad booked us on it,' I replied. 'Anyway, it'll be fun.'

'This isn't my idea of fun,' she remarked.

'You do not like art?' said Francesca, surprised.

Daisy shrugged. 'I do. But I like shopping more.'

'But shopping you can do any time, anywhere,' commented

Aidan. 'It's not every day you're standing in the courtyard of the Uffizi Gallery.'

'I'm just not into it,' shrugged Daisy. 'And I don't see why I should be forced to spend two hours of my life doing something that I don't want to do.'

'I did suggest you said all this to your dad,' I pointed out.

Because there wasn't much I could do about it now, was there, and, to be honest, it would have been much nicer for me to have come on my own if she was going to moan the entire time. I didn't know why Nick had insisted that she come, the poor girl seemed to have been forced to do things she didn't want to do the entire trip.

'Can't I go shopping and meet you back here after?' she asked, looking at me hopefully.

'Daisy, I'm responsible for you. I can hardly let you go wandering off on your own, can I?'

'But I go out on my own all the time in London. What's the difference?'

Francesca gave me a sympathetic look. 'Here,' she said, pulling several headsets out of her bag. 'While you decide, you can put these on. Then you can hear me wherever you are. It is very busy in there and it can be hard to hear me without.'

Aidan and I each took a headset, but Daisy didn't even make a move to take one.

'You could call Dad and ask him?' suggested Daisy.

'How old are you, Daisy?' asked Aidan, who already had his headset on.

'Fourteen, nearly fifteen.'

'Wow. So you like fashion, do you?'

'Yes,' she said, as though she was sussing him out. 'I want to be a fashion designer, actually.'

'Really?' said Aidan. 'Florence must be heaven for you,

then, with all these shops. Have you checked out the Gucci Garden, I hear it's very good?'

'We went there the day before yesterday. It was amazing. I got this bag,' she said, showing Aidan the leather shoulder bag that Nick had treated her to.

'Beautiful,' he said. 'Can I touch it?'

Daisy shrugged. 'Sure.'

Aidan stroked his hand across the bright yellow leather. 'So soft!' he said.

I smiled, despite myself. Aidan did have a way of making people feel noticed.

'I didn't know bags were your thing,' I said.

Aidan shrugged. 'I appreciate fine goods when I see them, that's all.'

Only then did I realise that I'd been overfamiliar. If Aidan and I were the strangers we were supposed to be, it would have been a very odd thing to say. How would I know what he was or wasn't into?

Luckily, Daisy didn't seem to have noticed. She just appeared to be over the moon that somebody was actually listening to her. Aidan had a knack for doing that. When he spoke to you, you had his full attention.

'Fine, I'll call your dad,' I said, taking my phone out of my bag and getting in a massive tangle with the earphones.

I dialled Nick's number, mouthing a 'sorry' at Francesca, who thankfully was good-natured about it, waving away my apology with a wry smile.

Nick didn't pick up, of course. He never seemed to, lately. I left him a message.

'Nick it's me. I'm with Daisy at the Uffizi. She really doesn't want to go in and says she'd prefer to go for a walk around the shops instead. Is that all right? She says she's allowed to go off on her own in London? Call me back asap because this is holding everybody up.'

I ended the call.

Daisy looked at me expectantly. 'Well? Can I go?'

'I haven't got permission from your dad yet, have I?'

'I can call my mum, let her know,' said Daisy. She twirled her own phone around in her hand. 'She won't mind, honestly.'

I didn't know what to do. Making decisions about what other people's children were allowed to do was not my forte.

'Florence is a very safe city,' said Aidan. 'There's hardly any crime, isn't that right, Francesca?'

'Yes,' Francesca agreed enthusiastically. 'I have teenagers myself and they come here alone and sit at a café or meet their friends.'

'They do?' I said, feeling better about it all.

'Of course,' said Francesca.

I looked at Daisy.

'And you swear you'll call your mum, right away, to tell her where you are and where you're planning to go?'

'I promise,' said Daisy, brighter now she knew she'd pretty much got her own way.

I was still worried, but the evidence suggested it would all be fine. If Nick had answered his phone, I'd know for sure, but he hadn't, so I had to work out what to do myself.

'You'd have to meet us back here. Right by this statue of Donatello. At eleven thirty sharp.'

'Sure,' said Daisy. 'Back here in two hours. Got it.'

'And don't go too far. Stick to the busy areas. The main streets. Don't wander off down any quiet alleyways or anything.'

Aidan gave me an empathetic smile.

'Promise,' said Daisy, already backing away.

My stomach swirled as I watched her walk away. I really, really hoped I was doing the right thing.

Chapter Nineteen

Once Daisy had gone, Francesca marched off in the direction of the entrance. I glanced at Aidan as we both adjusted our headsets. I was already wishing that I'd told him not to bother coming.

'Just us?' he said.

'Looks like it.'

What I had to hold on to was that this was possibly my last chance to find out what had happened to Aidan a couple of years ago, and although I'd tried to convince myself that I was doing it for me and Nick, so that I could focus on our relationship and on getting to know his family, deep down I knew that I was doing it for me, for my own peace of mind. And I'd decided that that was probably OK. Why shouldn't I put my own needs first for once? I wanted Aidan out of my life and out of my head and hopefully I'd have achieved both by 11.30 this morning.

'Reckon you can take video footage in there?' I asked Aidan.

Francesca, who clearly had ears like a hawk, replied instead, 'No videos in the museum!'

Aidan caught my eye and raised his eyebrows.

'Are you still at Holiday Shop? Working for that dickhead, Tim?'

'Yes. And yes.'

He looked surprised.

'He's been promoted to senior producer. My friend Lou is a director now. And I'm still exactly where I was two years ago. For now, anyway,' I said, thinking about my website idea.

We navigated the security to get into the gallery, an airport-like set-up similar to the one at the Galleria dell'Accademia. Once we'd had our bags checked, Francesca led us through what felt like the backstage area of the gallery. A series of corridors painted in white and grey, and lots and lots of stairs.

'You know, not getting promoted isn't something to beat yourself up about,' said Aidan. 'It's a tough industry. It's easy to get stuck.'

'I guess we can't all fall on our feet like you,' I said.

Aidan looked confused. 'What do you mean?'

'I hadn't put you down as a *Conde Nast Traveller* type.'

'It's a job, Maddie. And I get to travel the world and write interesting pieces that go onto glossy pages with beautiful glossy pictures. So what if it doesn't align perfectly with my values?'

Great. I'd made myself sound all bitter and twisted about his success.

'As long as you're happy,' I said, seemingly unable to lose the snippy tone.

It was like I'd turned in to Sophia Mark 2.

'The Uffizi Gallery was built by order of Cosimo the first, the Grand Duke of Tuscany,' said Francesca's booming voice through the headset.

Cosimo again, I thought.

'It was built on the site of an ancient church. If you look here, inside this glass, you can see the ancient floor and the altar.'

I paused to look down beneath my feet at some stone

ruins. When I looked up, Francesca and Aidan were way ahead and I had to hurry to catch them up. As we turned to go up another steep staircase, I could hear Francesca huffing and puffing in my earpiece, which was quite disconcerting when I couldn't actually see her! At the top of the stairs, I found them again.

'The gallery was designed by Giorgio Vasari. It is the second most important art gallery in the world. Maddie, can you tell me which is the number one most important art gallery in the world?'

It was like being back at the wine tasting all over again.

I held my hands up: my general knowledge really wasn't very good. 'Um, the Louvre?' I guessed.

'Correct!' said Francesca. 'The Louvre is the most important art gallery in the world and it is in fact twenty-four times bigger than the Uffizi.'

'Wow,' said Aidan. 'No wonder the only thing I remember about it is the Mona Lisa.'

'Same,' I said.

'It is very intimidating, no? Even here in the Uffizi, you cannot see it all in one day,' noted Francesca.

We were now in the first-floor corridor, which had the most perfect light streaming in through the windows on the right-hand side. On the ceiling were wood panels as far as the eye could see, each containing an ornate set of hand-painted frescoes.

Aidan stood alongside me.

'I was thinking about you last night,' he said.

Francesca was telling us about a series of paintings of popes, kings and queens.

'Were you?' I asked, keeping it casual, pretending to be mesmerised by the paintings on the ceiling.

His arm brushed against mine and it was as though every

single nerve-ending in my body was suddenly standing on end.

We moved around the gallery, stopping to look at beautiful paintings and sculptures, some of them over six hundred years old, with Francesca enthusiastically explaining the fascinating history behind them. An hour passed in what felt like a split second and part of me didn't want to ruin the experience by hearing Aidan's explanation for what had happened in the past. Because whatever it was, it wasn't going to change anything, was it? But as we followed Francesca into another room, stopping in front of a painting of seven different women sitting on a medieval throne, I had the feeling that it was now or never.

'This is the *Seven Virtues*,' said Francesca, who was standing just in front of us. '*Faith*, *Hope*, *Charity*, *Temperance*, *Prudence*, *Fortitude* and *Justice*.'

'I'm not sure I possess any of those,' Aidan whispered to me.

'I'm not sure you do, either,' I agreed, only half-joking.

I'd begun to remember what it had been like to be with him. How funny he was, how naturally the conversation flowed. This was not good.

'Six of these paintings are by the artist Piero del Pollaiuolo,' said Francesca. 'But one is the first work by Botticelli. I will be very happy with you if you can correctly guess which one.'

I stared at them. To me, one popped out immediately. It drew me in. The woman's dress was so detailed and clear, and her face looked more three-dimensional than the others.'

'That one,' I said, pointing at the first panel.

Francesca patted me on the shoulder. 'You are right, Maddie, well done. This is *Fortitude* and it was painted by Sandro Botticelli in 1470.'

'You're better at art than you are at wine,' commented Aidan.

'Seems so. By the way, did you doodle bananas to help me out?'

'Maybe,' he said, smiling at me.

I nodded. 'Thank you.'

'Any time.'

'I'll have to bring Nick's family here and show them that I'm not as clueless as they seem to think I am.'

Aidan frowned. 'Is that really what they think of you?'

I shrugged.

'And Nick used to be married to that overconfident one? Sophia?'

'Yep.'

'And he didn't tell you she was coming?'

I shook my head. 'Do all men lack basic communication skills?'

'I couldn't possibly speak for all men,' said Aidan.

I took a step closer to *Fortitude*. There was something very strong and powerful about the 550-year-old woman in the painting.

'So, are you going to tell me, then?' I said. 'About what happened. Why you left.'

'Ah, yes,' he said softly, standing so close behind me now that I could feel his breath on the back of my neck. His voice was sending tingles down my spine.

Focus, I thought to myself.

'So I think we got to my mum's diagnosis?'

I nodded. 'Yes.'

'I found out that the disease is usually passed down via the mother and while both men and women can develop the condition, men go on to have symptoms more often.'

I swallowed hard. Was Aidan losing his eyesight?

'That's when things started not adding up,' said Aidan. 'Neither Mum nor Dad mentioned that maybe I should get a test, and when I brought it up, they brushed it off. Said their doctor had told them it wasn't necessary, that it was very unlikely I'd have it and that since I couldn't do anything about it, there was no point in knowing unless I started developing symptoms.'

'That doesn't sound right,' I said.

'Exactly. Which is why I contacted my own GP and arranged the test myself.'

'Why didn't you tell me any of this at the time?' I asked.

We'd shared lots of things. Our disastrous relationships, our aspirations, our failures. So why not that?

'I should have said something,' said Aidan.' I wasn't used to talking about my feelings. I know it felt like I was, because it came more easily with you. But that was very unusual. And I went to tell you loads of times, but something always stopped me. I thought that if I did have the gene, it would mean an end to everything. You wouldn't want to have children with me, for a start, would you?'

'Aidan, we'd been together a month. Having children wasn't even something we'd thought about, let alone discussed.'

'I'd thought about it,' he said, looking at me in that intense way he had.

I swallowed hard.

'Now we go to see more Botticelli,' announced Francesca grandly.

Keeping Francesca in my eyeline, my mind was whirring. He'd seen a future for us. He'd thought as far ahead as children, something I hadn't dared consider. So what had gone so wrong?

'This is *Primavera*,' said Francesca, coming to a stop. 'Spring.'

The painting had a dark background but was bursting with colourful details: fruits, flowers, trees and plants. Francesca explained that in the centre of the painting was Venus, the goddess of love, set back from the others, and above her head, a blindfolded Cupid shoots his arrow. When the small crowd in front of us dispersed, Aidan and I stepped forward to take a closer look.

'Quite moving, isn't it?' said Aidan.

I nodded. 'I never realised that you literally have to be standing right in front of these paintings to appreciate them properly.'

Aidan looked at his watch. 'It's just gone eleven, you know. We don't have long.'

I understood. It felt like this would be the last chance for us to speak privately. If I didn't get the full story now, I might never know how all of this had impacted his decision not to turn up that night.

'What did the tests show? Do you have the gene?' I asked gently.

'No,' he said.

'That's good, right?' I said, relief rushing through me.

He nodded. 'But the strangest thing came out of it. When I told my parents about the test, my mum started crying. Balling her eyes out, right there in front of me.'

'Because she was relieved? Would she have blamed herself?'

'Well, that's what I thought, initially. But then came the bombshell. There was something they needed to tell me. Something they'd been meaning to for – well – thirty-one years.'

'What was it?' I asked.

'I'm adopted.' Aidan laughed hollowly. 'And they'd decided it was a great idea not to tell me.'

I felt as though the wind had been knocked out of me. Adopted? I remembered how close to his parents he'd been. How affectionately he'd spoken of them and how refreshing that had seemed.

'Fucking hell,' I said. This was not panning out to be one of the superficial excuses I thought he'd come up with.

'Yeah. It was a lot to take in.'

'And that all happened ...?'

'The afternoon I was meant to meet you to go to that exhibition. It was such a shock. Mum and I had never even fallen out, not really. I'd always thought I was exactly like her: we were both sensitive, and we had a sweet tooth and neither of us slept well and we liked being around people in a way that my dad didn't. But the stuff you think is in your genes? Turns out that sometimes it isn't.'

He tried to smile, but I could see from his expression how painful this had been for him.

'But it is from your mum. In that it's about the relationship you had. The cues you picked up on, from observing how she was with other people. Which is kind of the same thing, isn't it?'

'Maybe,' he said, as we followed Francesca into the Leonardo da Vinci room.

The light was very low, which Francesca said was done purposely to show his paintings in the best way: meditative and slow. With the stillness of the room, the subdued lighting, it felt like the perfect space for everything to finally fall into place.

London

Two Years Earlier

'Where are you off to?' asked Lou, perching on the end of my desk.

'Some travel photography exhibition. I mean, how "me" does that sound? Beautiful pictures of someone's travels? Check. Trayfuls of free champagne being handed out? Check.'

Lou looked dubious. 'That might only happen in films.'

'True.'

'I hope you're not hanging around here much longer?' said Lou, looking at her watch. 'Haven't you officially finished for the day?'

'Yep,' I said, tapping away.

I wanted to finish the script for the Balearics show I was helping Tim produce the following day. When I said helping, I basically meant that I was doing all the work so that Tim could take all the credit, again.

'Aidan can't get here until seven anyway,' I explained. 'He's got a meeting or something, so I thought I might as well hang around here rather than go all the way home and then back out again.'

Lou looked at me conspiratorially. 'What are your plans for the weekend?'

Lou and her husband, Will, were desperate to get me and

Aidan over for dinner so that she could grill him properly. But I felt as though I wanted to keep him to myself for now. Which sounded strange, and possibly a tad possessive, but we were still getting to know each other. Every time we saw each other, I felt more and more connected to him. And yes, I saw a future for the two of us, even though we'd only met just over a month ago. But there was still so much to find out about him. And before I subjected him to an onslaught of questions from my friends and family (not that I was in any hurry to introduce him to my parents and siblings, full stop), I wanted to make sure that things really were as good as they seemed.

'We'll come for dinner soon, I promise,' I assured her.

She sighed dramatically. 'Fine. Well, then, I'm out of here. Will has set me the very exciting challenge of clearing out the cupboards this evening. We really do know how to have a good time in our household!'

'Domestic bliss, eh? Why do I want it again?'

'Exactly! Enjoy the hot sex and excitement while you can because I'm sorry to be the bearer of bad news, but it doesn't last.'

I laughed. Although, secretly, I couldn't imagine ever not having hot sex with Aidan. I let myself do whatever I wanted, say whatever came into my head with him in a way I'd never quite felt comfortable doing before. He basically made me feel like the sexiest, most attractive version of myself. It was all pressing me up against walls and sweeping stuff off tables and joining me in the shower when I was supposed to be getting ready for work. Seriously, I didn't know how I'd got so lucky.

'I'll see you tomorrow, then,' I said, putting the finishing touches to my script.

I was planning to touch up my make-up and google stuff

for twenty minutes or so until he arrived. Maybe I'd do some research on the photographer whose work we were about to see – it might be nice to look knowledgeable about such things and to be able to make intelligent comments about the work rather than just gush about how much I liked it.

Half an hour later, I was fully made-up. My hair, which I'd worn down for most of the day but which had become more and more mushroom-like as the hours passed, was now pulled back in an annoyingly fluffy ponytail. I wasn't feeling particularly great about the way I looked this evening, but I supposed those were the perils of getting ready at work. You couldn't do anything about it if your outfit didn't look quite right in hindsight, or if you needed your hair straighteners, which you'd decided you couldn't be bothered to lug in on the tube but now bitterly regretted not bringing.

I checked my phone again: nothing from Aidan. He was probably minutes away, and it wasn't like we had to be there at any particular time. I googled thirty-minute meals, having decided that I ought to expand my repertoire if Aidan was going to continue to come to mine every other night.

At 9 p.m. I was starting to get worried. I'd tried calling several times, had sent a text, a WhatsApp and a voice note. He'd never once not got back to me when I'd messaged him, and he'd never once been late to meet me – in fact, I was the one who was always texting him, apologising profusely for getting caught up in the office, or stuck in traffic, or whatever it was. Except that now I was sitting alone in my office on a Friday night, all dressed up. It was so late that the cleaners had started vacuuming.

I absent-mindedly googled 'problems in London tonight'. Then 'tube issues'. Then 'bus crashes'. And then I sat there, wondering what to do, whether to just head home. Surely he wouldn't turn up two hours late expecting me to be here? How pathetic would I look for hanging around, anyway? With one last glance at my interminably silent phone, I turned off my PC and skulked out of the office, waving to the cleaners who I'd never met until now because even I didn't make a habit of working this late. Something was wrong, I knew it was. However this panned out, I had a feeling it was going to be bad.

I purposely left my phone in the kitchen that night, thinking that would stop me constantly refreshing the screen, but, of course, I convinced myself I needed a glass of water and I swung by the kitchen counter, illuminating the screen accidentally. Still nothing. Then I persuaded myself that I should have the phone near my bed in case somebody desperately needed to get hold of me in the middle of the night (you never knew, did you?) but that I would bury it in the bottom of my underwear drawer.

Later, as I tossed and turned, wishing sleep to come so that I could have a break from worrying about Aidan, I heard the ping of a text. I leapt out of bed so fast, yanking open the drawer, shovelling my way through knickers and bras and Spanx until I reached my phone. He'd texted. I gasped, opening up the message.

I can't do this now. I'm sorry.

I swallowed, felt like crying but didn't and read it over and over.

I texted back.

Talk to me. What's going on?

And then I spent the night with my phone cradled in the palm of my hand, waiting for a reply that never came.

Chapter Twenty

We'd thanked Francesca and were walking back through the colonnade of the gallery by 11.29. Aidan was hugging the sun in the courtyard and I was under the shade of the arches so that he kept disappearing from view, hidden behind a pillar, only to reappear a second later, smiling at me, looking even more devastatingly handsome than before. Aidan had had bad news the night we were supposed to meet. He'd been distracted, I was the last thing on his mind, I got it. To an extent.

'Couldn't you have called me?' I said. 'Not that evening. But later, once the shock had worn off?'

'I just … my trust was shattered,' he explained. 'I hated my parents in that moment. The people I loved most in the world had lied to me for over thirty years. And if they were capable of that, then so must everyone else be. And I was falling for you and it scared me. I felt completely paranoid, started convincing myself that what we had wasn't real, that you were probably hiding something from me, too, that you weren't who you said you were. It took some time to get over all that and to feel like myself again.'

I didn't know what to think. On one hand I could empathise. Sometimes, when I was a child, I used to fantasise that *I* was adopted and that one day my real, attentive, loving parents would swoop in and save me from my imposter mum and dad, who, although I loved, I wasn't sure wholeheartedly loved me. Not in the way I'd always dreamed of being loved. But, of course, that wasn't what I really wanted. And it must have been devastating for Aidan who had been so close to his parents.

'I'm sorry,' said Aidan. 'Although I know that doesn't cut it. Not at all.'

I kept an eye out, looking for the statue of Donatello, where Daisy had promised she would be waiting.

Aidan looked at me. 'And for what it's worth, I haven't had a relationship since.'

'But you were all about relationships!' I said, shocked. 'I was the one who was scared to throw myself into them. You were fearless. You went in head-first and you didn't look back, that's what you said.'

'That was before.'

I thought about the fallout from the end of our relationship; how it had affected me. Aidan had felt like a good thing in my life, a special thing, that I couldn't wait to tell everyone about. And when it all went wrong and I'd had to explain that actually I'd made a mistake, that I hadn't found the love of my life after all, it had been overwhelming. Utterly humiliating. And I think that in some ways it was why I'd thrown myself back into dating so soon. I'd been trying to convince myself that it didn't mean I was going to be alone forever, that there was somebody out there for me, there had to be. Whether or not they were the right person didn't matter in that moment because my goal was to not be alone. And then I'd met Nick.

'I came to your work, you know,' said Aidan.

I looked at him, shocked. 'What? When?'

'Once things had calmed down and my head was straight. A few weeks after I found out about my parents. I waited for you outside your office. I knew you finished at about five, so

I got there early, sat on a bench in that square opposite your building.'

'And what, you didn't see me?'

'I did see you.'

I shook my head, not believing it. He was there, at my office! It could all have turned out so differently.

'Why didn't you come over? Say something?' I asked.

'Because you were with Nick.'

I thought back, trawling my memories for a time when Nick had met me at work. He didn't usually because he worked in the city, nowhere near my office. And then it dawned on me. Our second date. The huge bunch of white roses he'd had delivered to my office with a note, asking me on a second date. Dinner at The Ivy.

'It was only the second time we'd met,' I said. 'I wasn't even going to see him again, because I wasn't ready to properly date. And I was still thinking about you all the time and didn't feel I was in the right headspace for it. But then he'd sent flowers to my work, asking me out for dinner that night. I'd had a shit day, Tim had been awful. I'd thought: why not? It's just dinner.'

'It felt like you'd moved on pretty quickly,' he said, looking away, down at the cobbles. 'And part of me didn't blame you because I knew I'd messed up by not calling you. I'd shut down, I'd had to, to protect myself.'

'But the other part of you ...?'

'Thought I'd had a lucky escape. Because, stupidly, I'd imagined that you'd be waiting for me. I'd pictured it all, how I'd come to your work and explain what had happened and how you'd listen and understand and just hold me, like you used to. But then I saw you with him. And this massive bunch of flowers. And it hadn't even been three weeks. I even wondered whether you'd been seeing Nick the entire time you'd been seeing me.'

'I hadn't. It's just what I do – I pretend I don't care that the person I was relying on most has completely let me down. It's not like I even wanted to be with someone else, I just had to prove to myself that I could be if I wanted to be.'

Aidan nodded.

'I assumed I'd pushed you away somehow,' I continued. 'And I came to the stupid conclusion that falling for someone that hard is dangerous and that there's a different kind of love, like what I had with Nick eventually. Slower, gentler. And that maybe that would be easier.'

'More within your control,' said Aidan.

I nodded. 'Yes. Exactly that.'

Somewhere down the street the opening bars of 'O Mio Babbino Caro' struck up. A busker on the violin. The two of us came to a stop next to the Donatello statue. It was past eleven thirty now. Where was Daisy?

'I'm sure she'll be here any minute,' said Aidan, reading my mind.

I checked my phone. Nick had not got back to me. Odd. He was only hanging around the hotel, he'd said. He was planning to have a coffee up on the roof with his mum. Maybe he'd left his phone in the room.

'It's well past eleven thirty,' I said, fanning myself with my hand. 'Why wouldn't she be here?'

She promised she'd be here on time. What if something terrible had happened?

'She's a teenager,' reasoned Aidan, 'they lose track of time, don't they? Isn't that what happened when they were late for the wine-tasting tour?'

'Don't get me started on that. Daisy may be an adolescent,

but Nick isn't. He was supposed to be there so that I didn't look stupid in front of his family.'

'Why do you care so much about what they think?' asked Aidan.

'I just don't think they can get their head round the fact that Nick wants to marry someone like me.'

'And here I am trying to get my head around the fact that you want to marry someone like him.'

I looked at him. 'What do you mean?'

'Did I just say that out loud?' he said, trying to laugh it off.

'Yes you did. So now you're going to have to elaborate.'

Aidan sighed. 'He seems like a nice enough guy ...'

'But ...?'

'But, when I see the two of you together, you seem different. More guarded, maybe. Like you're trying to be a different version of yourself.'

'That's only because his family are here. It's not like that usually.'

Or was it? Things were better when it was just the two of us, sure, but I still kept part of myself back, I thought. I didn't think he'd want to see pure, unadulterated 'me' with all my baggage and my anxieties and my need to please people all the time. And Nick, in comparison, seemed very 'normal' and together, if a little emotionally unavailable, so I didn't get the feeling he'd understand. If we could exist in some sort of parallel universe where it was just the two of us, maybe it could work, but when you threw families into the mix, it got complicated. Nick loved his family, they were important to him. Of course he was going to listen to what they had to say and I, in turn, was going to have to accept that they'd potentially be part of my life forever.

'I'm going to have to try Nick again. Maybe she went back to the hotel,' I said, dialling his number.

'Maybe. Although wouldn't he have told you?' said Aidan.

I wondered how I was going to word this: *have you seen your daughter? You know, the one I was supposed to have been looking after for the last three hours?*

It went straight to voicemail again. I held the phone in my hand, willing him to call straight back.

I paced up and down, into the courtyard and back under the arches, looking for Daisy, who could be coming from myriad different directions. Had she walked through the Piazza della Signoria, or would she come in from the other side, by the Arno?

'Why don't I stay here and you check back at the hotel, see if she's made her way there?' suggested Aidan.

'Are you sure you wouldn't mind?'

I'd probably feel better once I was actually doing something active, and she couldn't have gone far. The street outside our hotel was teeming with shops, so it would make sense that she'd headed back in that direction.

'I'll hang around for another half an hour or so,' said Aidan. 'I'm sure she'll turn up.'

I nodded gratefully. 'OK. If you're sure.'

Setting off in the direction of the hotel, I picked up my pace as I headed diagonally across the square.

'Maddie!' called Aidan.

I stopped and spun around. For some reason, it felt like a moment that had the capacity to change everything.

'If you want to talk more,' he said, 'you know where I am.'

Chapter Twenty-One

I hesitated before going into the hotel because I had no idea what I was going to do if Daisy wasn't there. The porter came out with his usual cheery demeanour and flamboyant Italian accent.

'Good afternoon, signora.'

'Hi,' I said, smiling at him even though all my facial muscles felt so tense I could barely move them.

I swung through the revolving doors, praying that the first person I saw would be Daisy. Sadly, it was Nick and Sophia. They were sitting in the hotel bar looking very cosy. Sophia had a coffee and was holding it neatly in the palm of her hand, laughing coquettishly at something Nick had said. Nick looked completely relaxed, slouched back in his chair, his shirt open at the collar. I watched them for a second or two. They were the perfect fit. I bet when Sophia and Nick used to enter a room, everyone would think: *Ah, yes. There's a couple who are meant to be together.*

I approached them. *Please let Daisy be in her room. Please let Daisy be in her room.*

'Hi,' I said, towering over them.

Sophia cleared her throat, putting down her coffee. Nick stayed in his slouched position, but there was something in his eyes, a sort of startled look, as though he'd been caught doing something he shouldn't have been. I wondered whether they'd been talking about me, whether that was why they both suddenly looked so guilty.

'Hello, darling,' said Nick.

Now it was my turn to clear my throat.

'Um, has Daisy been back here by any chance?' I asked, keeping my tone light and bright so as to not in any way cause alarm.

'Wasn't she with you?' asked Nick, confused.

'She was. But then she didn't want to go into the Uffizi. She was adamant about it, said she'd rather go window shopping.'

'Well, I hope you didn't let her?' said Sophia.

Fuck.

'I tried calling you,' I said to Nick. 'She assured me that neither of you would mind. That she goes out on her own in London all the time.'

'This is not London, Maddie. For God's sake!' snapped Sophia, standing up. 'So where is she now?'

This was hands-down the most awkward situation I'd ever been in. My mind started racing ahead to the worst-case scenario. What if she'd been abducted? What if we never saw her again and Nick and Sophia lost their precious daughter forever and it was all my fault? What if she was being held hostage by one of the predatory Italian men Peter was so quick to assume would be lurking on every street corner?

'I don't know,' I admitted. 'She said she'd meet us—'

'Who's us?' demanded Nick, who had also stood up now, the relaxed stance from minutes ago long gone.

'The other people on the tour. The guide, Francesca. Daisy was supposed to meet us at eleven thirty at the statue of Donatello.'

'And she wasn't there?' pressed Nick.

I shook my head. 'I waited for twenty minutes and then I thought I'd better come back here.'

'She might still be at the Uffizi,' said Sophia, who was gathering all her things together, her bag, her scarf. 'We'd better get down there, Nick.'

I was going to have to tell them about Aidan. Casual, I thought to myself. A fellow guest of the hotel simply doing me a favour.

'That guy from the wine-tasting tour said he'd wait,' I explained, cringing inside. 'You know that journalist guy? He was on the tour too and offered to wait while I came back here.'

Nick flashed me a look. 'So, right now, Daisy could be with some older man we barely know, essentially a complete stranger?'

'Look, I'm sorry, OK. She was very persuasive, and—'

'She's a teenager, Maddie, of course she's bloody persuasive,' said Sophia, raising her voice so that the concierge and a couple of hotel guests looked over with interest. 'Surely you're intelligent enough to work that out.'

'Right,' I said, trying to stay calm.

It was understandable that she'd be lashing out at me, but because it was Sophia, of course she had to be extra awful about it.

'I did try to check in with you before I let Daisy go,' I said to Nick.

'I must have left my phone up in the room,' Nick replied, giving me a dark look. 'Seriously, Madeleine, how could you be so stupid? You should never have let her go off on her own.'

'Come on, Nick,' said Sophia, sweeping towards the door. 'We need to go and find our daughter.'

Nick followed dutifully without so much as a glance in my

direction and I was left standing alone in the lobby as they rushed through the doors and out onto Via Tornabuoni.

I made my way miserably to the lifts, reaching our room in a daze. I'd really fucked up this time. Although Florence felt very safe, and there were people everywhere, so unless she'd completely wandered off the beaten track, it was unlikely that anything terrible had happened, wasn't it? She could have got lost, I supposed, but she could always ask for directions. She was sensible enough to be able to go into a hotel foyer or ask a policeman or something.

I let myself into the room. The cleaners had been in and everything was neat and pristine. The windows were still thrown open, as I'd left them this morning. I looked around, confused. There was no sign of Nick's phone. Not on the bed, nor the bedside table. His charger was plugged in under the desk, but his phone wasn't attached. I checked in the bathroom: nothing. I wondered if he'd been lying about having left it up here. But why would he do that? Unless he felt bad about something. After all, he'd been perfectly happy to let me go off with his daughter alone for over three hours without once checking his phone to make sure that everything was all right. Not that it was excusing my part in it all, far from it, but it was interesting to note that he'd gone to the trouble of lying about it. And it made me think about the other untruths that might have been covered up, on both our parts. Because if I hadn't been able to tell him about Aidan, then there were probably things that he'd kept from me, too. And suddenly the thought of marrying him made me sink onto the edge of the bed. I put my head in my hands feeling clammy and hot. What if I didn't want to marry him anymore? What would I do if I'd changed my mind?

London

Two Years Earlier

I flicked through Tinder, marvelling at the random faces popping up on my screen, none of whom did anything for me whatsoever. Seriously, was this what it had come to? Swiping left or right based on the static, often filtered images someone had chosen to share? They were clearly showing themselves in the best light, weren't they? What about the other stuff, the stuff they didn't announce/brag about? Exactly how bad was it?

'He's nice!' said Lou, fake enthusiastically, pointing at a man wearing a too-small suit, who described his favourite pastime as playing board games.

'I'll be the judge of that,' I said, swiping madly, left, left, left. This all felt very desperate and I wholeheartedly doubted I was going to meet the man of my dreams sitting on my sofa in my scraggiest leggings and sweatshirt combo looking at photos that said absolutely nothing about what the person was really like. I was only doing this to stop Lou going on and also as a distraction from thinking about the inevitable (the absent Aidan).

There had been nothing since his original text and it had been two weeks now. I was proud of myself for having managed to not text him for the last six days. I was going to have to accept, wasn't I, that for whatever reason, he didn't want to see me anymore. And it hurt. Badly. Which didn't make that much sense given the amount of time we'd known each other. Which was why I was prepared to try anything – *anything* – to make myself feel better. Like go on a stupid Tinder date.

'Can't we stop now and just enjoy the show?' I begged Lou.

We were watching *Married At First Sight Australia* and the couples were having to do a cruel honesty box task, resulting in them asking each other questions they'd always wanted to know the answers to and then instantly regretting it when the answer was even worse than they'd imagined. There were tears galore.

'You haven't even given it a chance,' said Lou. 'Look, what about him?' She thrust a picture of a smiley, blonde-haired guy in my face. 'Nick, his name is. He's a little bit older – in his late thirties – a divorcee, head of marketing at Sky and most importantly he doesn't look like a serial killer.'

'Is that really the most important thing, though?' I said, tutting. 'Am I really setting the bar that low?'

I didn't think my dream man would have been recently divorced. Who knew how messy it had been? But I wasn't looking for a dream man, I was looking for a quick fix for my heartbreak, plus maybe Lou was right and a date with someone else was exactly what I needed. He looked like the best of a bad bunch.

Two days later, I walked into a very nice but shockingly overpriced Japanese restaurant in Fitzrovia, one I'd never been to before and was never likely to again. Nick was waiting at a table – I recognised him immediately, which was a good sign. At least he looked like his photo. I took a deep breath and walked over.

'Hi,' I said, unsure what the etiquette was. Should I be shaking hands? Kissing him on the cheek? None of the above? 'I'm Maddie.'

Nick pushed back his chair, standing up. Great – he wasn't a foot shorter than he'd said he was.

He took the lead, pumping my hand as though we were business associates at a meeting. 'Maddie! So lovely to meet you. Take a seat, I'll get us some drinks. What do you like? Wine? Champagne?'

'Um, white wine would be great. Thanks.'

There was definitely something nice about him. OK, I didn't have that instant raw attraction I'd had with Aidan (the image of him hopping about in his skin-tight wetsuit was permanently etched on my mind), but Nick had kind eyes and he dressed nicely and he smelled lovely. He was quite posh and clearly privately educated, but I didn't think that mattered. Clearly this wasn't my future husband, and that wasn't what I was looking for. This would be a chance to lift my spirits and to prove to myself that I wasn't completely un-dateable.

'So, you work in TV, too, is that right?' said Nick, taking a large sip of water.

I wondered whether he was nervous. I wasn't, funnily enough, probably because it didn't feel as though there was anything at stake.

'Yes, for a holiday shopping channel called – very cleverly – Holiday Shop!'

Nick laughed. 'Sounds fun. You love travelling then, I presume?'

'Well, it's not exactly a prerequisite for the job. We don't go much further than Tenerife at a push, but yes, I love travelling. It's probably my main passion, if I'm honest. I have pictures on my walls of all the places I want to go in the world. What about you?'

Nick winced. 'I'm terrified of flying, so that kind of puts a dampener on things. And I like my home comforts too much!'

'Good for you,' I said, relieved that I was not looking for a life partner here. I mean, he'd need to want to travel.

'I do like a nice hotel, though,' he added.

'Boutique or luxury chain?' I quizzed him.

'Oooh, you've got me there,' he replied, mulling it over. 'I do like a gym and a pool, so I think I'd have to say luxury chain.'

'Interesting ...'

'You're a boutique person, aren't you?' he said.

I smiled. 'Maybe.'

I looked around the restaurant, which was full of the trendy media types who populated this part of London. The centre point of the restaurant was a dramatic open kitchen with polished brass and roaring flames and chefs in whites concentrating hard on creating the beautiful plates of food I'd seen being delivered to neighbouring tables.

'It's lovely in here,' I said. 'Thanks for suggesting it.'

Nick picked up the water jug and topped up my glass.

'Not to sound like a cliché, because I genuinely mean this: what's a beautiful woman like you doing on Tinder?'

I laughed, a little nervously, probably because how was I supposed to answer that?

I took a few sips of water to kill some time.

'Um, I had a pretty nasty break-up recently,' I said. 'So I thought I'd try something different. This is actually my first ever Tinder date.'

'Well, I'm honoured,' said Nick.

His eyes weren't big and brown like Aidan's but smaller

and blue and exuding a sort of quiet intelligence. I was enjoying myself more than I thought I would and it all felt very grown-up and calm and sort of serious but not in a bad way.

'What about you?' I asked him.

He grimaced. 'One word: divorce.'

I propped my chin in the palm of my hand. 'That bad?'

He nodded. 'Pretty bad. But it's nice to be here with you, Maddie. And here's to a lovely evening for the two Tinder novices,' he said, picking up his wine.

I did the same, smiling as we clinked glasses across the table.

Chapter Twenty-Two

The restaurant had a beautiful view of the Duomo, which was hands down the most impressive cathedral I'd ever seen. St Paul's had been my favourite when I was younger and when I'd daydreamed about getting married to whichever unobtainable local boy/boyband member I was currently crushing on, I'd imagined the ceremony taking place there. I'd be brimming with joy as I walked down the aisle on the arm of my new husband and we'd walk through the huge doors at the front and there would be well-wishers on the steps (I wasn't sure who) cheering and throwing confetti. This daydream was heavily inspired by photos I'd seen of Princess Diana on her wedding day. And if (strange to think it might be an 'if' now) I actually was to get married, the reality was likely to be much less idyllic than it had been in my fantasy. My family would have to meet Nick's for a start and I couldn't imagine two sets of people less alike. And my mum and dad would have to be in the same room, which had only happened a couple of times since they'd split up and was never easy.

'Impressive, isn't it?' said Rosamund, who had clearly been watching me watching the Duomo. I didn't think it was actually called that: the church itself had a name. But it was the huge dome with its terracotta roof that was most memorable. I'd read a bit about it in my guidebook: something about the revolutionary way they'd created the ceiling.

And about the huge gold orb on top once falling off and crashing onto the pavement below, somehow managing to avoid killing anyone in the process.

'Stunning,' I said. 'It must have taken hundreds of years to build. All that detail.'

Rosamund nodded. She poured us each a glass of water.

'Have you and Nick travelled much together?' she asked.

I thought this was possibly one of the most normal conversations we'd had since I'd arrived. Which was ironic, because I was full of doubts in a way that I hadn't been at the beginning of the trip. About Nick, but also about Aidan, who had come back into my life at the worst possible moment and yet had brought a lightness that I'd forgotten existed.

'A little,' I said. 'But, as you know, Nick's reluctant to fly, especially long haul.'

'Yes, he's terrified, poor thing. Always has been,' remarked Rosamund.

I was pretty sure Nick had told me he'd been skiing every year in some pretentious-sounding resort, and had clearly been forced to fly then, so why couldn't he force himself now? I'd even offered to book him on one of those fear-of-flying courses the big airlines do, but he'd point-blank refused.

'So how does it feel to have been married for forty-five years?' I asked.

Rosamund dabbed the corner of her mouth with a napkin. I wasn't sure why, because we hadn't eaten anything yet.

'I've been very lucky,' she said. 'But I knew very early on that he was the one. You just know, don't you?'

'Mmmn,' I said, nodding enthusiastically and trying to ignore the curl of fear in my stomach.

Bloody Aidan's face came into my head, of course. He was

absolutely not my one. When you meet 'the one' things go smoothly, don't they? You don't have one person ghosting the other, or one of you getting engaged to somebody else. It should be smooth and obvious from the beginning. No drama. No massive ups and downs, just a constant stream of it feeling nice and safe. Like it was with Nick. Except that maybe not being able to be myself didn't feel that safe. And, recently, it hadn't even felt particularly nice.

'Lost any teenagers lately, Maddie?' piped up Sophia from the other end of the table.

I looked at her. Was she really doing this, in front of everyone? Nick was no help, he wouldn't even look at me.

'I've already apol—'

'I'm only joking!' trilled Sophia, guffawing at her own non-joke, even though it was clear to us all that she was still absolutely livid with me.

'Oh hahahaha!' joined in Rosamund.

'What have I missed?' asked a baffled Peter.

'Nothing, Peter. Maddie managed to ... mislay Daisy earlier, that was all,' said Rosamund, being uncharacteristically tactful.

'It wasn't Maddie's fault, anyway,' said Daisy, loudly enough that everyone stopped their chortling and looked at her. 'I wandered off and lost track of time.'

'You shouldn't have been given the opportunity to wander off, Daisy, really,' remarked Sophia, looking pointedly at me.

Daisy, who must have been feeling guilty (either that or she just wanted to spice up the evening by causing a huge row), wasn't letting it go. 'Yeah, but I basically lied to Maddie and told her I went out in London all the time on my own and that Mum and Dad were fine with it. And I told her I'd call Mum to tell her where I was. Maddie tried to ring you, Dad, but you didn't answer your phone. As usual.'

'As usual?' repeated Nick.

Daisy shrugged. 'I can never get hold of you when I need to.'

'That's ridiculous, Daisy,' said Sophia, her eyes blazing. 'Daddy always puts you first.'

Daisy didn't look convinced. And it made me wonder that if Daisy didn't feel she was Nick's priority and I certainly didn't, who was? Himself, I supposed. There was a definite vibe that people looked after number one in this family. I couldn't believe I'd never noticed that about Nick before. I mean, he was generous and giving and loving in many ways, but now I came to think about it, he would also never do anything that he didn't want to do for the sake of somebody else.

Peter seemed to be finding the whole thing hilarious. 'So you've caused a bit of a drama today, have you Daisy Boo? Attagirl!'

'Don't encourage her, please, Peter,' said Sophia, who was clearly pissed off that everyone except Rosamund seemed to be missing the point, which was that I was a terrible, useless and incompetent person.

'Anyway, Maddie,' said Daisy, ducking into her bag, 'I made this for you.'

She passed me an A5 piece of cream card with something sketched on it in fine, grey charcoal. I recognised it immediately: the Piazza della Signoria.

'Daisy, did you draw this?' I asked, touched.

She nodded, her cheeks flushing pink. 'I noticed how much you like that square. And I just wanted to, you know, say sorry for getting you into trouble.'

I reached across the table and squeezed Daisy's hand. 'Thank you, Daisy. I think this is the loveliest gift I've ever received.'

As I looked at the sketch, I could feel several sets of eyes on me. I wondered what they were all thinking. And I wondered how a fourteen-year-old had managed to make me feel more 'seen' than all of them put together.

Dinner had thankfully come to an end and I was relieved to be away from Sophia and her stream of snippy comments as Nick and I made our way back to our room. I'd half been expecting him to say he was going for a walk or something, anything to avoid being alone with me. Things had been frosty between us since we'd argued about Daisy and whereas I'd usually be doing everything I could to smooth things over, I hadn't this time, and so it had gone on and on because I didn't suppose Nick was going to back down. Which wasn't great because it meant we had basically stopped communicating.

I pressed my lips together and went for it.

'Nick, can we talk?' I said, as we made our way down the corridor towards our room.

'I'm not ready to just at the moment,' he replied, sounding all stiff and distant.

'Is this still about Daisy?'

'Of course it's about bloody Daisy!' he snapped. 'You're going to be her stepmother. How do you think it looks when you can't even keep tabs on her for a couple of hours? It's embarrassing.'

I stopped dead. 'I'm embarrassing you now, am I? Really?'

Nick tutted. 'I didn't mean it like—'

'Of course you did.'

I was seething. I must have apologised about twenty times and still he was punishing me for doing such an awful job of caring for his daughter.

Nick tried to open the door, but the keypad kept beeping

insolently, flashing red instead of green. Not that I felt like going into the room with him anyway. I was on the verge of turning around and going out myself. A solo walk along the Arno sounded preferable to being holed up in a hotel room bickering about something that I couldn't change. Obviously, if I was in that situation again, I wouldn't let Daisy go, but couldn't Nick cut me some slack? Daisy had convinced me it would all be fine and she'd admitted that herself at dinner.

'Jealousy doesn't suit you, by the way,' said Nick.

I frowned, genuinely confused. 'Who am I supposed to be jealous of?'

'Sophia,' he replied. 'You keep looking at her apparently, every time she tries to talk to me. We're always going to have Daisy in common and we will always need to talk, so I'm sorry if it makes you uncomfortable, but that's the way it's going to have to be.'

Nick went into the room and I hung back, using my foot to prop open the door. I didn't want to go in. Every part of me was telling me to leave, that this person was not the Nick I'd first met, who'd been so chivalrous and easy to be around. If this was what being with his family did to him, I wished it had happened sooner so that I would have known.

'This has come from Sophia, hasn't it?' I said, still hovering in the doorway. It would feel too claustrophobic in the room. 'She's putting these ideas in your head.'

I heard the lift ping open and glanced down the corridor. Aidan was walking towards me. He was wearing a pristine white polo shirt and black jeans and his eyes sparkled as he smiled at me, as though he was genuinely happy to see me, something I hadn't felt from Nick for what seemed like ages. I felt like taking my foot out of the door, letting it close behind me and walking into Aidan's arms. I had never forgotten how it felt to be held by him.

And then I took a deep breath and tore my eyes away. I went into our room, dropped my bag on the floor and sat on the end of the bed. Nick was in the bathroom; I heard the shower turn on. I listened hard to the beep of Aidan opening his door and the slam as it shut behind him.

Chapter Twenty-Three

Rosamund and Peter's official anniversary lunch, which had come at a particularly bad time, was taking place in the hotel's restaurant that afternoon. Nick was still giving me the silent treatment and I couldn't stop thinking about Aidan. All those misunderstandings. The traumatic stuff he'd been through, how bad it had all felt for me, too, and how I'd thought I'd been going mad to feel that connected to someone after four weeks. But he had felt it, too. I hadn't imagined it.

I tried to tune into the conversations happening around the table. It was the usual: which wine to order; how Rosamund had *had* to fire her cleaner; how much homework Daisy wasn't doing when Sophia and Nick were paying a small fortune in school fees.

Suddenly, Peter started banging his glass with his fork, so loudly that I thought it was going to shatter in his hand. I clearly wasn't the only one who'd noticed (well, you could hardly not): half the restaurant were looking over with interest.

'Speech!' guffawed Nick.

'Go, Peter, whoop, whoop,' yelled Sophia.

I caught Daisy's eye and I wasn't sure who was more mortified by the whole spectacle, me or her. She raised her eyebrows and I winced back.

'As you know, we are gathered here in the delightful city

of Florence to celebrate the forty-fifth wedding anniversary of myself and my lovely wife, Rosamund. Four and a half decades and two children later and we're still going strong.'

Everyone cheered. I clapped in that way you do when it looks like you're clapping wildly but actually your hands aren't properly connecting and you're making barely any sound. I didn't want to add to the din they were making.

'I've bought you a little gift, darling, to say thank you for putting up with me for all these years.'

'Oh Peter, you shouldn't have,' said Rosamund, looking as though he absolutely should have.

Peter scuffled about under his chair producing a beautifully wrapped rectangular box. He placed it on the table in front of Rosamund. Sophia immediately started cooing, stroking the wrapping paper with her long, blood-red fingernails.

'Did you wrap this, Peter?'

'God, no,' he said.

Rosamund began unpicking the paper, enjoying the fact that several pairs of eyes were trained exclusively on her. She really drew it out, pausing to make eye contact with Peter, struggling over a piece of Sellotape. At this rate, the main course would be served before she'd even opened it. Finally she had one end open and was able to pull out a green jewellery box with Cartier emblazoned on it.

'Blimey,' I said, not meaning to have spoken aloud.

'Oh, Rosamund. Open it,' urged Sophia, whose voice had gone all husky at the sight of the Cartier logo.

Rosamund used her thumb to pop open the box, revealing a beautiful, white leather, diamond-encrusted ladies watch. Even Rosamund seemed lost for words.

'Well done, Daddy,' said Nick, looking impressed.

'Put it on, Rosamund, put it on!' squawked Sophia. 'Isn't it stunning, Daisy?'

A disinterested Daisy gave her grandmother a thumbs-up.

As Rosamund slipped the watch on her wrist, there was no doubt it was beautiful. She tipped it this way and that, letting it sparkle in the light. I was surprised a waiter hadn't come bustling over thinking she was doing Morse code.

'Do you remember when you bought me those Cartier earrings for my thirty-fifth birthday, Nick?' asked Sophia.

He chuckled lightly. 'I certainly do. I've still got the credit card bill to show for it.'

'Oh hahahaha!' said Sophia.

I made a point of not giving Sophia any reason to deem me 'jealous' again by looking everywhere but at her. When I happened to glance across at the door, I saw Aidan had just arrived. A waiter showed him to a table in the corner. He had his laptop with him and set it up, catching my eye over the top of it. I watched him order a drink – a beer, I bet, something Italian.

As everyone fawned all over the watch and Rosamund basked in her moment of glory, I began to feel very hot. I became aware of my heart racing and when I took some deep breaths to try to relax, I started noticing my breathing, too, which felt shallow and erratic. Everything went a bit fuzzy and I knew I needed to get out of there. It felt like the beginnings of an anxiety attack, but why, when I hadn't had one for years?

I pushed my chair back, scraping the legs on the floor, and stood up, gripping the edge of the table for support.

Nick looked up at me, concerned. 'Everything OK?'

I nodded. 'Just need some air,' I blurted, grabbing my cardigan from the back of my chair.

'Well, don't be long,' said Nick, 'the food will be here in a minute.'

I nodded, not trusting myself to speak and headed for

the door. I didn't want to catch Aidan's eye as I left, but it was impossible not to. That's how it felt, anyway, as though gravity was pulling me towards him. I whipped my eyes away and focused on getting out of there and up on to the roof, where hopefully I would start to feel like myself again.

Chapter Twenty-Four

I leaned on the wall, looking out towards the Arno and the rooftops and then closing my eyes, hoping that would calm my mind. My breathing felt easier, it had done the second I'd stepped out of that dining room. I wiggled my fingers – they felt normal again, not laced with pins and needles like they had been a few moments before.

I took some deep breaths, gulping down the air which felt cleaner up here, as though it was coming straight from the Tuscan hills. Nick's face kept popping into my head – kind, smiley Nick, not the version I was seeing here in Florence. And then Lou came into my mind for some reason and I remembered what she'd said early on, when I'd first introduced Nick to her. She'd said he seemed nice, but that I didn't seem anywhere near as happy as I'd been when I talked about Aidan. I'd shrugged it off at the time and had declared what Aidan and I had had toxic. Not real. A brief affair and, of course, those always felt more intense because you hadn't really had time to learn all the bad stuff about each other. But I was big on first impressions – I trusted them. And it scared me when I remembered how I'd walked into the restaurant that night and had seen Nick sitting there when really, despite my best efforts, it was Aidan I wanted.

'Hey.'

I turned around, already knowing it was him. His voice was unmistakable; the Home Counties accent with an estuary twang, the way it seemed to be on a particular frequency so that when he spoke it resonated deep inside me.

I opened my eyes as he came to stand next to me.

'Are you all right? You looked very pale when you walked past me just now.'

I nodded. 'I just felt anxious for a minute there. Like I couldn't breathe.'

Aidan looked concerned. 'Was it a panic attack? You said you used to get them, right?'

'Maybe. I haven't had one for ages, though.'

Aidan nodded. 'What made you have one today?'

I bit my lip. 'This trip has been … a lot.'

Aidan leaned on the wall. 'It has,' he said.

If I stayed here much longer, I was going to say or do something I'd regret, I knew I was. There was just something about Aidan that made me want to blurt out the truth, even when the most rational part of me was emphatically telling me not to.

'I have to get back,' I said. 'It's Rosamund and Peter's actual anniversary today. There's a big lunch and I—'

'Have you changed your mind about Nick?' asked Aidan, his voice gentle.

Before we'd come to Florence, I had been happy. Not in the way I'd been when I'd first met Aidan, when I'd had this constant fluttery feeling in my chest and thought about him every minute of every day and every moment I wasn't with him was like some kind of torture. I'd never felt like that about Nick, even in the early days. But it had been nice. And uncomplicated.

'He's good for me,' I said.

'He's not.'

'Well, he's stuck around, so that's something.'

Aidan sighed. 'Maddie, I—'

'When you love somebody, you have to let them see every part of you. You should want to share everything with them, even the bad stuff. If you'd just called me to explain what was happening, then I could have been there for you. Listened to you, helped you work it out. But you shut me out without a single word and that's not OK.'

Tears were pricking the backs of my eyes, but I refused to let Aidan think he'd got to me. I never wanted to let people see me cry over them.

'I've changed,' said Aidan softly. 'I can learn to let someone in again.'

'Why now?'

'Because of you. Because ever since I saw you again the other night, I've not been able to get you off my mind. Then again, who am I kidding? I've never stopped thinking about you.'

'It's a bit late now. I'm engaged to somebody else!' I said.

'But what if you weren't?'

Aidan reached out and took one of my hands. I looked at our fingers, entwined again. It felt painful, because of all the time that we'd lost, but it also felt like the right thing. The *only* thing.

'What if we were to try again?' he asked. 'I know I hurt you really badly and that I messed up and that I could have handled things a hundred times better. But it can't be a coincidence that we've found each other again. I feel like we've been given one more chance. Don't you feel that, too?'

I took a deep breath. I'd have to be honest, it was now or never.

'I do,' I said.

But downstairs was Nick.

'But it's too late,' I added, glancing down at my engagement ring.

'Does it have to be?' asked Aidan.

How could I call it off now? Nick would be so hurt, or at least I thought he would be. I realised, then, that I didn't really know him as well as I should. He kept so much of himself tucked away and I was happy to let him do that because I was doing the same thing.

'I'd better get back,' I said, making a move to leave.

'All I ask is that you think about it,' said Aidan softly. 'Take your time to properly think it through. And don't let anybody rush you, me included.'

I nodded. I remembered how patient Aidan had always been. How that perhaps it wasn't the stability of someone like Nick I needed, but someone who really listened to me, who liked me for all that I was, the good and the bad. Was it time for me to take a leap of faith? To be brave and take a chance? Maybe I'd end up with no one, but surely that would be better than ending up with the wrong person.

Chapter Twenty-Five

I felt light-headed and fluttery as I made my way back to the restaurant. When I thought about Nick waiting for me, my stomach swirled. I'd come to Florence to meet my future in-laws and would be leaving with the realisation that it might be over between Nick and I. Tomorrow evening we'd be back in London and I would have to decide whether to end things, which, of course, I was dreading. I hoped he'd be OK. And actually, given how things had been going over the last few days, he might even be a tiny bit relieved. Because I could feel him pulling away, too. I thought he probably wasn't quite ready to accept it, but I was, and terrifying as that felt, I knew I had to follow my heart and do this for me, instead of trying to do what was best for everyone else. Because, really, much as I hadn't wanted it to be, it had always been Aidan.

I knew something was wrong as soon as I walked into the dining room and everyone stopped talking over each other and stared accusingly at me. Rosamund's gaze was like ice, even more so than usual, and Nick's face was a bright, tomato red. I caught Daisy's eye and she winced at me – it was like she was giving me a warning, which I took to mean: retreat, retreat.

What on earth was going on? Had someone overheard my conversation with Aidan upstairs? I didn't see how, we were definitely the only ones up there and we would have heard the door to the terrace open.

I carried on over to the table, feeling even more reluctant than I had a few seconds before. Everyone watched as I scraped back my chair and sat back down. The atmosphere was tense and loaded. I cleared my throat as if I was about to speak, but I had nothing to say, not in front of an audience, so I took a mouthful of wine instead. Our mains had come while I was upstairs and I already knew I wouldn't be able to stomach the ornately decorated fish dish in front of me.

'Where have you been?' asked Nick, sounding as though he needed to loosen his collar.

'Upstairs,' I said lightly. 'Getting some air. I felt a bit faint.'

'With that journalist guy, were you?' said Peter.

Shit.

'What do you mean?' I asked, trying to play innocent.

'Sophia's just been filling us in,' said Nick. 'About your little romantic trysts with him. What the fuck is going on, Maddie?'

I began to break out in a sweat and grabbed a linen napkin to dab my brow. Bloody Sophia, I might have guessed she'd be involved.

'Well?' demanded Nick.

There was no way I was doing this in front of his family, who were clearly all baying for my blood. If I'd imagined the worst possible way to tell Nick about Aidan, then this would have been it. How could I explain – in front of his mother and his ex-wife! – that I hadn't just mysteriously starting doubting my relationship the moment we set foot in Italy. That it wasn't just about Aidan.

'Nick,' I said, turning to face him, my calm demeanour belying the fact that I felt as though I was about to pass out with nerves, 'this is between you and me. If you want to talk, let's do it in private, OK?'

He hesitated and then he threw his napkin dramatically on the table.

'Fine,' he said, scraping back his chair.

Avoiding eye contact with everyone else, I followed him silently out of the restaurant.

Nick stomped over to the open fireplace where I'd seen the loved-up couple chatting over wine when we'd first arrived. What a weirdly romantic spot for a relationship to end.

'So what's going on?' demanded Nick, slumping down into an armchair.

I sat opposite him, perching on the edge of the seat. I took a deep breath. For the first time, I was going to have to be the one to end a relationship. I was much more familiar with being on the other end. The dumpee. When someone didn't want to be with me anymore, I knew exactly how to act and how to (eventually) make myself feel OK afterwards. Rejection was something I was used to; rejecting somebody else was scary and new. I gathered my resolve.

'I do love you, Nick,' I started. 'Very much. But not in the way that I probably should love someone I'm planning to spend the rest of my life with. And if I'm being completely honest – with myself, as well as with you – I've never been sure, not one hundred per cent. '

God, that felt difficult to admit, and of course, I wished I'd come to this realisation sooner.

Nick sighed heavily. 'Has it got something to do with that journalist guy, then? Is Sophia right?'

I bet Sophia had been in her element when she told him what she suspected.

'In a way,' I said. 'The thing is, I know him – Aidan

– from before. We were dating just before I met you. And the ending had been ... sudden. I shouldn't have been on Tinder in the first place when I was still hung up on somebody else. And going out on a date with you was probably not a great idea, in hindsight. I wasn't looking for anything serious, not at all.'

'So I was a rebound thing, then, is that what you're saying?' he said sadly.

I cleared my throat. There was no nice way to put it, was there, no matter which soft, flowery words you used?

'I really liked you. I did,' I said, remaining as strong as I could. 'And when you proposed to me in Paris, I was swept away by it all. But part of me wanted to slow things down, and I hadn't known how to say it. I should have found the strength to explain that I was doubting whether it was what I wanted.'

Nick slumped further down in his chair. He looked gutted and it was all my fault.

I took a deep breath. It was done, now. I had to keep my resolve. I reached out to take Nick's hand.

'I've loved every minute of the time we've spent together. But somewhere in my head there's always been Aidan. And I've never really been able to forget him. And I'm really sorry that I didn't tell you sooner.'

My heart was thumping so hard in my chest, I felt sure Nick could hear it.

'So you knew he was going to be here in Florence, then, did you?' asked Nick.

I shook my head. 'I hadn't seen or spoken to him for years.'

Nick shook his head.

'I'm so sorry, Nick. I thought I could do this with you. I wanted to, more than anything.'

Nick looked at me. 'And you're sure? You don't want to wait until we get back to London? Give yourself some time to think about it?'

I squeezed his fingers. 'I just don't think I can picture my life with you anymore.'

He nodded. 'If this is really what you want,' he said, 'then I'm not going to try to stop you.'

I smiled at him the best I could under the circumstances. My face felt flushed from the open fire roaring next to us but also from the fact that this was possibly one of the worst moments of my life. I hated disappointing people and I'd not just let Nick down, I'd dropped him from a huge height. The poor guy had had no idea what was coming when he'd booked me a train ticket to Florence, but then, in truth, neither had I.

'Be happy, OK?' I said, swallowing hard.

I didn't think he needed me balling in front of him and I suddenly had a modicum of compassion for everyone who had ever dumped me in the past. This was *hard*.

Nick reached out to tuck a strand of hair behind my ear. 'You too, Mads. You too.'

Chapter Twenty-Six

As I waited for the concierge to call his brother-in-law in the Oltrarno area of the city because apparently he owned a small pensione that might have a very reasonably priced room I could stay in for the night, my phone pinged. There were a few people it could be, some I wanted to hear from more than others, but annoyingly, it was Tim.

HOW ARE YOU GETTING ON WITH THE FOOTAGE?

Without overthinking it, I typed a message back.

Tim, I'm afraid I don't think it's fair for me to be shooting footage when I am on annual leave and for no additional pay. I am on a break from work and therefore do not wish to be thinking about actual work. I know Florence quite well now, though, so if you'd like me to come back and shoot some footage some other time, I'd be happy to. See you on Monday, Maddie.

I pressed 'send', regretted it for about a second, shrugged and called Lou.

'What's up?' she said. 'Are the in-laws still being a nightmare?'

I left it a beat or two because it was the first time I'd said it out loud and it kind of got caught in my throat.

'I've split up with Nick.'

Lou, for once, was silent.

'Hello? Can you hear me?' I said.

'Of course I can. I'm just letting this momentous news sink in. What on earth's happened?'

The concierge gave me a thumbs-up and I gave him a thumbs-up back.

'Where to start? Aidan and I have been talking. And he's never forgotten about me either and I think he might be my "one" and we're probably going to give it another shot.'

'What?' exclaimed Lou.

'Oh, and I told Tim where to go. Politely, obviously.'

The pianist started up, it was that time of the evening. More Vivaldi, I thought.

'Oh Mads. This sounds a lot. Are you OK?'

'Not sure. But I will be.'

'What are you going to do when you get back to London? Do you want to stay at mine for a bit?' asked Lou.

God, I hadn't even thought about that. I could hardly go back to Nick's place, could I?

'Would that be OK?' I asked, grateful.

'Absolutely. Is somebody playing the piano?'

'Yep.'

'When are you back?'

'I've re-booked my flight for tomorrow morning. I'm off to a pensione for the night.'

'Very *A Room With a View*.'

'Right?'

Lou sighed. 'I know you probably feel terrible right now, but if you think about it, you've potentially just avoided making the biggest mistake of your life. And I, for one, am proud of you for stepping up and going after what you want.'

I pressed my lips together, wondering whether to say anything.

'You've never liked Nick, have you?' I asked, keeping my tone light.

I supposed it didn't matter now whether she did or she didn't, but I wanted to know. It was something I'd always suspected but had never called her out on because I hadn't been ready to hear the truth. Lou was very astute about stuff like this and I thought that if she'd had some insight into why Nick and I might not be right for each other, I'd find it impossible to ignore. And I'd so wanted to want to marry him. Or at least, I'd tried really hard to want it.

'I don't dislike him,' said Lou gently. 'I was just never sure he brought out the best in you. I never thought you had enough in common. You didn't seem particularly connected, you know?'

That I could take.

'The only good thing to come out of it is that I never have to see his wanky family again. Turns out the only one I care about is Daisy. She's lovely, actually. I'll miss her,' I said.

My phone beeped as a text came through from Tim.

'Tim's just texted. I'm too scared to read it,' I said.

'Fuck Tim. I met my friend Katrina for dinner the other night and she's heading up a new travel show for Channel 4. I told her about you and she said to send in your CV. If you're interested? Since you're on an empowerment roll?!'

I watched other guests coming in and out of the doors of the hotel, some with suitcases and tired faces, some dressed up for dinner.

'Are you there, Mads?'

'I'm here.'

'So will you go for it? The job?'

'Actually – and this is a bit radical – I've been thinking of going freelance. Not right away, I'll need to save a bit more money first. But I've got an idea, Lou, and I'm really excited about it. I'll tell you all the details when I see you.'

Lou screeched so loudly that I had to temporarily hold my phone away from my ear.

'Sorry, but I can't take all this in,' she yelled, sounding

genuinely shocked. 'What's happened to the Maddie I know? Do they put something in the waters in Florence?'

I ended the call and got the details of the pensione from the concierge.

'Oh, and can I please settle the bill for room 315?' I asked him, getting my card out.

He tapped away on his computer.

'All paid, madame.'

I frowned.

'I thought they were going to pay at the end? Can't I pay half at least?'

'The bill is settled, there is nothing to pay, madame.'

'Right,' I said, annoyed that they'd got in there first. Then again, at least I wouldn't have to max out my credit card to pay for a hotel room that – I could conclude – was no nicer than some of the places I'd stayed in for half the price.

I was just about to leave when I realised I still had my engagement ring on. I stared at it for a moment or two, holding out my hand to observe it from a distance.

'Would you mind keeping an eye on my stuff?' I asked the concierge.

He was already on the phone but nodded a yes.

I walked towards the restaurant, pulling off my ring as I went. I'd give it to Nick and if I felt like I could, I'd say goodbye to the others. It would be a shame to leave things on such a bad note, although I supposed it was too late for that.

Rosamund saw me first.

'Don't worry, I'm not staying,' I said, looking at everyone one by one. Daisy smiled at me, at least. 'I just thought I ought to give you this, Nick.'

I handed him the ring, pressing it into the palm of his hand.

Sophia laughed out loud. 'Can you believe the audacity of this woman?!'

'Mum!' said Daisy. 'Stop being so horrible to Maddie. She's a nice person. And I, for one, am really sad that she won't be part of my family anymore.'

Strange that she'd turned out to be the only person I felt some sort of affinity with, despite our rocky start. I thought it might be because I could see so much of myself in her.

'Thank you, Daisy. And I am going to treasure the picture you gave me.'

And then I turned to Rosamund.

'I hope you enjoy the rest of your trip and that this hasn't disrupted things too much for you.'

She gave me a steely look in return and I rattled on before she had a chance to start laying into me.

'And, Nick, I'll be in touch when we're back in London.'

He cleared his throat. 'Fine.'

'Bye, Daisy,' I said. 'Good luck with everything.'

'You too,' she said.

And then I turned and walked away, noticing how the further away from them I got, the more my shoulders fell from my ears and the more my jaw unclenched. I was free of them and it felt great. And whether or not things worked out with Aidan, I knew I'd done the right thing by not being with Nick. His family might have tried to make me feel as though I wasn't good enough for them, but it had ended up having the opposite effect.

As I pulled my suitcase through the doors of the hotel, slipping the doorman a twenty-euro note as I went, I felt stronger and more hopeful than I'd ever been before.

Chapter Twenty-Seven

I stepped out onto Via Tornabuoni, taking one last, longing look at the Gucci store and checking the directions the concierge had written down for me on the hotel's headed notepaper: the pensione was over the river in Oltrarno. It should be about a ten-minute walk, he'd said.

As I slipped the paper into my bag, I pulled out my phone before I could check myself, opening my contacts, finding Aidan's (now reinstated) number. My thumb hovered over the 'call' button. I badly wanted to talk to him, but I'd promised myself I wouldn't do it until I got back to London. I needed time to process everything, to work things through properly. To be one hundred per cent sure, this time, that this was what I wanted.

I set off towards the Arno, deciding it was easier to walk in the road where there was more space, even if it was bumpy on the cobbles.

'Need some help with that?' said a voice I knew all too well.

I tried to keep my cool, glancing across at Aidan, who had fallen into step beside me. He was wearing a checked cotton shirt open at the neck and and he had the same sparkling, hopeful eyes he'd always had.

I'd done the right thing, I knew I had.

'Pretty sure I can manage,' I said, grinning at him.

'Well, at least let me walk with you. Just in case. I hate

to say it, but I reckon your suitcase has seen better days,' he said, grimacing at its noisy, wobbly wheels. 'Where are you headed?'

'The Pensione Valentina.'

'Very romantic,' he said.

I daren't look at him. I knew what he was thinking. I was doing my best not to think about it, too.

We turned left and then right, finding ourselves beneath a beautiful arched corridor underneath one of the former palaces that were dotted around on every other corner of Florence. A flower market was packing up for the evening and I could smell the scent of the pretty wild flowers and olive trees as we passed. Lanterns were hanging above our heads, bathing us in a warm, buttery light.

'I've called off the engagement,' I blurted out.

I marched off ahead, anxious, suddenly, that he'd changed his mind. What if he'd got carried away up on that roof, like I had at the top of the Eiffel Tower?

'Maddie, can we stop a sec?' he called after me.

I stopped, hesitating before turning around. Whatever he had to say, I was going to have to face it. I'd got over him before, I supposed I could do it again, if the worst came to the worst.

'You've ended things with Nick?' he said, looking as though he couldn't quite believe it.

I nodded.

'I wasn't expecting that,' he said.

'Neither was he,' I replied.

Aidan came closer, not stopping until there was hardly any space between us at all. He reached out and ran his fingers along the length of my arm, from my shoulder to my wrist.

'Are you OK?' he asked.

'I think so,' I said, melting into his shoulder, letting myself remember what it had been like to touch him. I breathed in the scent of him.

'So what does this mean for us?' asked Aidan, his voice low, his breath warm on my neck.

I didn't care about the locals passing us, bulging bunches of flowers in arms, or the tourists taking photos of the pretty arches. Following my instincts for once, I clasped his head between my hands, rose up on to the tips of my toes and kissed him lightly on the mouth, just for a second or two. He put the flat of his hand on the small of my back, pulling me in to him, and kissed me back, first on my eyebrows and then on the tip of my nose and then, finally on my lips. Harder this time, with no holding back, as though he was making up for the years we'd been apart. I never wanted it to end.

'Is this really all happening?' he asked, pulling back at last and looking at me with a kind of awe.

I nodded, laughing, breathless, also not quite able to believe it. 'I think it really is.'

Epilogue

Aidan had grown up on the outskirts of London like me, in a non-descript road flanked with slightly tatty semi-detached houses a bit like the one we'd lived in when my mum and dad were still together.

'I used to ride my bike up and down this street for hours in the summer holidays,' said Aidan, throwing his arm easily around my shoulders and pulling me close to him so that he could kiss the top of my head.

'I bet you rode like a maniac,' I replied, enjoying the crunch of golden leaves beneath the heels of my boots.

I loved this time of year best, the lead-up to Halloween and fireworks night, when the air felt breezy and crisp but a little bit smoky and you felt like sitting in cosy pubs nursing a glass of red (which Aidan and I seemed to do a LOT).

'I want to say I was very careful ...' said Aidan, laughing to himself, 'but I think my mum was probably relieved when I got home in one piece.'

I slipped my arm around his waist so that there was no space between us.

'How are things between you, now?' I asked him, running my fingertips under the hem of his jumper and stroking the cool skin just above his waistband.

'Better,' he said. 'I'm beginning to understand why they didn't tell me. We've talked it through and I might not agree with it, but I get that they had my best interests at heart.'

I nodded. 'It wasn't a decision they took lightly, was it? I bet they'd been agonising over it for years.'

'Yeah. They said they had.'

'What about your mum's vision?'

He shrugged. 'No worse for now. I think it's a case of watching and waiting.'

We reached a house that looked sunnier than the others. Brighter and more inviting, with pink curtains and a neat front garden with a bench in it and a bird box and a knackered-looking Ford Fiesta parked in the driveway.

'This is us,' said Aidan.

I hesitated.

'You do realise this is my second *meet the parents* experience in less than six months?'

Aidan nodded. 'Nervous?'

'A little.'

'You do know my mum's not anything like Rosamund, right?'

I grimaced. 'Promise?'

Aidan stopped and took my head in his hands, looking at me. 'Have I told you how happy I am that you're in my life again?' he asked.

'Um, just a couple of times,' I teased.

'And did I mention that I am completely, madly, out-of-control in love with you?' he asked, stroking my cheek-bones with his thumbs.

I pretended to consider his question carefully. 'You might have mentioned something ...'

And then the door flew open and a woman wearing an apron with a map of Majorca on it and pink velour slippers was standing there beaming at us. She threw open her arms. 'You must be Maddie,' she said.

I laughed, holding out my arms, too. Her hug was warm

and inviting and I immediately felt safe and accepted, which was a lot for a first impression and kind of everything I'd ever wanted.

'Do I get one of those?' asked Aidan, jokingly elbowing me out of the way so that he could hug his mum, too.

'Now, come and meet Ken and then we'll have some lunch. Aidan said spaghetti carbonara is your favourite, so that's what I've done. I hope he got it right?' she asked, looking at me anxiously, as though I was going to say no; as though this wasn't one of the nicest things ever to happen to me.

'Spaghetti carbonara is perfect,' I said, following her into the house and smiling at Aidan over my shoulder.

Acknowledgements

Thank you so much to everyone involved in producing this book – it was a dream to write, partly because I adored these characters (Rosamund and Sophia in particular were so much fun to create!) and also because obviously I just *had* go on a research trip to Florence, which I declare is possibly the world's most perfect city.

As ever, I'm so grateful to the whole team at Orion Fiction, who championed this story from the off and who have helped me mould it into the book it is today – special thanks to my editor, the lovely Rhea Kurien, and to Charlotte Mursell, Sanah Ahmed, Francesca Banks and Lucy Cameron. And as ever, I am so grateful for the support of my brilliant agent, Hannah Ferguson, and the whole team at the exceptional Hardman & Swainson.

So many thanks to my friend, Alexandra Mackenzie, who along with Margaret and Johanna introduced me to the delights of Loch Lomond, a place I hadn't imagined to be so beautiful. And also to Alexandra for being the perfect and very patient companion for a research trip to Florence, which felt extra special because it was the first time I'd left the country since before the pandemic – I loved it there so much that I missed my flight home! Thanks to the beautiful Milu Hotel on Via Tornabuoni, which was perfect in every way, not least because it was diagonally opposite Gucci (even if my budget could only stretch to a pair of socks!).

They kindly organised a plethora of brilliant tours for us – special shout out to Katy, Rose and Anne, who made our wine-tasting tour in Chianti the highlight of our trip.

And, of course, thank you to all my lovely family and friends who are forever supportive and excited for me, especially Mum, Matthew, Robbie, Alyson, Janet and Louise. To the writer friends I've made who are invaluable sources of support, especially the Debut20s, the Debut21s, the Screenwriting crew and The Troubadours! And to my sweet Gabriel, who never complains about the fact I've got my laptop out again! And to my dad, who I know would be very proud.

Credits

Lorraine Brown and Orion Fiction would like to thank everyone at Orion who worked on the publication of *Five Days in Florence* in the UK.

Editorial
Rhea Kurien
Sanah Ahmed

Copyeditor
Jade Craddock

Proofreader
Francine Brody

Audio
Paul Stark
Jake Alderson

Editorial Management
Charlie Panayiotou
Jane Hughes
Bartley Shaw
Tamara Morriss

Contracts
Anne Goddard
Dan Herron
Ellie Bowker

Design
Nick Shah
Rachael Lancaster
Sandra Chiu
Charlotte Abrams-Simpson
Joanna Ridley

Finance
Jasdip Nandra
Nick Gibson
Sue Baker

Marketing
Javerya Iqbal

'Wonderfully escapist'
Beth O'Leary

Could one split second change her life forever?

Hannah and Si are in love and on the same track - that is,
until their train divides on the way to a wedding.
The next morning, Hannah wakes up in Paris and realises
that her boyfriend (and her ticket) are 300 miles away in
Amsterdam!

But then Hannah meets Léo on the station platform,
and he's everything Si isn't. Spending the day with him in
Paris forces Hannah to question how well she really
knows herself - and whether, sometimes, you need to go
in the wrong direction to find everything you've been
looking for ...

Sometimes love is just around the corner ...

Rebecca isn't looking for love. She's perfectly happy with her high-flying city job, gorgeous flat overlooking Hampstead Heath and fortnightly fling with the hot CEO. She's certainly not interested in the hot actor neighbour who's just moved in opposite ...

Jack is still looking for his big break. It turns out being the star talent at drama school doesn't give you a golden ticket to Hollywood, after all. The last thing he needs is any distractions right now – especially not the uptight, power-suit-wearing girl next door.

They might live only a few metres away from each other, but their worlds couldn't be further apart, plus opposites don't really attract ... do they?